Thomas Russell Sullivan

Roses of Shadow

A Novel

Thomas Russell Sullivan

Roses of Shadow
A Novel

ISBN/EAN: 9783337349134

Printed in Europe, USA, Canada, Australia, Japan

Cover: Foto ©Andreas Hilbeck / pixelio.de

More available books at **www.hansebooks.com**

ROSES OF SHADOW

A NOVEL

BY

T. R. SULLIVAN

"Why should poor beauty indirectly seek
Roses of shadow, since his rose is true?"

SONNET lxvii.

NEW YORK
CHARLES SCRIBNER'S SONS
1885

CONTENTS

ROSES OF SHADOW.

I.

A DOZEN years or more ago, the figures do not
matter, before the invading host of traders had
pitched its tents in one of the noblest avenues of
the modern Athens, the " Ægean " Club still inhab-
ited a cosy red-brick house on the lower side of
Boston Common.   The stone portico with its Tus-
can columns, the wrought iron balustrades, the
heavily slated roof and ugly little dormer-windows
have been swept away, and the club, well known
as one of the oldest in the city, stretches itself anew
in more luxurious quarters.   It was not a large
club in those days ; three or four hundred members
there were at most,—doctors, lawyers, literary men,
men of business, with a few idle souls who listened
well,—somewhat incongruously grouped, as in most
clubs from time immemorial.   About the old place,
nevertheless, there was an air of jolly fellowship,

that is said by certain solemn gray-beards to be lacking in the new one. But club men of five-and-forty who can look back ten years, even to think of what they had for dinner, without sighing, are rare indeed.

The word dinner is a reminder that its hour was a merry one at the old " Ægean." Men dropped in between five and seven to dine, two or three together, in a large room on the second floor overlooking an irregular enclosure behind the house; the servants called this patch of ground "the garden," but there flourished in it only dusty grass and vines with a restless dwarf of a fountain, that kept a gilt ball bobbing up and down its tiny jet all the summer time. After dinner, coffee and cigars were to be had in the library or, weather permitting, on the stone balcony fronting the street and the double row of great English elms in the mall that bounds the Common. What sunsets those were to be lazily admired or ignored according to the digestive mood of the moment! The new club-house turns its back upon them.

In the twilight of a warm May evening, three young men chanced to have the balcony and the fading panorama of the sky to themselves. Inside, the waiters were flying about to fill orders, amid the tinkling of bells, the click of billiard balls and the confusing clamor of a political discussion, wherein ten worthy citizens animated by the best of motives, were striving to express simultaneously their ten conflicting views; but, undisturbed by

this Babel of familiar sounds, these three sat alone
with the twinkling stars and their tobacco, and
watched for some time without comment the stream
of human life that kept its restless course along the
street below them. At last one of the three was
provoked into breaking abruptly the seals of
silence; two girls, let loose from some shop, happened to pass by on the other side, and one of
them threw a mischievous backward glance at the
group on the balcony.

"Pretty face, that!" The speaker roused himself
so suddenly that his hand struck the balcony rail
and sent his cigar flying.

He was rather short, rather stout and rather
dapper, and it pleased him to affect an English intonation; as the cigar fell he looked after it and
good-naturedly cursed his own awkwardness.

"Hunter lost his heart again?" asked one of his
companions who sat behind the others a little in
the shadow.

"No," answered the third, a handsome fellow,
with a minute, dark moustache that he was per-
petually twisting, "only his cigar! Here, Hunt,
console yourself!" and he passed his cigar-case.

"Thanks, but I did lose 'em both, Elliston.
Both? All three, for the face is gone now."

The man in the shadow growled rather scorn-
fully, and the conversation was left for Elliston to
resume, which he presently did.

"What a curious thing city life is!" he began.

"Apropos of what?" broke in Hunter.

"Well, of your face in the crowd. Ten to one, you will never see it again. Every day hundreds of strange people pass in and out of our lives. This street is like a kaleidoscope; whenever it stirs there comes a new combination."

"Well, really, you know," said Hunter, "always seeing nobody new would be demned stupid, you know! You might as well live at home! Eh, Marvin?" and he turned to the man behind them.

Marvin answered Elliston over Hunter's head. "I am not so sure about this kaleidoscope business, Jack," said he. "Did you ever make experiments? One combination, at least, repeats itself often enough."

"What's that?" Elliston asked.

"A blank!" Marvin answered. "That's a simple figure! No doubt the more complex ones would follow, if—"

"If you only followed 'em up!" put in Hunter. "Recipe: to make new faces old ones, follow 'em up, Jack, follow 'em up! And begin now,—look there!"

He pointed with his cigar to the slender figure of a girl, who, as he spoke, crossed the pavement below and narrowly escaped collision with the light wheel of one of those almost noiseless vehicles built for the most reckless form of rapid transit. Reaching the opposite curb, unconscious of her danger, she passed on in the crowd, looking neither to right nor left with brows knit as if she were lost in thought; she was very simply, even shabbily dressed, but the men only noticed her pale, tired, little face that under other conditions would have been beautiful.

"Whew!" said Hunter, "that cub all but ran her down! What a little beauty it was though!"

"Bless us, Bob, I believe you!" said Elliston. "Her face was lovely! Strange, too! It was like —" but he left the sentence unfinished.

"Like whom?" asked Marvin, whose eyes were still following the girl's retreating figure.

"No matter, old boy, you would be none the wiser if I told you; I'm forever seeing these chance resemblances. Choice combination though,—worth watching for again!"

"Choice enough, if Marvin noticed it!" said Hunter.

"Yes," said Elliston, "he isn't often taken that way. I believe when we are all married and settled, Marvin will be found here alone, left sitting, like what's-his-name's New Zealander—"

"Yes, smiling at your ruined lives!" interposed Marvin, looking solemnly at the stars as if his friends' destinies were written in them. Elliston laughed.

"By the way, though," said Hunter, "I had almost forgotten! Who was that devilish fine figure of a woman you were walking with the other day, Marvin?"

"I?" asked Marvin. "Where?"

"Oh, come, you can't play that! In one of the suburbs! Belmont, wasn't it?"

"Nonsense!" said Marvin, gruffly, still staring at the stars. "I never went there in my life."

"So you have forgotten it," Hunter persisted, " or perhaps you didn't know you were there. You seemed to have lost yourself. For once, you looked almost good-natured."

"That settles it!" said Marvin. "It was some-body else—my double, I suppose."

"Your double! He's a lucky dog, then! Take my advice, and cultivate him; he keeps good company."

"What was she like, Bob?" asked Elliston, whose curiosity was now thoroughly aroused. "Come, tell us."

"Well," returned Hunter, reflectively, "she was tall and dark,—dark-haired and dark-eyed—yes, a brunette, decidedly. She had a very trig get up, don't you know; her raiment was of a foreign cut —quite the latest thing from the other side, I should say, but there was nothing loud about it, either. She was really most uncommon good style, Jack. The sort of girl to make cold mutton attractive, now, I give you my word."

"Hear him!" said Elliston. "Bob Hunter eloquent! What next?"

" But my heart was stolen away, don't you see?" said Hunter, "there was a kind of a what-do-you-call-it about her—a heap of mischief, don't you know, in her eyes!"

"Tall and dark!" cried Elliston. "That sounds like—" But before the name, which must have

been the right one could escape him, he felt the
warning pressure of a hand—Marvin's hand—upon
his shoulder. A very gentle pressure it was, and
darkness having now fairly overtaken them, the
slight movement needed to make it passed unnoted
under Hunter's very eyes; a pleading pressure,
almost pathetic in its significance to Elliston, in
whose heart it struck a tenderly responsive chord.
"Don't!" it seemed to say, "don't give this imper-
tinent little brute my secret, for it is one!" The
bond between these two was that of an intimate
friendship somewhat curious in its nature, on Elliston's side amounting almost to affection, on Marvin's to little more than tolerance. So the former
now stopped short and made no sign, only looking
askance at Marvin, inwardly amazed. His friend
sat like a graven image with eyes fixed upon the
firmament; but Elliston still felt the hand resting
lightly on his shoulder.

"Well," said Hunter, impatiently, "well, who
was it?"

"Miss Jewsbury!" said Elliston, with a mischievous look at the tormentor's eager face.

Marvin withdrew his hand, chuckled, sent a great
puff of smoke heavenward and burst into a
triumphant laugh.

"Pshaw!" said Hunter in a nettled tone, "I
thought Jack really knew!"

Hunter, some years before, had proved a social
failure; but having developed at a tender age a
marked talent for money-making, he had become

an authority and a power in the stock-exchange.
His self-complacent little soul accepted the situation; and he was accustomed to give out that he
had weighed society in his delicately adjusted
balance and found it wanting. Balls, parties, and
all other innocent devices tending to a reunion of
the two sexes he classed alike in the same category
—they did not pay. A man of business, he argued,
should be steeped in business; he should be ever
ready to grasp even the fleeting leisure moment in
his Midas-clutch and make it golden. But to err is
human, and this amiable philosopher had lately
shown signs of lamentable weakness—a doubt in
or an inability to follow the tenets of his own
creed. Within a few days Elliston had caught
Hunter at the theatre, cheek by jowl with a certain
Miss Jewsbury, heiress and woman of fashion; one
or two other good fellows had also noted the incident, and had agreed that Hunter was displaying
"a tendency" that they saw no harm in discussing
in shady corners under the rose. Elliston, with less
discretion, seemed now about to indulge in open
satire at the stock-broker's expense; for to him at
least Miss Jewsbury's charms were strictly imper-
sonal in their nature; physically she was as unlike
Hunter's portrait of an unknown beauty as any
woman could be.

Hunter, thus fairly caught in a trap of his own
setting, at once turned the talk into another channel
and began a comic story to which Marvin listened
good-humoredly, while Elliston listened not at all.

His mind, on the contrary, was wholly absorbed in
the new phase of Marvin's character now
suddenly revealed to him. Among his friends
Gilbert Marvin had always passed for one who
from sheer apathy of soul would never marry. A
lazy indifference to all but his own comfort, great
composure of manner, and a habit of referring
every doubtful problem to the dictates of his reason
had gained for him the nick-name of "the Stoic."
He was rather proud of the title, and, having a
moderate fortune, some taste for books, with a
strong distaste for hard work, contented himself
with living up to it. He had been five years out
of college; he had been abroad, had studied law
and had even been admitted to the bar; then he had
decided that he would rather not play with a profession. His age was twenty-seven; in figure he
was robust and broad-shouldered; his face was not
remarkably handsome,—blue eyes and a yellow
moustache just saved it from the other extreme,—
but it was a good face; and he was a good, straight-
forward fellow, who had never in all his life known
a sick moment, never, it was said, a moment of
enthusiasm. To Elliston, therefore, the touch of
this man's hand at a critical moment seemed to
amount almost to a confession of weakness. It
was, at any rate, the most spontaneous and confidential advance in their somewhat one-sided friendship that Marvin had ever made. " What does it
mean ? " Elliston thought, while Hunter's rivulet of
humor trickled mildly on to the vanishing point;

" is it only to spite Bobby that I must not breathe
her name? Or is the old boy caught at last?
Upon my soul, I believe so!" And he began to
fit together little bits of corroborative circumstan-
tial evidence, that coincided like the pieces of a
Chinese puzzle. Suddenly Hunter's monotonous
tone was merged in an expressive chuckle, and a
deep-toned growl of amusement from Marvin
warned him that it was time to join in the laugh. It
is easy to counterfeit the hilarity that is born of story-
telling, as all who are not story-tellers well know;
and neither of Elliston's companions had the least
suspicion that he could not have repeated a single
word of Hunter's tale. Yet fearing perhaps that
his sincerity might be called in question, Elliston
now rose nervously, walked toward the nearest
window, and thus gave the signal for breaking up
the party. Mechanically the others followed his
lead, and they went into the house together. The
great dingy smoking-room, so noisy a while ago,
was now deserted. In one corner a group of ill-
assorted chairs marked the scene of the wrangling
debate over the affairs of the nation, that had been
prematurely adjourned *sine die;* the round table
under the reading-light upheld a confused heap of
current literature—journals, reviews, magazines,—
that had been flung at it from all sides; smoke was
everywhere; the walls were discolored by it, the
furniture, rugs, hangings had absorbed it, and it
oppressed the air like an exhalation.

"Ah," said Elliston, "here are the new reviews!"

He was an architect, enthusiastic in his profession as in everything that concerned him at all, and he went at once to the table to consult the latest technical authorities. Marvin following, began to pull over the papers listlessly. Hunter, meanwhile, made his way to a half-open door leading to the library, whence there issued the sound of voices; on the threshold he ran into the arms of a burly fellow, red-haired, red-faced and red-bearded, who came out of the inner room, grinning like a merry-andrew.

" What's up, Doctor?" Hunter asked, as there followed a shout from within.

" Only a new engagement—just out!" replied the tawny medical man, whose name was Dudley.

" Well, speak up man, who is it?"

" Ambrose—lucky devil! I shouldn't have thought it, although—"

" Ambrose engaged!" said Elliston, suddenly throwing down his paper, and advancing. "To whom?"

" Miss Bromfield!"

" Helena Bromfield?" Elliston spoke the name with a sort of gasp. He thought afterward that he would have given a year of his life for a sight of Marvin's face when the announcement was made; for it was this name that had just trembled on his own lips out there in the darkness. He turned, but it was too late; his friend's looks had already regained whatever degree of composure they had lost, and now Marvin joined them, about to speak, if Hunter had not saved him that trouble.

"Don't know her!   Money, isn't there?"

"Rather!" said Dr. Dudley, with an expressive defiance of grammatical laws. "Ask Marvin; he knows the family; or ask Ambrose."

Even as he spoke the library door swung open, and there entered the fortunate suitor, Maitland Ambrose himself, attended by a noisy troop of friends; a man under thirty, tall, muscular, well-proportioned, with a classically outlined face; not a hero's face; not the face of a demi-god, but the earthier, athletic type that has come down to us in statues of the Phidian age.   Low-browed and square-jawed, with thick, black hair, tightly curling and showing here and there a tinge of gray, he was the fighting gladiator in a dress suit—outwardly, no less, no more.   By women he was always called phenomenally handsome, and most men reluctantly admitted that he was so.   Intellectually clever, brilliant even, he had distinguished himself in college and was now the most promising of young lawyers, with a rising reputation that ensured his success in society; all this, to the great delight of his father, a commonplace mercantile man, who had married a superior woman and had grown old prematurely.   This was his only child and his idol; the son's pleasure was the father's first thought; he would have gone without life's necessities himself to give his boy its luxuries.   This homage Maitland accepted as a matter of course, and carried himself at home and abroad with a certain arrogance that had threatened for a time to mar his fortunes. But nothing succeeds like success; criticised, sneered at, Maitland Ambrose may have been, but only with bated breath; his enemies were few, his friends many; and his followers were legion.

Neither Marvin nor Elliston could boast of this man's friendship; yet both knew him intimately. This sentimental paradox is one of the phenomena of American club life. Men cannot sit together an hour or more daily, year in and year out, by twos or threes or fours as chance wills it, without acquiring, little by little, a pretty definite knowledge of each other; particularly when the hours of intercourse are dinner hours and therefore apt to be unguarded ones. *In vino veritas* is a truth worn threadbare every week in a club dining-room, where your neighbor, who is icy over his soup, melts at the *vol-au-vent*, and nibbles his salad with a communicative warmth, of which he will repent upon the morrow, if he remembers that he dined with you. Thus, Ambrose was very well known to these two, who met him pleasantly enough upon occasion in the club-house, but outside of it never exchanged a word with him. They stood somewhat aloof until Hunter had finished his boisterous greeting; then Elliston made Ambrose a civil speech and Marvin silently shook his offered hand; after which they quietly fell back into the outer circle of the group in which the engaged man had now become the central figure.

He threw himself down into an arm-chair with a

serene expression in his face, like that of a martyr
undergoing torment, whose conscious heroism is its
own reward.   The myrmidons at once renewed their
interrupted attack, this time under Hunter's lead.

"Come now, Ambrose," he said, "tell us all
about it.   How did it happen ?"

"Never mind, my dear boy; it can never happen
to you!" was the quick retort, provoking a general
laugh that only acted like a spur in the side of
Hunter's intent and did not discomfit him in the
smallest degree.

"Oh," he said, lightly, "you take a great deal for
granted.   Every dog has his day, and mine will
come.   No woman ever held the same mind above
a week, and you have been engaged—how long?"

> "Souvent femme varie,
> Bien fol qui s'y fie!"

murmured Dr. Dudley, who in the hospitals of
Europe had gained a smattering of many tongues.

"Women are so freaky, don't you know!" continued Hunter, who spoke no language but his
own; "there was one who made sheep's-eyes once
at me, and then—"

"There was Beauty too, Hunter," said Ambrose,
"and her Beast!"

Another laugh greeted this apt allusion, and this
time Hunter looked a little ruffled.   "No, but
seriously, you know," said he, "a girl told me only
the other day, at a party I was decoyed into, that
she hated lobster, and then ate a whole plateful—
three claws too—that another fellow brought her!"

"I know who that was!" piped a squeaking, effeminate voice from the other side of the room.

These unlucky words were received with peals of laughter, during which Hunter turned scarlet, then white, and answered nothing; for it was the voice of little Phil Jewsbury to whose sister's caprices the stock-broker was already accounted a willing slave. When there came a lull Dr. Dudley threw him a crumb of consolation.

"Don't mind Phil," said he. "We made him drink a quart of Barsac at dinner. The very roots of his tongue are loosened!"

Mr. Jewsbury protested that he needed no such apology, and was thereupon admonished by Hunter to "shut up."

"Oh, *I'm* happy, Bob!" was his sarcastic reply.

"Happy!" repeated Ambrose, who felt, perhaps, that his interests were in danger of being slighted. "You'll never be that till you have followed my lead."

"Not then, perhaps," said Dudley. "A happy marriage is like an honest politician—rare!"

"Much you know about it," Ambrose continued. "Poor devils! Not one of you understands what happiness really means."

"Bah!" spoke up a man who sat behind him. "I can tell you."

"Hear! Hear!" was the general shout as Ambrose turned upon the speaker.

"Oh, it's you, Bruni," said he. "Well, you have the floor."

Bruni, as many will remember, was an Italian artist who had drifted over to America in his youth, and had won by hard labor a local reputation; a man just over forty, with great black eyes and a leathery, oval face; he was small and thin, too,—so thin that he looked as if a strong east wind would waft him away; his first wife, of his own nation, had died when she was little more than a girl; his second choice, an American, was still in the bloom of health, yet Bruni passed all his evenings at the club, the very prince of night-owls. He spoke with a slight foreign accent and the right word was often long in coming.

"It is a dream," he said; "a vision, a phantasmagoria, your happiness—always in anticipation, never in possession. You long for, it may be, a ray of light; and your very longing is a prism that refracts it into seven primary colors. Remove the prism, gratify the longing, it is a ray of light—that is all!"

"Cynic!" said Ambrose, with a good-humored smile.

Bruni wheeled his chair forward into the circle. "No, no," he said. "What I tell you is the truth. When I was a boy I toiled ·night and day to see Paris; I went there, and I found it a city of enchantment. I made it my home, and little by little the glamour wore away; nothing can ever bring it back. ·Paris is a city—no more to me than this one. So in everything. You admire a picture. Well, don't buy it. Let it hang on the other fellow's wall—he has forgotten that it is there. Why, the Venus Victrix would have become a block of stone even to Pygmalion— if he had owned her!"

"Pygmalion! Pshaw!" Ambrose returned. "He was one of you artistic chaps that fell in love with his own work, and more fool he. It's not a question of the fine arts, but of lovely woman, who is infinitely variable. *Vide* Dudley, and a better man before him!"

"Ah!" said Bruni. "You have a cricket in your head. What do you call it here? A caprice! You are happy. You think so?"

"Think? I know!"

"Good. You have found your Beatrice,—then possibly some one else has lost her. Good, again. He is the man I envy. He is happier than you."

"Oh, I don't grudge him his happiness," said Ambrose, laughing.

"He's a better man than you, I'll swear," continued Bruni. "He will have a hard pull of it, but he will see it through. He will go home and stir his fire; the smoke will get into his eyes, but he will dream over the embers long after you have forgotten Beatrice. What's a fire to a married man? He never sits over it. His romance has come to the word 'Finis!' He throws down the book and picks up an essay on toleration; for man and wife tolerate each other, as brothers and sisters do."

"And this is Bruni, the *galantuomo!*" said Dr. Dudley, with affected sadness in his tone.

2

"Put him out! Put him out!" said Phil Jewsbury. "Shocking! Married man, too!"

"Yes," replied Bruni, "like any other. We are
all the same—all human."

"Well, Ambrose," said Elliston, "you are done
for—shelved with 'Waverley' and 'Ivanhoe' and
all the old love-stories. Which of us goes next?
That's the question."

"Ask Marvin," said Hunter, while Elliston
mentally cursed his own too ready tongue.

"Ask Hunter," said Marvin, toward whom all
eyes but Elliston's were now directed.

"Oh, mine is an old story," Hunter retorted,
"but yours—"

"Pshaw! Marvin is safe enough," said Elliston,
ill at ease.

"Perfectly! Perfectly!" muttered Bruni, who
was now lying back in his chair and watching
Marvin through his half-closed eyes.

"Don't you believe it!" insisted Hunter. "A
sly dog is Marvin, as I can prove."

He paused thus upon the very threshold of his
tale, hoping, perhaps, for some word of remonstrance to ensure the interest of his hearers. He
looked at Marvin, who neither spoke nor moved.

Ambrose laughed incredulously. "Prove it,
then!" said he.

Elliston for Marvin's sake was now on pins and
needles. He felt that his friend's calmness was for
once assumed, and that Hunter's version of the
encounter in the suburbs was the last thing he

wanted to hear. Moreover, Hunter had already proved sufficiently accurate in his word-painting; what if that portrait of his were to be recognized anew by every man in the room? Decidedly, the vulgar little beggar must not be permitted to go on!

With the evident intention of making the story a long one, Hunter was beginning: "Well, you see, it was only the other day in the country—" and Elliston, in despair, was meditating a wild plunge at his throat, when suddenly Bruni curled up in his chair with a gurgle and a gasp, and then, rigid and unconscious, dropped sidelong into Phil Jewsbury's arms.

Instantly every man started to his feet in alarm. Amid the general confusion, Dr. Dudley, whose bearing at once became comically professional, took charge of the patient and bore him to the nearest sofa, accepting in this the silent aid of Mr. Jewsbury; the latter, apparently stirred to the heart's core, turned pale as death and trembled in every limb.

"Is he dead?" he asked, hovering over the Italian's prostrate form, while the anxious group closed in behind them.

"Dead! No! He has fainted," said the doctor, impatiently, as he loosened the scarf about Bruni's neck. "Get some water, will you? Stand back, here! Give the man a chance to breathe."

Phil Jewsbury made a dash through the door for a great water-cooler that stood in the adjoining room, and the doctor threw up a window with emphasis. As they turned away, Bruni opened one eye with a delighted look at the row of solemn faces now keeping their respectful distance; then he twinkled back into unconsciousness again.

"Here's the water!" shrieked the trusty messenger, reappearing.

"Don't make such a row!" was Dr. Dudley's brutal speech, as he cocked up Bruni's heels in approved fashion. He must have taken the titter of suppressed mirth behind him to be all at Jewsbury's expense, for he went gravely on with the process of resuscitation.

Jewsbury joined the others, and finding a smile on every face was hysterically amused without knowing why.

The doctor wheeled about angrily. "What are you laughing at?" he asked. This was the last straw. A shout arose that fairly shook the room, and Dr. Dudley in amazement saw one man after another distort himself as in a convulsion, and then, reverting to the sofa, there beheld Bruni sitting up in damp disorder, holding both his shrunken sides.

The medical man gave one inarticulate gulp of chagrin, and stalking to the mantel-piece rang the bell violently.

"What will you drink?" he inquired, with due submission.

The waiter entering from the hall, took his list of orders wearily, and crossed the room to go out another way. At the door he recoiled in dismay; for Jewsbury in his emotion had left awry the stopcock of the water-cooler, and the inner room was well-nigh deluged. This exhilarating incident acted upon the mirth like oil upon flame, keeping the company aglow with genial warmth till the return of the waiter with his jingling glasses. A facetious toast in honor of the doctor was then drained in bumpers.

"Only one of Bruni's cursed jokes," he growled in acknowledgment. "I might have guessed it. Holloa! Here's one glass over. Who has left us? Ambrose!"

"On duty!" said Bruni; "and he did not give us time to drink his health."

Marvin rose and buttoned his coat about him. "I must be off, too," said he.

Elliston jumped up. "Are you going home?" he asked. Their eyes met, and Marvin looked at him steadily a moment before he answered.

"No; only up to the card-room. There's a gang at it, I believe. Will anybody come with me?"

Dudley pulled out his watch and pleaded a professional engagement; Hunter and Jewsbury were exchanging stories, each laughing at his own; Elliston made no reply, but Bruni professed himself ready for cards and brandy-and-soda to all infinity.

The two went up stairs slowly, arm-in-arm. Elliston, homeward bound, lingered in the hall, looking after them thoughtfully. "Strange!" he muttered. "He never plays here. Does he think I want to question him? Bruni's fit was curiously apropos. Could he have known?"

II.

" POOR MARVIN ! "

AFTER an hour or two of varying fortune at
the card-table, Marvin yielded his place to
a new-comer, and withdrew with a cheery " good-
night;" hurrying down to the coat-room, where the
hall-boy sat sound asleep at his post, he quietly
took his hat, and left the house. As he crossed the
street he looked up at the lighted windows with a
sigh of relief, and then turned his steps toward his
lodgings, which were near at hand. The night had
grown suddenly cold, and there was a scent of rain
in the air, but he was moving just now in an atmosphere of his own that kept earth's vapors from him.
Mechanically, like one who walks in sleep, he
crossed the familiar threshold and stood in his unlighted rooms. Once there, safe from the hostile
eye of man, he seemed to come to himself, for he
shivered a little, closed the windows, kindled a fire
and stretched out his hands toward the friendly
blaze. As he did this, a smile stole over his face.
" Good fellow, Bruni," he muttered. " Better than
he dreams. Clever speech of his about a fire—it
does comfort a man." Then he struck a light and
looked around him.

22

It was a large square room with a low ceiling that he might almost have touched by raising his hand. The windows were small, deeply recessed and divided into many panes; to reinforce their scanty supply of light the walls had been covered with paper, once a creamy white, now mellowed and dimmed by the " careful and reasonable use " of smoke-emitting lodgers. The furniture, which was Marvin's own, was rather stiffly disposed about the sides of the room, with blank spaces here and there, as if there were not enough of it to go round. An oblong table in the middle, and an arm-chair, warranting bodily comfort by its fair proportions, were the only objects that did not seem adherent to the walls. Under both chair and table the gray carpet, elsewhere of faded gentility, was worn threadbare. Two giant bookcases held an array of noble names in honorable retirement behind their glass doors; other names of lighter import were represented in the little squads of books drawn up, for the time being, in various halting-places about the room. The favorite prints of an earlier generation hung upon the walls, with now and then a foreign photograph, recalling Marvin's few months of European travel; there were foils, too, and wire masks, boxing-gloves and a bit of rusty armor; and over the door leading to his chamber was stretched a strip of black cloth with the legend " G. MARVIN " painted thereon in letters of staring white,—a souvenir of college days. Above the mantel-piece, looking forth upon him from a tarnished frame, were the features of his remote ancestor—Roger Marvin, able advocate and jurist of New England's later colonial time; a rather thin-lipped, austere old fellow of fifty, he seemed, with sharp, black eyes and hair in powder, some of which had shaken down upon his claret-colored coat. In spite of Marvin's blue eyes and of his fuller facial outline, he bore a strong resemblance to this portrait that was not only a treasured heir-loom but also the acknowledged master-piece of a famous hand. It was a picture that arrested atten-tion, and, flashing out like a rich jewel in the plainest of settings, it lent warmth and color to a room that was singularly deficient in the indefinable home-like quality that women always ascribe to "little things." Here, the only little things were ash-receivers—fitting symbols of the place. For every bachelor apartment is a kind of *columbarium*, where he who holds the key deposits day by day the ashes of his heart. And yet, every woman, married or single, when she is graciously admitted to such a retreat invariably waits upon the threshold with a sigh, looks about her and says : " He is too comfortable ! "

Marvin, standing there with his back to the fire and the portrait, was oppressed with a sense of dreariness he had never known before. He bal-anced himself first upon his toes, then upon his heels, humming all the while the airiest of tunes; but it would not do. To pass his counterfeit gayety off upon his neighbors had been easy enough; he found it harder to cheat himself. At last he shrugged his shoulders impatiently, and going to the table, wrote his name with his forefinger in the dust that had settled there; but even this novel pastime failed to distract him, though he repeated it once or twice with an unpleasant sneer upon his face. So he followed his thought where it had flown long before him to an old-fashioned escritoire that stood in a corner near the window. Opening this, he took from it two or three letters around which there hung a delicate perfume like the scent of withered roses; they were all of recent date and in the same handwriting, and seemed alike commonplace in their tenor as he passed them in review. The first was an invitation to dinner, stating merely the day and hour upon which he would be cordially received; the second thanked him for some trifling bit of information. He read these hastily, crumpled them up and flung them into the fire, lingering, however, over the third, which was a little longer than either of the others —but only a very little. It ran as follows:

"TUESDAY, 5TH MAY.

"MY DEAR MR. MARVIN:

"Let our walk be to-morrow if you have nothing better to do—and after I have admired your famous oak trees, will you help me to perform a small act of charity? I have a poor woman to visit in Belmont,—much-dreaded duty, for I am unsympathetic, as you know. May I count upon your escort to bring me through the trial cheerfully? Will you not dine with us, too, upon our return? I am sure that papa will be delighted to see you.

"Always cordially yours,
"HELENA BROMFIELD."

"Always cordially yours!" The words were hardly a week old, and now she was another man's! The pretty, fashionable formula that meant absolutely nothing fairly enraged him, and now for the first time he admitted to himself that he had fallen in love. Hopelessly, too, there was the pity of it. And she had led him on. She had proposed this walk—had arranged it all. This very note was an encouragement; in writing it she had advanced as far as a well-bred woman could to meet him. He remembered his triumphant thought when he received the lines and tried to read between them: "She gives me a chance—she may be mine for the asking!" Well, he had not asked her. And now the whole scene flickered back in the fire there before him. The warm, bright, spring afternoon; the stroll under the linked arms of the great prehistoric oaks just budding into young life again. What a light there was on everything! What a chirping and twittering and scolding went on overhead! And when they stopped and stared about not a feather could be seen. Even the violets seemed to turn pale and shrink from them; but, all at once, two little yellow birds flew out from a stunted cedar and kept fluttering on in front as if to lead the way; and a great robin stood up and peered at them out of the grass as they crossed the noisy little brook on stepping-stones. They laughed and chatted of a thousand things; yet all the while he was saying to himself: "She is mine if I ask her! . Shall I?" Then he was left, pacing up and down

with his cigar, two draggled ducks and a sleepy
white cat for company, before a tumble-down house
by the roadside, while she, on her errand of mercy,
lingered there within; and then it was that selfish
doubts and fears of losing his independence began
to creep into his mind. Was he ready to make his
first thought a life other than his own? Was not
marriage at its best a fearful risk,—a step forward
in the darkness, not to be taken rashly? Why not
wait and think it over? There was time enough.
Was she not all but won already? He *would* wait!
So out upon the road, in the little hollow, where
they were to climb the slope leading through
Waverley meadows to the turnpike, a silence fell
upon them. Who knows? He might even then have
opened his sealed lips and owned himself enslaved,
if up there, close at hand, a certain chestnut horse
with Bob Hunter on his back had not ambled by
upon the highway. He smiled, the prying rascal,
half turning in his saddle; he had seen them.
Truly it was absurd! The stern philosopher, suffi-
cient unto himself, whom man delighted not nor
woman neither, caught gathering nosegays with a
silken nymph in Arcady! Most absurd—unreal!
He could not recognize himself. He would wait
until to-morrow—to-morrow he would come to his
senses, and then—

The log upon the fire parted and the ends fell
smouldering under the andirons. The clock struck
one in the church tower, two streets away; he
went to the window and looked out; there was a

moaning of the wind, and great rain-drops
pattered against the pane. Was it one of these or
a tear that had fallen upon his hand? He had
come to his senses here alone in the night, when
it was too late. Pshaw! No matter! He turned
back to the fire and thrust the open letter into
the coals; the paper changed color and writhed
like a living thing in torment; a yellow flame
flashed up—"always cordially yours"—it was
gone. He laughed; he was happy, he was free;
he knew his own mind now; nothing could ever
change it. And yet—and yet—there was nobody
like her—nobody in all the world. Even Hunter
knew that—had he not seen the "heap of mischief"
in her eyes? Weakness, weakness! He was
tired, no wonder that he yielded to it now;
but he was a man and not a child; he would go
to bed, turn his face to the wall, sleep, and all
would come right in the morning. What speech
was that his favorite hero, the giant Frenchman
of '93, made upon the scaffold? "Danton, no
weakness!" A good word to remember. But yet,
there was nobody like her—nobody, in all the
world.

Down in the street, Bruni, plodding home alone
from his brandy and his card-playing, looked up at
the lighted window, and, forgetting that this was
the man whose lot he had called enviable, shook
his head and sighed: "Poor Marvin!"

And Marvin, sleeping lightly, dreamed that he
was not a man, but a child, gathering star-flowers

in a wide, neglected garden, where a great angel
with snowy wings led him by the hand and pointed
to a shining city, lying beyond the wall, under low-
arching trees, very far away.

III.

THE next morning, which by a swift caprice of the northern spring, came in all smiles and sunshine, a new Marvin, his wit turned the worldly side without, sat at breakfast with the newspaper spread out before him. Like many another honest single gentleman, this one was always reluctant to converse before eating, and he preferred that the first meal of his day should be served in strict seclusion; the cloth was therefore laid in his own apartment over a small round table, near a window. Through this semi-transparent medium the audacious sunbeams now forced their way, treating everything they touched with a kind of disrespect that revealed hidden imperfections and cast mocking shadows where none were before. Even the painted semblance of grim-visaged Roger Marvin did not escape their harlequin trickery; for now and then a nimble sprite of the sun leaped back from some glittering object on the table, to play about the compressed lips as if he would force them to relax a little; but the son of the Puritans was inflexible and smiled not even in seeming.

30

Marvin read the morning news, munching his roll all the while with a good appetite; then, cup in hand, he rose and moved over to the fire-place to drink his coffee standing. There was no fire, but he had a habit of surveying life serenely from the hearth-stone, after the manner of a domestic animal. He stood there now in an attitude of composure; but it was the composure of an actor who has just passed through his first trying situation, and waits, with his face made up, for the next act to begin.

Presto! The curtain was rung up and he looked upon the world again. There came a knock at the door, and Elliston entered with an un-accustomed nervousness of manner that was at once dispelled by his friend's kindly greeting. He who would confide nothing wished the other to think there was nothing to confide; a little warmth, and the light fog of suspicion would clear away.

"Have you breakfasted?" he asked, pointing to the well-furnished table and the vacant chair.

"Hours ago!" said Elliston. "Do you think I have time to 'chew the cud and be silent'? I am deep in business already."

"This, then, I take to be a business visit," said Marvin, finishing his coffee and putting the cup down.

"Strictly," answered Elliston, as he took a chair, leisurely. "Give me a cigarette, please. I have a scheme."

Marvin lighted his friend's cigarette, then his own. "Unfold it," said he.

"Well, my family are settled now in our country place at Winton River Mills,—they went, you know, just before tax-time to circumvent the city fathers—and I am in the throes of a new house that I am building up there for one of the aborigines; he has written me a stormy letter, and his wrath must be appeased. An affair of a day or two under the paternal roof. I am going this morning."

"Well," said Marvin, laughing, "what is it? Can I lend you the money for your fare?"

"Bless you, no, it's not that! But you're looking rather under the weather—Dudley noticed it last night."

This was a blunder; but Marvin was perfect in his part and made no sign.

"Two mistakes in one evening," he said, with another laugh. "Dudley should go West! I am strong as a horse—look at me!" and he pommelled his chest with his clenched right hand.

"A hollow mockery," answered Elliston. "You need change of air. Come up to our shanty with me—there's a train at 10.15."

"Impossible—" Marvin was beginning,—then he suddenly thought, "Why not go, be in the best of spirits, play the part out to the end?" and he suited his words to the thought. "Impossible—at least, by that train!"

"Ah!" said Elliston, who had expected a blunt refusal. "When is there another? Let us see!" and he consulted the newspaper.

But now Marvin hummed and hawed, and had

important business to keep him in town—he who led the most indolent of lives—and did not think he could go, after all. Then Elliston insisted; and so, after some discussion, it was finally arranged that he should postpone his departure, meeting Marvin at the station after a two-hours' interval, during which it was probable that these urgent affairs could be transacted and dismissed forever.

He went away in the merriest of moods, and Marvin smoked a cigar with great deliberation, then gathered up his luggage with care and precision, dawdling about as though he had the day before him; after which, being somewhat pressed for time, he wrote a hurried line to a florist, ordering a handful of his wares to a given address with the card which he enclosed. And this was the important business that required his immediate attention.

Soon they were gliding out together, southward and westward over the ringing rails, across the broad, blue basin, where the river lingers a little to murmur a protest half playful and half plaintive against the encroaching bulwarks of the city, before it suddenly swerves, and is borne with a resistless current under long, low, wooden bridges, by rotting wharves and crumbling warehouses, through the traffic-stained harbor out into the sea. Next, they came to green patches of unreclaimed marsh-land, lying between them and the river-bank; then, to quiet villages and bustling country towns full of dust, small trade and churches; and still the same river, silent now and dwindled to a ribbon of

mottled blue and brown, wound in and out on one
side or the other of the railway. At last, on the
edge of a wood, at a little station, not twenty miles
from town by rail, but more than fifty by boat upon
the river, the train, turning from the main line and
moving slowly, seemed almost to brush its way
through the interlacing branches—then crossed a
rumbling viaduct high up over the stream, and
finally stood still and panted in a little hollow that
lay like a green cup dropped down among the hills.

There were no other passengers left in the train,
which backed noisily away the moment Marvin and
Elliston alighted. The village of Winton River
Mills began with the station where they stood,—then
came the two weather-beaten paper mills whence it
derived its name; beyond these, a broad, shady
street, curving round the base of one of the hills,
soon found itself a country road again; overhead, a
church-porch stood out against the dark pines of
the grave-yard, and the other hills were white with
apple-blossoms. Within these narrow limits lay
the quiet village, that looks to-day much as it did
then, as it has looked for more than thirty years.
For the railway, that disturber of the peace, enters
the little valley, finds it a stupid *impasse* leading
nowhere, retraces its course and goes the way it
came.

A patient horse attached to a weak-jointed wagon
stood in the shadow of the station. The driver,
white-haired and solemn, with a blade of witch-
grass in his mouth, nodded gravely to Elliston as

they took possession of the vehicle, and the horse started off with a jerk as though he had suddenly found a definite aim in life. They were soon rattling upon the wooden bridge over a dam, where a sheet of glassy water gliding quietly down into a brown pool seemed to make undue commotion there; then they turned away from the village street, and drove through a cool, green lane by the riverside. The driver asked Elliston what the weather was in town; and Elliston told Marvin that the hill behind them was called White Knob.

"Yes," said the driver, "from there you can see Mount Monadnock. Haw! up!" These last words in response to a reckless plunge of the horse, while Marvin mentally wondered if there were any hill in Massachusetts without its shadowy Monadnock on the northern horizon.

Both river and village were out of sight when they drew up before an irregular wooden house, low-roofed, with only a clean-cut privet hedge between it and the road.

"This is the place," said Elliston, as they dismissed their conveyance. "You see I did well to call it a shanty; the Governor really must let me put up a decent house here. Now for the tribe!" They passed through the hall and one or two of the lower rooms, meeting everywhere an air of comfort and the "neat disorder" that betokens well-bred women; but none of the tribe were to be seen. At last they roused a somewhat hard-featured maid-servant, who informed "Mister Jack"

that the members of his family were all away and
would not return until dinner-time.

"And Miss Gérard, too, Sarah?" Elliston asked.
Yes, Miss Gérard was with them. He next inquired how the kids were; and Sarah, comprehend-
ing this reference to his two small sisters and
smaller brother, who, with "Mister Jack" and a
boy of twenty away at sea, made up the younger
generation of the Elliston family, replied that all
were well; this, with a sigh, as if it would relieve
her to have one or two of the "kids" laid up with
some mild disease, and then she added:

"And there come a letter from Master Tom this
morning."

"Ah," said Elliston "that's good! Now, then,
Sarah, this is Mr. Marvin. Show him to his room
—the lower one on this floor—and give us no end
of luncheon immediately."

"And who is Miss Gérard?" said Marvin, suddenly, later in the afternoon, when they were driving
back from a pacifying visit to Elliston's simple-
minded patron, who had been slow to grasp what he
called the young architect's "chicken-fixings." "Is
she a regular incumbent, or only a 'casual' like me?"

"Oh," said Elliston, "she holds the office of
Governess Extraordinary in our simple household.
She came to teach the younger ideas how to shoot
their mother tongue and make ducks and drakes of
the multiplication table. My mother petted her—
has made a companion of her; and now we do, all
of us, what fate and Miss Gérard ordain."

"Gérard," repeated Marvin. "That is a French name!"

"Canadian," said Elliston. "Her father was a French *emigré*, I believe; she may be, for aught I know, the daughter of a line of kings. She chose, however, to come to us unheralded, except by a certificate of good character from her last place. We live in a practical age."

"Is she young?" Marvin asked. "Is she pretty?"

"My dear fellow, I have tried to tell you who she is. What she is, you must decide yourself. To pass judgment upon books or women, you know, is dangerous; I do it only, as the man says in Punch, 'as often as I can avoid.'"

"Very fortunate, too, for the books and the women," Marvin replied.

And now, as they drew up before the house again, a woman, in simple dark blue attire that fitted her to perfection, advanced to meet them in the door-way. "Fine figure at all events," said Marvin to himself, noting this in one glance out of the corners of his eyes. Then he was formally presented, and, looking up, received his first impression of Mademoiselle Denise, or, as she was commonly called, Miss Isa Gérard.

"About thirty—yes, all of that!" he mused, as after bidding him welcome she turned to Elliston again. "Brown hair—wishy-washy—might as well be no color at all! Fine eyes,—gray eyes. She is too pale, though, and her lips are thin." Then she smiled, and he thought her decidedly pretty; but there came two odd little wrinkles at the corners of her mouth, and the smile seemed to make her look older after all. " Upon my word, Jack's right!" was his last reflection. " Young or pretty? Hang me if I know!"

She spoke her few commonplace words in a well modulated voice, with a shade of self-consciousness in its expression; of French accent, however, no trace could be detected. Then she moved gracefully away as Mrs. Elliston appeared at the door of the drawing-room. Jack's mother was an impressive person, who had been a beauty in her youth and was handsome still; she was of the world, worldly, and to have money in plenty was the highest aim in life she had ever known. This shallowness of soul betrayed itself continually in her conversation and in her manners; even when she meant to be most cordial she seemed to be thinking of something else. She was delighted now to see Mr. Marvin; it gave her pleasure always to meet her son's friends. How well her boy Jack was looking; his father would be here presently— indeed, it was time for him now—and dinner would be ready in fifteen minutes.

Marvin went to his room and entered the hall again just as Mr. Elliston, the elder, appeared upon the outer threshold. He knew Marvin already and liked him; his greeting, therefore, was of the heartiest. They would keep him for a long visit,—as long as he could endure country life. Ah, Mr. Marvin liked the country! Well, it was refreshing after a busy day in town—but then he was speaking to a man of leisure. Did Mr. Marvin know what it was to have the care of three mill corporations in trying times like these? Enough to fag a man out, eh? Well, he was fagged out,—or would be so, at least, but for this breath of heaven's own air. God made the country and man made the town—present company excepted, man was an ass! His handsome face looked tired and care-worn, Marvin thought; but he was apparently in the best of spirits, with a kind word for everybody, and did not even check the younger children, who were rushing about in the peculiarly frisky mood that overcomes childhood and kittenhood at nightfall. "Ah!" he said, suddenly, "I forgot the letters that I found at the station," and he drew from his pocket a handful of papers, some of which were worn and tumbled. As he turned these over hastily, a letter fluttered down to the floor at his feet; Marvin, being nearest him, stooped to pick it up, and saw that it was addressed to Miss Gérard, who, apparently divining that it was hers, held out her hand with a smile.

"Wait a moment," said Mr. Elliston, before Marvin could deliver the letter, "I want you to make a note of this young woman's admirable business training; how she came by it I can't imagine. Miss Gérard, you must know, has charge of our domestic economy; she is the good fairy who writes our household cheques and pays the bills. Invariably she encloses a stamped envelope, addressed as you see, for the receipt; the trades-

men bless her, so do we; you should see her desk
with its files and pigeon-holes,—method, method to
a fault! Miss Gérard should have been a man."

The subject of this rather doubtful compliment
colored a little as she answered:

"And you expect Mr. Marvin to say he's glad
I'm not one! But he hardly knows me yet."
Marvin had been staring at the envelope, which
was directed in an irregular, scrawling hand.
"See!" she added, "he would like to give me
lessons in penmanship—I am sure of it!"

"No," said Marvin, "I like the hand. There
is character in it."

"Are you trying to read my character?" she
asked. "It will take too long. May I have the
letter, please? That is, if you have fully noted
my admirable method."

"Oh, I beg your pardon—"

"*Merci!*" she said, sweetly, and pocketed the
letter instantly.

"Show me this wonderful desk of yours," continued Marvin.

"They say you are a man of leisure," she
retorted, "it would not interest you."

"You shall see it, never fear," said Mr. Elliston.
"But dinner is ready—let me marshal the clan.
Will you take Mrs. Elliston in?"

The children, save only Miss Annette, a silent
little maid of fifteen, were whisked mysteriously
away to the regions overhead, and they sat down
six at table. The conversation, conducted by the

Ellistons at first with a scrupulous deference to their guest, soon became general and familiar; for Marvin, though he could talk well, was rather prudent in speech at all times; so, having expressed in due course his well-ordered opinions upon the state of the weather, the crisis in European affairs, the negative quality of the morning editorials and the literary merit of the latest novel, he found himself ready to lend a receptive ear to that recital of petty domestic events in which every household indulges and in which every stray bachelor finds a melancholy charm.

" Where have you been all day? " Jack asked of his mother, who was presiding with a languid grace that Marvin thought attractive.

" Paying visits," she replied. " We drove first to West Winton. The new hotel is perfect—Jack built it, you know—" she said in parenthesis to his friend; " the view from the piazza is lovely, and the table excellent, I am told."

" Who on earth has turned up there? " inquired Jack.

" Your uncle tried it for three days, my dear. But we did not find him, after all; he went yesterday."

This eccentric old bachelor, John Musgrave, was half-brother to Mrs. Elliston, and, so to speak, her main-stay. His name was always on her lips, and his opinions, however unsound or antagonistic, were golden ones to her. The reason was simple enough. Mr. Musgrave was single, at sixty, and she

was his nearest relative. He had retired from active
business with a large fortune; that he would retire,
too, at no very distant date, from the shifting scenery
of this work-a-day world, leaving her a handsome
allowance, and his favorite nephew, her son Jack,
the remainder of his vast estate, was an event whose
coming shadow she had schooled herself to contemplate with the utmost serenity. Like the royal
personage referred to in " Macbeth," this sainted
brother "died every day he lived," and was en-
shrined as often in his half-sister's heart. She
knew just what depth of mourning should be
ordered for him, and how long it should be worn.
Many a time, in fancy, she had seated herself with
bowed head and clasped hands to hear the reading
of that last will and testament, with its earnest of
joy, comfort and plenty echoed down the vale of
her declining years. Yet the delight of such an-
ticipations she never admitted, even to herself. We
have turned a ray of magic light deep down into
this good lady's heart, remember; she is not to be
blamed for what we could not see without it.

"The jolly old bird!" said Jack, irreverently
referring to his uncle. "I nodded to him across
the club dining-room, last night."

"Oh, Jack! and he hasn't seen you for a fortnight! You should have spoken to him."

"Yes, but I didn't," he replied. "No matter!
Did he like the hotel?"

"Oh, yes," said Mrs. Elliston. "At least, so far
as one can judge! What did he say about it, Isa?"

"Something about the chutney," replied Miss Gérard, "a new kind, with an unpronounceable name,—I can't think what it was."

"Less photographic than usual," said Mr. Elliston, laughing.

"What?" she asked, innocently.

"Your memory, that's all."

"Oh," she answered, "I have no memory for disagreeable things. I tried chutney once, and disapproved of it."

"Quite the reverse with my uncle," said Jack. "And he stood the hotel three days! Upon the whole I think he liked it. Go on with the afternoon's adventures."

"Well," said Mrs. Elliston, "we found everybody at home. The Whateleys have come—and the Featherings have painted their house a hideous color—a sort of pea-green,—and Mrs. Ambrose kept us to luncheon—and, oh, Jack, do you know that Maitland is engaged?"

"Yes," said Jack, scowling. "Heard of it last night."

"Miss Bromfield is very charming," pursued Mrs. Elliston. "What she saw in that creature, I can't think."

"What he saw in her would be more to the point," said Mr. Elliston. "Many a woman marries a man simply because he asks her."

"Nonsense!" returned his wife, "women do nothing of the kind. If that were true there would be no single men. As to Miss Bromfield, I am

sorry for her; but of course she knows her own
mind.   Maitland is certainly good-looking; they
will make a handsome couple.   Have you met her,
Mr. Marvin ? "

" Miss Bromfield ?   Oh, yes,—often."

" Ah, then it was an inspiration on my part," said
Mrs. Elliston.

" What was ? " asked Jack.

" Mrs. Ambrose said Helena was coming there
to-morrow, so I asked them all to dine here the day
after; and Mr. Marvin and Miss Bromfield are old
friends."

" Oh," said Jack, carelessly, "is that all ? "   And,
dinner being nearly over, he rose and went in
search of his pet cigars.   His father and Miss
Gérard were discussing memory, "the warder of the
brain; " and Mrs. Elliston still harped upon Miss
Bromfield in a confidential aside to Marvin.

" She is so thoroughly a lady," was the key-note
of her spoken praise.   " So obviously an heiress,"
was the sign written on the score within.   " When
she came home from Europe, I said all I could to
make Jack fall in love with her.   Perhaps I said
too much.   I am afraid you have a bad influence
upon Jack—they say you are not a marrying man,
Mr. Marvin.   Don't make an old bachelor of him,
I implore you; one in a family is quite enough.
And when he is married, I hope it may be to just
such a dear, sweet, lovely, refined girl as Helena
Bromfield—a daughter-in-law any mother might
be proud of!   Now, Mr. Marvin, don't you agree

with me? Even your hard heart must have melted
a little; I don't see what you young men are
thinking of!"

"Confound all women!" Marvin thought; and
then aloud, in dulcet tones, he confessed himself
blind, obstinate, prejudiced,—in short, the uncanny
thing his hostess desired him to think he was.

"Now then, mother, when you have done conspiring," said Jack, "here's Marvin aching for a
smoke and too polite to say so."

At this broad hint the ladies withdrew hastily,
and brought the dinner, begun so ceremoniously,
to a lame and impotent conclusion. After one
cigar, Mr. Elliston followed them; the others
smoked on, talking lightly and freely of many
things. Marvin was in capital humor, and he
spoke of Miss Bromfield once or twice with such
an assumption of nonchalance that all Jack's sus-
picions of the night before were put to flight.
"What an ass I made of myself!" he thought.
"There is no disappointment in this case, after all!"
Then he proposed a game of billiards; and after
that and another and a third, they went back to the
drawing-room to find Mrs. Elliston, buried in
shawls and sofa-cushions, dozing over a novelette in
the Revue des Deux Mondes, while Elliston *père*
and Miss Gérard were finishing a game of chess
that had lasted all the evening. In a few moments,
the hostess hoped Mr. Marvin would find his room
comfortable, bade him good-night and glided away.

This little talk so confused Mr. Elliston that his

opponent quietly checkmated him forthwith. " Bless
my soul ! " he cried, drawing out his watch. " Half-
past ten! I had no idea it was so late! Jack,
lock up the house. Good-night, everybody!" and
he was gone.

"And will you light my candle, please ?" said
Miss Gérard.

They went out into the hall, where the candle-
sticks of various designs stood on a little round
table at the foot of the stairs. She chose a silver
lily leaf and blossom, with a curling stem for the
handle and a bud for the extinguisher; but the
candle had never before been lighted, and as she
passed a window on the second landing a puff of the
night wind blew out the spluttering flame. She
gave a little shriek, and Jack went up to the rescue.

" I am so afraid of the dark!" she said, as the
taper was rekindled. The light shone full in her
face, and she looked down at Marvin, smiling and
shivering a little.

"We stand ready to defend you," he responded.

"Just like you men !" she returned. " You are
always ready to do anything—even to turn night
into day!" And she went away laughing, half to
herself, as it seemed.

Jack lighted another candle and led the way to
Marvin's chamber on the ground floor. He satisfied
himself that the room was in order, gave Marvin
the light and turned to go.

"Jack!" said his friend, abruptly. "She *is*
pretty ! "

"Miss Gérard?" said the other. "Yes—perhaps." He had reached the door, but he came back. "Does she remind you of anybody?"

"No," said Marvin, "not that I remember." At that moment a little night-moth fluttered into the flame and fell dead on the candlestick in his hand.

"There!" said Jack; "that is very like her!"

"Oh!" Marvin answered, with a laugh; "she will die harder."

"Yes," said Jack; "I meant the flame. Goodnight." And the door closed behind him.

Now, in the dead of night, there occurred a curious thing resembling a dream, though it certainly was not one. Marvin, without knowing why or how, suddenly found himself wide awake after an interval of forgetfulness, dreamless and profound. He held his breath for a moment, looking and listening with senses sharpened by the darkness as a blind man's are. There was no moon; and, just outside his window, a strip of veranda, overshadowed by a clambering vine, made the gloom of night oppressive. The window was open; the light breeze brought in a faint, soft murmur of the vine-leaves, that was broken all at once by the sound of voices, pitched low, almost to a whisper, but evidently close at hand. Marvin's heart beat violently; a strange numbness stole over him, and for a few seconds he lay there powerless to move. Then, as the thought of a desperate hand to hand struggle with midnight marauders took definite

shape in his mind, he determined to face his disagreeable duty manfully without delay.   He started
up in bed; then waited again, this time in amused
surprise; for one of the disturbing voices was unmistakably a woman's.   And, hark!   Yes, surely,
it was the voice of Miss Gérard.   Not a word could
be distinguished, but, as if to make assurance
double sure, there came again that low, sweet, half-
abstracted laugh of hers, just as he had heard it on
the stairs.   Then silence.   Then the rustling of the
leaves.   He waited and waited, hoping for some
further sound or sign; but there was nothing.   He
rose at last, crossed the room and looked out upon
darkness, night, and the stars,—that was all.   He
lighted a match, consulted his watch, and found
that it was nearly half-past twelve.   " Not so very
late, after all," he said, and so went back to bed and
slept till morning.

Six o'clock, and the sun already high in heaven!
A little brown bird flew down to perch as near the
window as he dared, and proclaim it in a merry
matin song.   To lie in bed another moment Marvin
found impossible; and when he was fairly up and
dressed, there was no staying in-doors apart from
all that fragrant sunshine with no brick-and-mortar
taint in it.   Marvin remembered that he knew
nothing yet of the Elliston domain.   Now was the
very time to explore it.   So he strode out upon the
lawn that stretched away before him to a moss-
grown wall under a row of maples; on one side

was the road and the hedge, with an old mulberry
tree overhanging the house. He waited in the
shade a moment, looking up at the chamber
windows; the nearest one was wide open, and on
its inner ledge stood the silver lily that he had last
seen in Miss Gérard's hand; but now, the candle
was burned low,—so low that the extinguisher upon
it almost touched the socket. "She is afraid of the
dark," he said to himself, laughing. And, suddenly
reminded of his waking dream, "What was she
doing, then, down here in the dark?" he thought;
"Who was with her? Was she here at all?"
He went back to the veranda. A little rustic bench
stood there, pushed back, in an angle of the wall;
but thick dust lay upon it and the dust was undisturbed. He turned away and caught the gleam of
something white—a paper, dropped by chance into
a tangle of the vines. An open letter, in Miss
Gérard's handwriting. Before he was aware of it,
he had read one line: "You do not care an atom
for me if—" What cowardly thing was this that
he was doing? Reading words he had no right
to see. Contemptible! He thrust the letter into
his pocket, blaming, as man will, the innocent cause
of his misdeed. Curse Miss Gérard! He wished
he had never seen her, and went his way.

At the other side of the lawn, hedged in by
dwarf evergreens, was a mound of turf with the
marble figure of a woman poised upon its summit;
a mild and ineffective piece of work, that Marvin
would have taken for a family portrait, but that the

4

young person bore a sickle and a sheaf of grain.
Avoiding the stables that lay just behind the house,
he went on through a bit of old-fashioned garden,
all tulips and pansies and edgings of smooth, shiny
box, coming at length to a garden of Nature's own
tending—a wilderness of long grass, buttercups,
clover, daisies, with here and there a wild geranium,
out before its time. In the midst a gray rock rose
like a mammoth porpoise curling over in a summer
sea. Marvin gained this stony haven after a plunge
through the morning dew, and saw immediately
before him a loop of the inevitable river—so
narrow here that the trees met over it, and the
sluggish water, chameleon-like, had taken the color
of their leaves. He pressed forward through the
clinging underbrush to a narrow path upon the
river's brink. Following this, a few feet up the
stream he discovered a birch-bark canoe, chained
to the trunk of a tree that grew close upon the
water. The very thing for him. But the chain was
securely locked, and there was no paddle. He
knelt down, pulled the canoe in and looked at it
wistfully; then, at the sound of a voice that had
grown to be familiar, he dropped the chain, walked
on rapidly, and at a turn in the path found Miss
Gérard gracefully reclining upon a low wooden
bench, with an open book in her hand. She had
been reading aloud, to herself, apparently—for she
was alone.

"I beg your pardon," he stammered.

"For nothing," she said, hardly changing her

position. "I rejoice to find you are no sluggard. Is it not a lovely morning?"

"You were studying," said Marvin, who had not yet recovered from the small surprise.

"No,—only reading aloud. I always do that when I grapple with a strange tongue. It improves one's accent. I found this in the library. See, it's very light reading." And she handed him the book.

It was a play of Calderon,—"Life's a Dream!" Marvin read the title aloud,—"La Vida Es Sueño!"

"Ah," she said, "you speak Spanish!"

"I have been in Spain," he answered. "I can ask for supper and a night's lodging—that is all."

"You are very accomplished—for a man!" said Miss Gérard. "I shall make use of you. Correct my inflections—they are wrong, I know."

She took the book again, and began to read.

"Hold, enough!" cried Marvin, desperately. "Have pity on my ignorance. This is worse than Greek to me."

"It is of no use, then," she said, laughing. "I have forgotten all I ever knew."

"You have been in Spain," he answered.

"No; there were some Spanish books at the convent where I went to school, and one of the sisters taught me a little. I found this play, and the name attracted me. 'Life's a Dream.' A good subject for a comedy—or a tragedy, either, isn't it?"

"Yes," said Marvin, "I suppose so. I don't care much for the theatre."

" Of course. I said last night there was no poetry
in you !"   She shut the book rather impatiently,
and, rising, took a few steps down the path away
from him.

Marvin laughed. "How women jump at their
conclusions !" said he.

" To be sure they do—and they are right nine
times in ten," she answered, turning on him.   " A
man hesitates and hesitates—takes a step forward or
back, as the case may be, and returns to his stand-
point, after all.   'He who deliberates is lost.'   That
proverb was made for men—the pronoun proves it."

This hit him harder than he liked to admit, so
he at once asserted that she was all wrong.   "And
as for poetry," he went on, " why must it go smirk-
ing about before the foot-lights, plastered with
rouge ?   Am I to be written down a Philistine,
because to canvas and green fire I prefer the real
thing ?   The world may be a stage, but there are
no scenes like this in any theatre."

" This is well enough," she said.   " If you like
it, I can do better for you.   What time is it ? "
Marvin showed her his watch.   " Quarter of seven.
We shall not breakfast for an hour.   Come ! "

They walked back to the canoe; she took a key
from her pocket and told Marvin to unlock the
chain; then she produced the paddle from its
hiding-place under the bank, and, steadying the
frail bark, bade him jump in.

" But you—" he said, hesitating.

" Oh, I must be your pilot. I know the stream,

and there are ugly shallows; besides, I would not trust you with the paddle—I am not sure that you can use one."

"You are very accomplished—for a woman!" Marvin said, laughing, and obeyed. "Where are we going?" he asked as they drifted away.

"There is a great rock at the next turn called 'The Giant's Skull,' and beyond that—" she paused, for they were sweeping now over long grass that seemed to float upon the water, and she was steering very cautiously.

"Beyond that?" repeated Marvin, when all was clear again.

"Beyond that lies the world," she answered.

Then for a few moments they went smoothly on in silence, while Marvin watched the dripping blade of the paddle as it rose and fell quietly under the guidance of her practised hands.

"Admirable!" he said at length. "May I ask where you acquired this uncommon skill?"

"In Canada," said Miss Gérard. "But this is nothing; here there are no rapids. See!" and she turned the canoe toward the opposite shore, where a huge granite boulder lay, half in the water, gray and dark under a forest of young maple leaves.

"Curious!" said Marvin. "I wonder if those seams in it are glacier lines, and if it stood here once on some great pedestal of ice, that slowly dripped away."

"It has a hideous likeness to a skull," said his companion. "Stone is only earth condensed; per-

haps some giant really did carry that for a time
upon his shoulders.   He would have been a man
worth seeing!"

"One with poetry in his soul, I suppose," pursued Marvin, derisively.

"No," she replied; "a man to be afraid of.
There are none now."

"Musset's trouble," said Marvin.   "You are
come too late into a world that is too old.   Give
me time, though.   I'll be as alarming as I can."

"You are growing poetical already," she said,
with a merry little splash of the paddle.   "I see all
this is having its effect upon you."

"Well, I like it," he admitted.   "I am only a
poor fellow of to-day—not a giant of the stone
age."

They were drifting now, in clear, deep water,
along a narrow reach of river toward a wide gap in
the trees upon the left bank.   As they came into the
open sunlight, Miss Gérard, with a swift stroke or
two, brought the canoe close up against the farther
shore under a group of pines.   She sprang out,
and Marvin followed her up a steep slope over
sticks and stones and brambles, till they reached a
little wooden belvedere, roughly built of bark-
covered boughs.   "There!" she said; "I promised
you the world, and it lies before you."

He looked down over a wide, green valley,
broadening away like a great curvilinear triangle
with the horizon line for base.   The river lost itself
in a wooded hill-side, after winding for a mile or

more through pale meadow-lands and freshly
ploughed fields of a rich chocolate color; higher up
along its banks, half-buried in their feathery elm
trees, stood isolated farm-houses, mere spots of red
and white in the landscape; farther on, rose the
roofs and spires of a small inland town; and beyond,
where the falling curtain of blue sky looked worn
and faded, there hung a soft, smoky cloud, under
which, at the river's mouth, lay the city, undis-
cernible.

But this enchanting prospect and the light speech
of his companion seemed to produce upon Marvin
an effect, the reverse of that she had intended. He
stood there scowling, and the longer he looked the
gloomier he became. " If the world were all like
that!" he said at last, in a low tone, unaware perhaps
of its sombreness, until her mocking answer roused
him.

"So!" she said; "you are a man with a
sorrow. Oh, don't deny it! To think that there is
poetry in you, after all! Who is she?"

He was alert enough now. "The question of
Vidocq!" he answered. "Yet Vidocq failed sometimes; and so, it seems, does Miss Gérard. My
sorrow is a poor, commonplace thing,—not even my
own; for it is only the melancholy doubt and wonder
that comes to every man, when he has brushed away
the first bloom of life and has discovered the hard rind
underneath. Doubt of the future! Wonder that
the past should have added his enigma to all the
unsolved riddles of the world!"

She believed, or pretended to believe. "Why was I born?" she said, "Is that all? Then give the riddle up. 'Take the cash, and let the credit go.' The world is what we make óf it ourselves."

"And afterward?"

"Afterward? That is rubbish. There is no afterward. If I die here, I am put into the ground. If I fall into that river, I am swept out to sea,—to-morrow, it may be. No matter! To day is mine—all mine. No one shares in it."

"Every man for himself, and no devil to take the hindmost!" said Marvin. "That seems to be your principle of action. Many of us live by it, perhaps, without saying so. All very well for one, but how about the rest? Do you rule out me—and others?"

"Others!" she said, almost fiercely. "Let others take care of themselves—I have done it—I mean to do it! Who was it that compared mankind to a basket of vipers, each struggling to be uppermost? I am in that basket!"

"At the top?" asked Marvin, lightly.

"No thanks to any one, wherever I may be!" Her harsh, unfeminine tone grated unpleasantly upon Marvin's ear. He shrugged his shoulders and said nothing. Then she added, more softly, "Don't you think we have gone far enough? Let us paddle back in our canoe."

"Not our own," he suggested.

"Yes, mine," she replied, with a little toss of her head in the probable direction of the Elliston abode. "They gave it to me."

" Then you must permit me to be grateful," said Marvin ; " even though gratitude is undreamt of in your philosophy."

She paid no heed to the implied reproof, and, as Marvin insisted upon taking his trick at the helm, her mind had no room now for abstract questions. They retraced their course upon the river, while she supplied him with steering directions and condemned his awkwardness, admitting, however, that the masculine biceps was not without a certain efficacy in stemming a current. So they reached the mooring safely and strolled leisurely up through the grounds, lingering at first, because it was Miss Gérard's daily task to provide a garland for the breakfast table. She would have only wild flowers, she said, and sent Marvin deep into the long, wet grass to pick them. It was not till they were fairly out upon the lawn and in sight of the house, that he remembered her letter carefully stowed away in his pocket.

" By the way," said he, " I have found something —something of yours. Guess what it is ! "

" I am no Yankee," she replied ; " and I have missed nothing ; if the thing is of value, keep it,— at your disposition, as Señor Calderon here would say."

" It is of no value," he rejoined ; " at least, to me. See ! " And he produced the letter.

All the color left her face ; even her lips looked absolutely bloodless.

" Where did you get that ? " she asked ; and the simple question seemed an effort.

" Here—on the lawn, this morning." And he pointed to the very place, down under the veranda in the vines.

She took the letter and turned it slowly over and over, looking hard at the folded page.

" Well ? " she said at last without raising her eyes.

" Well ? " repeated Marvin.

" What is your price, I mean. They say all men have one."

" Price ! For what ? " he asked, hardly able to believe his ears.

" The contents of this and your knowledge of them,—your ignorance of the knowledge."

Marvin drew himself up. " I am no barbarian ! " he said, coldly. " You forget, I am not a man to be afraid of,—nor am I a thief ! "

She looked him full in the face. " You could pick this up and see nothing ! That is hard to believe."

Marvin bit his lip. " No ! " he said. " I saw one line—only one ! But I am none the wiser ; if you have a secret, it is safe."

" On your honor," she asked, " is that true ? "

" Oh," he answered, angrily, " must I swear it ? "

" No," she returned. " I believe you—and I beg your pardon for my rudeness. The letter does contain a secret,—or rather, it alludes to one,—a certain family matter that I could not bear to have known. I wrote it last night. It must have blown down from my window. Please say you forgive me."

Her eyes met his with a gentle, pleading look ;

she held out her hand and Marvin took it, though he only half believed her. "Of course," said he.

"Without malice?" she asked, for his tone was not all that she desired.

"Do you think I am a brute?" was his blunt rejoinder.

"I think I am half afraid of you. Without malice?" she insisted.

"Without malice!" he answered heartily, and they went into the house.

IV.

THE morning Jack and his friend devoted to a
long ramble about the country. A few steps
from the house they plunged into lovely woods,
rich with the native American wildness that all the
jewel-like greenery of England can not match; and
so they might have gone on for hours. But walking without an object Jack thought slow work, and
before long they took to the open fields, scrambled
up the rough side of White Knob, saw Monadnock
and returned by the high road. In the afternoon
came a formal drive with the ladies; and, at dinner-
time, when Mr. Elliston appeared, tired and dusty,
with the look of the town in his face, he held
among his letters one for his guest. Why did Marvin's cheek wear a conscious color when he took it?
To be sure, the handwriting was Miss Bromfield's;
yet it was a mere line, thanking him for his beautiful flowers; rather coldly and distantly worded, he
thought—and, the moment he was alone, tore the
thing to atoms. He rejoiced when a game of whist
—ladies' whist—was proposed in the evening; for
this gave him an opportunity to be distrait without
much fear of discovery. So long as he made no

revoke, his partner could but smilingly defer to his superior skill; and he revoked but once, even then detecting it himself in time. The truth was, he could not forget that he must meet Miss Bromfield on the morrow, and he dreaded this meeting; he felt that he would rather run away; that his lot would be happier, if they might never meet again. But the first was, of course, impossible; the second highly improbable, to say the least. So, after all, he could only lie awake in the dark and curse his luck. Even that resource, too, was soon denied him; for he slept, and this time his sleep was undisturbed.

Day came, the day of the dinner, as he could not help reflecting the moment he awoke. But in that contemplative shaving-time when poets are said to write their best verses and all men's thoughts are purest and freshest, he grappled with himself and took a firm resolve, to wit: that this ill weed, this parasite so lately fastened upon his heart, should be rooted out and should trouble him no more. He could not have the woman; his longing for her was unmanly—the desire of a child for the moon. Twice already he had come dangerously near to setting himself up as a target for criticism— a laughing-stock of fools. Another and severer ordeal awaited him; and this once passed, he could walk unchallenged among his fellow-men. Would not the hidden wound itself begin to heal at the touch of the friendly cauterizing iron? He answered, Yes. And girded his loins for the encounter, hopeful, defiant, strong.

His spirit shone through him at the breakfast table, where he conversed far more freely than was his wont at that hour of the morning. "Such a pity he is not a marrying man," Mrs. Elliston thought. "His manners are most agreeable. I wonder if something can't be done about it." Then she thought of her boy Jack and sighed; then of her impending dinner-party and sighed again. Just at this moment up there came a message from the cook, to the effect that certain indispensable provisions, prime factors in every household, were suddenly ascertained to be "out." Mrs. Elliston held up her hands in dismay. What was to be done? Without the missing quantities no dinner could be given at all,—and this was the eleventh hour !

"It ought to be called the cooks' hour," said Jack, "for they are always out in it."

"Oh, Jack, how can you ! They serve us shamefully in the village,—nothing there is fit to be eaten."

"Now, mother, did you ever see a farce called, 'A Bull in a China Shop ?'"

"Never; and what has that to do with—"

"Everything ! Its hero is one Bagshot. Delightful character ! Ever ready in every emergency with, 'I am here—trust in me—all is not lost !' No family should be without its Bagshot,—in me behold yours !"

"What do you mean ?"

"I say but one word—Waterside."

"Your hotel! To be sure; I never thought of it!"

"Marvin has not been there; we talk of driving that way this very morning. Give me a list in black and white and you are saved."

"I will write the list," said Miss Gérard.

So the soul of Mrs. Elliston was disquieted no longer, and the two men were despatched upon their errand of supply. As they drove into the yard of the Waterside Hotel, Jack was respectfully saluted by a groom who stood at the porch holding a thorough-bred horse that seemed impatient for his rider.

"Ah, Jerry," said Jack, "is that you?"

He had spoken to the horse, who turned his brown eye full upon him, and then graciously wrinkled up his nose for a caress.

"Mr. Musgrave is here, then?" Jack said to the groom.

"Yes, sir; he comes and goes like, as you might say. And Jerry, here, is eating his head off, sir, mostly."

Jack laughed. "What a queer old bird he is! You know him, don't you?" This to Marvin.

"Oh, yes," his friend replied; "by sight; as everybody does." The fact was that at the club he had been honored more than once with an introduction to Mr. Musgrave. But that person of note was always meeting so many people. His circle of acquaintance was filled already, and the young men were coming along so fast. How could he undertake to recognize a new face in the throng until he knew that the effort would be worth his while ?

Forth he came now, grave, stately, yellow and in faultless riding trim; he wore no beard upon his sallow face; his thick hair, a sable silvered, was cut close, affording scanty shelter for his rather large, prominent and decidedly ugly ears; his eyes, large, too, and black and piercing, were set deep under brows regular as lines of charcoal; he was very tall, and his erect figure bore lightly its sixty-years' burden; but two great wrinkles on each side of his nose accentuated that aquiline feature, and his neck was unmistakably old.

He was very fond of Jack, and bade him what was meant for an affectionate good-morning; then he turned a cold, glittering eye upon Marvin, drawing on his glove the while.

"Good morning!" Jack returned. "No sort of notion you were here! Mr. Marvin—my uncle, Mr. Musgrave,"

"Ah!" said the great man, whose bronzed skin and metallic inflexibility gave him an East Indian, heathenish look like an idol's; and without another syllable he graciously deposited two delicate gloved fingers in Marvin's cordially proffered palm.

Marvin was anything but "emotional"; yet his blood tingled when he found that his hand thus grasped a deliberate insult. He felt like doubling up his fist and striking out with it straight from the shoulder; but, of course, he had no thought of doing so. He only turned away and smiled at his own irritation. Meanwhile, the man of millions, if not of manners, springing gracefully into the saddle rode away, only waiting to bid Jack tell his mother that he should join them at dinner that evening. Upon the delivery of this message at the luncheon table the last cloud upon Mrs. Elliston's spirits cleared away.

"Your uncle has come back? How very fortunate! I was in the depths at being caught with a vacant place at table. Mr. Ambrose—old Mr. Ambrose —is called away on business. Just like him—at the last moment! Now your uncle—"

"Will make these odds all even," said Jack. "Good! He is better company than Pa Ambrose."

"Yes; your uncle always exerts himself so at a dinner. Remember, Jack, you are not to live and die a bachelor; but if you must, take your uncle John for a model. He has never grown old." And the good woman seemed to grow young again herself as she spoke the words.

From one or two trifling hints that had been given out, Marvin inferred that the agreeable duty of en-tertaining Miss Bromfield would fall to him in the character of old friend. In his present mood of defiance this was exactly the thing he desired. He donned the world's armor, therefore, when the time came, in his most scrupulous manner, as if he were determined that the sombre garb of society should sit upon a man for once with a festal look. Having allowed a full hour for his warlike

5

preparations, he was early in the field, and found
Mrs. Elliston and her distinguished half-brother
alone in the drawing-room.

"You know Mr. Marvin, I believe," said the
hostess.

"Ah!" was the stately answer, followed up by
the fingers—two fingers—of the morning.

But Marvin stood up like a man, and gave him
two fingers in return; so that Mr. Musgrave's
astonished muscles, avoiding an awkward predicament, involuntarily closed around them with something like a grip.   A quiet passage at arms between
these two that no one else ever dreamed of.   But
the victory lay all with the prentice hand; Mr.
Musgrave never needed another introduction to it.

Speedily now he remembered not only their
meeting in the morning, but also that Jack had
often spoken of his friend, Mr. Marvin.   The new
hotel?   Oh, yes, he liked it; very fairly planned it
was, on the whole; though, of course, Jack had
much to learn.   Some of our best people had taken
rooms there.   Captain Bromfield and his daughter
were to try it in a week or two.   Hers was not a
face that interested him, though she was called a
pretty woman.   But then, her face was not her
fortune.   Shrewd fellow, that Ambrose,—one of
the persistent kind.   Did Mr. Marvin know him?
Slightly, eh?   Well, his grandfather was—

But, here, just as the Ambrose family tree was in
danger of being torn up by the roots, Miss Gérard
appeared in a dress so simple and yet so becoming,

that Marvin, who could not for his life have told whether the material were crape or lawn, fell to studying its effect, and wondering in what its art consisted. She had joined them, and was parrying lightly with a feathered phrase some complimentary rapier-thrust of his companion. Then the room began to fill up, Mr. Musgrave was called away, and Marvin found himself alone with her in the curtained recess of a window, waiting out that awkward ante-prandial moment when the prudent man utters not his good things, but holds them in reserve. Suddenly came a stir at the door, and his heart gave a great bound. Helena Bromfield! There she was, dressed in creamy white, smiling, radiant, lovely,—lovelier even than on that far-off day—a week ago was it, or a year?—under the oaks at Waverley! And Ambrose was a shrewd fellow—one of the persistent kind.

" Mr. Marvin, I believe you can't repeat a single word I have been saying," says Miss Gérard.

True, he cannot, but he does not tell her so. His laughing denial is interrupted by a whisper from his host : " Mr. Marvin, will you take in Miss Bromfield?" He shivers a little as he crosses the room ; it is trying, certainly, to stand before her with one absorbing thought, that spoken would make him a thing of pity. But the first step—the step that costs—is over. Her arm rests lightly upon his, and his secret was never so safe as now. Had he just stifled a man instead of a sentiment his look could hardly be more unconsciously serene.

" It was very thoughtful and kind of you to send me those lovely roses," said · Miss Bromfield, when he had found her chair at the host's left, and they were fairly seated.

"Oh," replied Marvin, with studied carelessness, " blame the florist, not me. He did it." A certain rigidity of manner clung to him always, and she did not observe that it was more marked than usual.

" I thank you all the same," she said, simply. " Maitland was much pleased at your taking the trouble."

" Maitland! Trouble!" growled Marvin to himself, as he glanced across the table where Ambrose was yielding gracefully to the fascination of Miss Gérard and smoothing out meanwhile the petals of a great purple pansy that he wore in his button-hole. " I wonder who gave him that," Marvin thought. Then he turned to Miss Bromfield again.

" I suppose it would be proper to say that I am glad of your engagement," he began.

"Oh, no," she said, "please don't do that. It would be rather like a compliment, and you can't pay compliments gracefully, you know."

" Entirely true," he answered, laughing, "and your apology is accepted. Yes," he added, as he saw by her eyes that she was thinking not of him, but of Ambrose, " he stands fire well, doesn't he ? You should have seen him a night or two ago, at the club."

" Oh, but I heard about it," said Helena, "and

about Signor Bruni, too,—that was just like him,
poor man."

" Poor—why ? "

" Because—" and she hesitated.

" He is married, I know, but—"

" But ! " she repeated. " Is not that misery enough
from your point of view?"

" Much more than enough, but then—"

" Then that is why Signor Bruni is unhappy,"
she said, dismissing the subject and turning away
to Mr. Elliston.

Directly opposite to Helena had established itself
the majestic form of Mrs. Ambrose (Ma Ambrose,
Jack Elliston called her), resplendent in purple
and gold. She was an oppressive and Juno-like
person, who dealt in magnificent commonplaces.
Marvin, left a moment to his own devices, gazed at
her in silent admiration. He had never sat at meat
with a duchess, but he said to himself, so might a
duchess look, so might she comport herself. He did
not know that had opportunity been given her she
would have pinned him into a corner and demanded
to be told his favorite poem. For it was her misfortune to be of a literary turn of mind. Upon her
library table at that very moment lay a little vellum-
covered volume of verse, privately printed upon
india paper, with very wide margins. " Windfalls by
A. A." She was A. A.

" Don't you dote upon a round table ? " cut suddenly in upon Marvin's meditations. He had
entirely forgotten for the moment his left hand

neighbor, Miss Flossie Feathering, a belle of three
seasons back. Mr. Musgrave had brought her in
to dinner, and she had been entertaining him with
her small talk, not too good-natured—never of things
but of people, and chiefly of her dearest friends. In
her defence it should be said that the old pagan had
seemed to the last degree diverted. " Don't you
dote upon a round table?" asked Miss Feathering.
" *I* do—it brings us all out so! Have you been
here long? And have you heard anything about
the Whateleys' garden party?"

" I am not likely to hear of the Whateleys' garden
party," said Marvin, " for I dislike them—garden
parties, I mean."

Miss Feathering looked at him with saucer eyes.
" What a queer man!" she said. " I never could
understand you at all."

" Is it necessary that you should?" he asked.

" Yes," she answered. " I always want to get at
people; I always say everything that comes into
my head, and I want everybody to do the same
for me."

" You had better give me up," said Marvin.

" No, for I think you're very interesting. You're
one of my enigmas—like Signor Bruni."

" Bruni!" said Marvin, who had hardly known
the Italian before that night at the club. " What is
it about Bruni? Why is he unhappy? His pictures
sell; he must be coining money."

" Money! That's all men think about. His
wife makes him perfectly wretched."

"What's the matter with her?" asked Marvin, puzzled.

"She has taken to lecturing," said Miss Feathering, solemnly.

"Oh," said Marvin, "I thought all wives did that."

"You know I meant in public," she replied. "How would you like to have your wife flying about the country and figuring in all the newspapers? Going in for dress reform, too, and writing pamphlets! Odious creature! Is that your idea of love, honor, and obedience?"

Marvin could not answer that it was; but as his reflections upon this important subject seemed to have been somewhat vague, Miss Feathering promptly volunteered the result of her own.

"A man's wife should sit always in the other arm-chair," said she. "Now, don't you agree with me, Mr. Marvin? I am sure yours will never be like Mrs. Thornton Hooker, who always leaves a room, they say, when her husband enters it. Have you heard how she is going on with young Wylie? I hope she's not a dear friend of yours,—"

Her voice sank into a low murmur, like the cooing of a dove. She was not to be shaken off. Marvin listened without committing himself, his eyes fixed the while upon the purple flower Ambrose wore. Suddenly Miss Feathering found her tale tiresome, and changed the subject.

"A delicate touch, isn't it?" she asked, catching the direction of Marvin's eyes.

"What do you mean?"

"Haven't you noticed? See!" And with a look she called his attention to the flowers in Miss Bromfield's dress,—pansies, too, of the same deep purple. Just at that moment Helena looked down, touched one of the curling petals and glanced across the table with a faint smile. "Delicious!" whispered Miss Feathering. "Life is old, but Love is young —so very young! How impossible all that seems, doesn't it, to you and me?"

And Marvin, his glass at his lips, only smiled in answer, while Ambrose with his flower signalled back a tender message and, ostrich-like, thought he had escaped detection.

Curious scraps of conversation were borne in upon Marvin's ear as another vacant moment became his.

"Character," explained Miss Gérard to Ambrose and to Mrs. Elliston, "is the result of experience. There is no heredity—we are slaves of circumstance —all."

"Yes," was Miss Feathering's soothing word to Mr. Musgrave, "woman's sphere is to obey; she should follow, man should take the lead."

"Browning heavy?" exclaimed Mrs. Ambrose to Jack Elliston. "Pray, have you read all his works?"

"No," said Jack, meekly.

"Ah!" returned A. A., the appreciative and the gifted; "I have."

"I know all about Bruni now," said Marvin to Helena, for at his right hand there was a lull.

"Ah," she answered, lightly; "then you are just the person for me. Go and look at my portrait that he is painting. I can't trust papa and Maitland. I want criticism from a remote point—from a friend of calm and judicial mind. Do go, and tell me precisely what you think."

"Excuse me, I would rather not," said Marvin, bluntly.

Helena changed color a little, looked at him curiously and laughed. She was amused and not offended.

"Just like you!" she said. "I might have known you would refuse. But why? It is a trifling service."

"Because friendship and criticism are like oil and water; they will not mix—at least in my organism. If I should fail to like the portrait, as is more than possible, I must either tell you a pack of outrageous lies or admit the truth and give my reasons; thereby, of course, bringing our friendship to a remote point indeed."

She colored again and looked annoyed. "Why?" she asked.

"Because I believe that few men and no women can stand a strong dose of the truth, however thickly it may be sugar-coated—truth dealing with their own qualities, I mean."

"Even admitting this," said Helena, "as I do not, it was only a bit of painted canvas you were asked to consider. There would be no need of personal criticism."

" Ah," replied Marvin, " the portrait is you—you are the portrait! No such work of art is ever destroyed without a special act of Providence. Good, bad or indifferent, it will hang before you all your days and the evil I say of it will live after me. I speak from bitter experience. Long ago, I uttered a harsh word of a certain likeness of one of my relations—a most estimable woman, who called me in as one of the family. I merely said that the picture should be cut out of the frame and burned. But the loathsome thing still hangs in her drawing-room; whenever we meet there, her eyes turn from me to the portrait; her lips move ; she is repeating my honest *dictum ;* and her invitations have grown infrequent to a significant degree."

" Do you think I could be so sensitive—so unforgiving ? " asked Helena, laughing.

" You are a woman," he answered, shrugging his shoulders.

" And you are—a bachelor. You shall not see my portrait now."

" Then that is settled," said Marvin; " we can't quarrel about it. You must forgive me—you who are charitable. We will talk of something else, of your patient—the one we went to see, and whom I did not see."

" In Waverley ? " she asked ; and the color began to steal up into her face a little. But Marvin did not notice it.

" In Waverley," he said, without flinching. " Has she recovered ? "

"Oh yes," replied Miss Bromfield, speaking rather more quickly than usual; " she went back to town a day or two afterward and is hard at work again. A letter from her came to-night just as we were starting. See! They say all women are curious, but I've not opened it."

Marvin took the envelope and saw that it was addressed to Miss Bromfield in a delicate feminine hand.

" Ah! a young woman."

" Yes," said Helena; "I thought I told you— only nineteen."

Marvin handed back the letter with an air of indifference. What possible interest could he have in the writer? She was evidently not a subject for charity; and even were it otherwise, charity he left to older and richer men and to women. Miss Bromfield held the morsel of paper in her hand a moment, looked down at it and sighed.

" You are certainly the least curious of women," Marvin said. "The letter contains an enclosure, and you have kept it a whole hour without breaking the seal."

" I will be honest," she returned, "and confess that I know what the enclosure is. No one is looking; let me show it to you." And tearing open the letter she took from it a small photograph and laid it down upon the table between them.

The likeness was in miniature, half the size, perhaps, of the palm of Marvin's hand. It showed him the face of a young girl, fair-haired, and dark-eyed, apparently, wonderfully pretty at all events. Marvin, looking carelessly down at it, was suddenly interested by a certain sadness in the expression and also by a singular consciousness that he must have seen the face, or one very like it—in a former state, probably, or in some waking dream.

" Who is this ? " he asked.

" Why, the patient ! " said Miss Bromfield. " I knew she would interest you."

" I have seen her somewhere," said Marvin.

" Oh, that's impossible ! She has been here but a short time, and has been ill, too, as you know."

" I have seen her," Marvin repeated.

" Of course you have; I may as well give in at once, for there's no convincing a man. You have seen her." And Helena caught up the photograph quickly, for she had not desired to draw the attention of the table to it, and she observed that Miss Gérard's keen eyes were bent their way.

" Where ? " thought Marvin. " Where ? " And then he asked, as if groping for a clue, " What is her name ? "

" Men are never curious," said Helena. " But I don't mind telling you, if its only to put you down, for the name is one you have never heard. Ruel— Amy Ruel ! She came here with her father from Canada, in search of good luck, poor child—for that is what they need. The father is a man of talent and a hero—a sculptor, struggling for recognition. Could anything be more hopeless? He will do nothing but good, honest work and that, it

appears, is not easily sold. Bruni says his things
are really fine, and that some day he will be famous.
Meanwhile, his daughter has to support herself by
—Ah! What is the matter?"

The matter was, that in some unaccountable
manner a champagne glass had suddenly broken in
Miss Gérard's hand, scattering itself in little, glittering flakes about the table. Around her plate
flowed a small deluge. There was an awkward
moment in which nobody moved, and then one of
the servants came forward to collect the fragments.
Miss Gérard drew back a little, and discovered upon
her hand an ugly cut, from which drops of blood
were just beginning to ooze.

"Oh, Isa!" cried Mrs. Elliston, who saw it at the
same moment.

But Miss Gérard was already on her feet, with
her handkerchief bound about the wound. "It is
nothing," she said; "pray excuse me for a little
moment." She left the room, and Mrs. Elliston
followed her immediately.

"Oh," said Mrs. Ambrose, with a long breath, as
she fanned herself into composure. "It gave me
such a shock. Poor child! How pale she looked!
And so do we all. As for Mr. Musgrave, he is
positively livid."

A faint flush stole up into the great man's cheek
as attention was thus drawn its way. "It was sufficiently startling," he replied. "I can't exactly see
how it happened."

"The glass is very thin," said Jack; "one has

only to press a little—so," and he would have
broken another glass by way of demonstration, if
Mrs. Ambrose had not caught his hand.

"Ah, yes," replied his uncle, absently; "that explains it;" and dismissing the subject, he leaned over
the table, and said: "About saddle-horses, Mr.
Ambrose. Miss Feathering thinks,—" and so, little
by little, the suspended animation of the company
was restored.

In a very few minutes Mrs. Elliston came back,
bringing Miss Gérard with her. To seem absorbed
in each other was clearly the duty of all the
guests save two, and by what might be called a
sleight of mind process, this duty was gracefully
performed. After some time, Marvin ventured to
look across the table, and he observed two things:
that Miss Gérard was still very pale, and that she
wore upon the wounded hand a gray glove that
was a trifle too large for her and that hung about
her wrist in picturesque folds.

"How becoming that glove is!" whispered Miss
Feathering. "I could believe she did all that on
purpose if—"

"If?" repeated Marvin, as she hesitated.

"If I had not been watching her,—take care!"
she exclaimed, as Miss Gérard looked over at them.
"More anon."

They had come to the coffee; a moment later,
Mrs. Elliston gave her signal, and the ladies rose.
Miss Feathering, a little later than the rest, let fall
her fan at Marvin's feet. As he handed it back:

"More anon," she said again, with a meaning look at Miss Gérard's vacant chair. Then she touched her lips with the tip of her fan and rustled away.

"That means envy, I suppose," said Marvin to himself. "The glove was too becoming. All women are alike,—all contemptible."

Ill-natured thought, unworthy of Marvin's stoical philosophy. But he was already in danger of forsaking his sect and turning bitter as Diogenes.

"Strong or mild?" asked Jack, as he passed the cigars; and Marvin took a strong one, and puffed away at it grimly, while the others stretched themselves out in their chairs, and suffered their talk to relax a little like their muscles. Ambrose, after more than a thimbleful of cognac, filled and refilled his wine-glass (fine old twice-round-the-world Madeira it was), and then the talk seemed to turn all his way. Marvin sat watching him through his cloud of smoke with a disgust that deepened as the room grew murky. He was by no means squeamish; but even broad humor, it seemed to him, should have its measure of restraint, and this element Ambrose chose to ignore. What the fellow said was not even witty, and his way of saying it was positively brutal. A gentleman remains a gentleman none the less for a glass more than is good for him; but nothing is more treacherous than veneer; put an unwonted strain upon it, and presto! it is gone in an instant, exposing the sham. Maitland Ambrose seemed to have departed with the ladies, leaving an ugly changeling, with the manners of a stable boy, in his place. "And he is just engaged," Marvin thought. "He's not half good enough for her. She must have been bewitched to fall in love with him. Titania with the ass's head!" Meanwhile, Jack and his uncle either found, or pretended to find, Ambrose diverting. Mr. Musgrave, indeed, was expanding like a tropical plant in a forcing-house; yet another five minutes and he would blossom to the full with geniality. Mr. Elliston, at first, tried to talk Ambrose down; but failing signally in this attempt, he retired with Marvin into the background, so to speak, and at the first favorable moment made a move toward the drawing-room. Thither accordingly they went, to find Miss Gérard posed gracefully at the piano, with her hands wandering in faint, improvised harmony over the keys. She looked up as the door opened, and smiled.

"Miss Gérard wants to prove that she is not disabled," said Mrs. Elliston. "Now we will have the song, my dear."

"Oh, not now," she answered.

"Yes, now," cried all the men at once.

She yielded instantly, with a bewitching little shrug of the shoulders.

"Shall I play the accompaniment?" asked Miss Feathering.

"On no account," she returned, for the moment forgetting to be civil. "Will some one give me a little more light, please? Thank you," she added, as Mr. Musgrave caught up a great, twisted, silver candlestick, and carrying it across the room, set it down before her. He stayed at her side, too, turning over the music and waiting upon her with a stately, old-time elegance.

It was a florid Italian air, with a plaintive refrain,—

> "And will ye come no more, no more?
> O days of yore
> Will ye no more return?"

Her voice was a mezzo-soprano, of not too tender a quality; but she gave the song vigorously, with all the skill, perhaps, that it deserved. Miss Bromfield was then called upon; she had no notes, but would do her best without them; and very simply and very sweetly she did it. Hers was a quaint love-song of old France, one that the great hero-king, Henri of Navarre, is said to have composed for some purpose of his own,—

> "Charmante Gabrielle,
> Percé de mille dards,
> Quand la gloire m'appelle
> À la suite de Mars,—
> Cruelle départie!
> Malheureux jour!
> Que ne suis-je sans vie,
> Ou sans amour?"

Her voice lacked the power of the other, but there was something in its tone that went straight to the heart. The words died away; no one spoke, no one moved, for the music went on softly, falling

6

and rising again like the murmur of a night breeze; and the song, when she resumed it, seemed to come out of the distance like an echo,—

> " Partagez ma couronne,
>   Le prix de ma valeur,
> Je la tiens de Bellone,
>   Tenez la de mon cœur !
> Cruelle départie !
>   Malheureux jour !
> C'est trop peu d'une vie,
>   Pour tant d'amour ! "

" Exquisite !" said Mrs. Ambrose, just touching with her handkerchief the corner of one eye. But for the half-light of the room a tear would surely have glistened there. Then came another moment of silence that to Marvin seemed a small eternity. He was thoroughly uncomfortable now. Why could not she have chosen another song ? The first note of this had conjured up for him a certain dark expanse of rippling water, with a shrouded moon peering out over a clump of chestnut trees, and the call of a nightingale growing fainter in the distance —the lake of Geneva, where he met her for the first time three years ago ; and there, seated in the stern of the boat, while his dripping oars rose and fell, she sung this song under the night and the stars. Had Ambrose ever heard it before, he wondered. He looked at Ambrose, who sat, as it happened, close beside him. The man was half asleep— actually nodding ! Soft music had lent its influence to that of the choice old Madeira and the fine

Havanas; and to these three the fortunate suitor
had succumbed, sinking back into a favoring shadow.
Marvin trod upon his toe considerately if somewhat
savagely, rousing him in time to echo the expressions
of delight over Helena's singing; and just then
Miss Bromfield joined the little group.

Ah! It was all clear enough now. Here was
Maitland Ambrose back again, no more the man of
that after-dinner scene than our Hamlet of last night
is Hamlet to-day in the morning. No wonder she
had fallen in love with this handsome, agreeable
fellow, whose five wits were all on the alert to please
her. But she sent him away with a whispered word
and stopped Marvin, who had tried to go, before he
was fairly out of reach.

" Geneva!" said Marvin, in lieu of applause.

" Yes," she answered. " I thought you would
remember. What an enchanting life we led there!
And how obstinate papa was! He would insist
upon setting off fire-crackers on the fourth of July.
I could do nothing with him that summer."

" But you always had your own way," said Marvin, " in the end."

" In the end? Oh, yes; I always do."

" What woman wills, Heaven wills," Marvin quoted.

" And man should will," she returned; then, as
the others were chattering busily, she drew a little
nearer and said, in a lower tone, " I have discovered
how you came to see my *protégée.*"

" What do you mean?" he asked.

" When I showed you the photograph at dinner

you declared that you had seen her. 'I thought it most unlikely, and I think so still. But now I have the missing clue. What you saw was a resemblance —one of those chance things that come and go in a face unexpectedly. While you were smoking I found it too."

"In whose face?" Marvin inquired.

"Over there—across the room. Do you see?"

"Miss Gérard? It can't be!"

"It can't be—but it is. Look."

Miss Gérard was standing with Miss Feathering at the piano, turning over a heap of music. She looked up suddenly as Helena spoke, and the light from the great candlestick fell full upon her face.

"Upon my word," said Marvin, "there is a likeness. I saw it then. Strange!"

"Yes," said Helena, "it is very strange. A mystery, and I mean to unravel it."

"How?"

"Simply by showing Miss Gérard the photograph, and asking her if the likeness is mere chance or something more."

"Ah!" said Marvin, with a somewhat doubtful intonation. He was really wondering how straight-forward an answer Miss Gérard would give to the question; for he had somehow acquired a vague suspicion of her, dating perhaps from their passage at arms over the letter in the garden.

"But I can't do that now," Helena went on, "and who knows when we shall meet again? You are to be here to-morrow?" she asked, abruptly.

"Yes," he replied, "for a day or two longer."

"Then you shall ask her for me! You will, I am sure. The question can do no harm and may do much good. My poor friends are strangely silent about their affairs, but I am inquisitive because I long to help them. Don't refuse me this favor as you did the other one."

So the little portrait found its way into Marvin's pocket and he, to his own surprise, found himself promising to make the inquiry and report upon it. A moment after he wished he had not yielded. Why could not the women, this one of all others, let him alone? If he had complied with the first request this latter could not have been exacted of him. But at all events he possessed the likeness of the unknown beauty; there was some compensation in that.

Then followed more chatter and more music. Miss Feathering played to the rapturous delight of her hostess an intricate piece of melody, that did infinite credit to her own powers of endurance. Miss Gérard begged off when her turn came and was graciously excused. Then, with Helena once more at the piano, nothing would satisfy Mrs. Ambrose but a second hearing of King Henry's little love song; and again the listeners were hushed into a silence that seemed breathless as the sweet, time-honored music cast its momentary spell upon them.

> "Que ne suis-je sans vie
> Ou sans amour?"

Had the melancholy words fallen directly from

the king's lips they could hardly have been heeded better. And Marvin fairly ground his teeth in gloom. How much longer was this sort of thing to last? Were these people never going? What an ass he had been! What an ass he was! If he could only kick Ambrose straight across the drawing-room and then turn round and kick himself! Pshaw! It was all—

But now, breaking in upon these jovial reflections came a stir in the room and a rustling of garments. The leave-takings at last! Marvin rose to bid good-night in his turn to the departing guests; but intimate friends among the gentle sex have many last words that must be spoken even when they do but part at night to meet again in the morning, and it seemed as if his turn were to be long in coming. So, the room being warm and he somewhat restless, Marvin moved over toward a large French window that stood opportunely open, as it were pointing the way to the veranda. To reach it he was obliged to pass behind the piano, and there in his flight his foot fell upon some soft, yielding object, evidently out of place where it lay. He stooped, fumbled a moment in the dark and picked up three purple pansies tied together with a bit of ribbon. The little love-knot Helena had worn— he knew it instantly. Charming token! She had caressed it at the dinner table! He looked at it now contemptuously, turning it over and over in the candle-light; then he had a quiet laugh all to himself at his own ill-temper. How amusing it all

was! Devilish amusing—yes! And moved by a
strange impulse he put out his hand and held the
flowers a moment in the flame of the candle. The
poor little posy sputtered and shrivelled into
nothing instantly. The guests were still parting
and re-parting: he had his back to them, they
could not see. He laughed again at his own
expense; and here his laugh was echoed in a low
voice close at his elbow. He looked up; just outside in the shadow stood Miss Gérard; it was she
who had opened the window before him to slip out
as he would have done; and his small scene in
dumb show had been going on under her very
eyes! He stood there helpless, confused and
angry while she came back into the room aglow
with mischief.

"What are you doing with the pansies?" she
asked; "don't you know they are Miss Bromfield's?
I shall tell her you have been making a burnt
offering of them—or an *auto-da-fé!* Which?" She
was darting by him, but Marvin made a stride forward and stopped her.

"For Heaven's sake—" he said, in a whisper.

She stood still and played with her closed fan.
"Oh," she murmured. Then she looked at him
gayly. "I was only joking."

"Of course, and I was joking, too!" said Marvin.

"From the moment that it annoys you—" she
went on, dropping prettily into the French idiom.

"It does not annoy me," said he; "let us go on
with the joke; tell her by all means."

" No, it has gone far enough. Good-night," she said to Helena who came toward them. They chatted a moment; the pansies had not been missed and nobody alluded to them. Mrs. Ambrose sounded a warning note in the hall.

"Good-night, Mr. Marvin," said Helena, "remember your promise."

"What promise?" wondered Miss Gérard to herself behind her sweetest of smiles ; and then she stole silently away through the deserted dining-room and so out of the scene. When Marvin looked for her she was gone. Miss Feathering had gone, too, without sharing her morsel of gossip saved up from the dinner-table. Much Marvin cared, though, for that.

He lost no time in making his escape into the friendly gloom of the ground-floor chamber, where his one candle did little more than render darkness visible. He put the light down, and going to the open window threw his left arm up against the casing and leaned his head upon it, looking out at the night. It was black and still—not so very still, though—at a window overhead some one was softly singing. Miss Gérard, of course! She was trying already that refrain of *le grand guerrier:*

> "Que ne suis-je sans vie
> Ou sans amour?"

Sans vie ou sans amour! Marvin caught the words as they fell, and hummed them in his turn, marking the time upon his forehead with the knuckles of his clenched fingers ; he changed his

position, looked down at his open palm and found
it full of ashes—the last shreds of the royal purple!
"Idiot!" he muttered, closing the window with a
slam. "'Go, get some water and wash this filthy
witness from your hand.'"

V.

"THE best laid schemes o' mice an' men," sings the Scottish bard, "gang aft a-gley"; and even fair women, whose will is heaven's will, and should be man's also, get their own way less frequently than one likes to think. "Remember your promise," Helena had said to Marvin, referring, of course, to her whim about the photograph; but this, and the tête-à-tête with Miss Gérard that it involved, were to be set aside indefinitely, for that young person appeared no more below stairs during Marvin's visit. Word of her illness darkened the breakfast hour the morning after the dinner-party; and the depressing effect of her absence clearly demonstrated her importance in the household. Even Jack was gloomy; the entire family seemed to be under a spell, that was not altogether dissipated at the word of the village doctor, who had been promptly summoned, and who had declared that Miss Gérard would be herself again in a day or two. Marvin's spirits fell with the others; why, it would have puzzled him to explain. In Miss Gérard's presence he was alternately attracted and repelled by her; when she was out of sight he

90

missed her. Pondering this, he concluded that she
was interesting merely as a study—a woman to be
afraid of, no doubt; but, then, all women were so.

Two days later he returned to town alone. Jack,
being detained by unforeseen professional difficulties,
in vain tried to detain him too; but he was not the
man to change his plans.

His rooms were stifling; every aperture, in his
absence, had been carefully closed to keep out the
dust, which none the less clothed all things as with
a garment. He stamped about, flinging open doors
and windows; and when it became possible to
breathe, he threw himself down upon the sofa, and
drew toward him a black-and-tan table in Chinese
lacquer, upon which the news of the last few days
had accumulated. The morning paper, it appeared,
had been faithfully delivered; this was a circular,
and that another; here was a tailor's memoran-
dum of "account rendered." He tossed them
all away. Then he found a few words that surprised him.

"MY DEAR MR. MARVIN: I want to see you for a moment or
two about a matter that concerns me deeply? Will you look in
some morning—for breakfast at two bells, sharp? My daughter
is away and we shall be alone.
           "Yours faithfully,
                 "ANDREW BROMFIELD."

What under the sun, now, could this mean?
Why should Helena's father call upon him for
advice at this time—or at any other, for that matter?
He read the note again. Undue solemnity in the

old bird's tone, he thought. "A matter that concerns me deeply," he read once more, and smiled.
Who did not smile at the thought of dear old
Captain Bromfield? Punchinello, they used to call
him in the navy. There was no offence in the
nickname, it was rather a term of endearment,—a
tribute to his rosy visage and his easily awakened
mirth, that drew his nose so very near his chin.
His figure, too! With a hump it would have been
Punch's own. How he shook when he laughed,—
and he was always laughing. Born in the shadow
of New England pine trees, he had stolen out into
the sunshine at a tender age, to go flashing through
existence like a valet in Molière. With a heart as
light as a cork that dances upon the waves, he followed the sea, and followed it literally round about
the world; in time it seamed his cheeks and
whitened his hair, but that was all; it left him
young as ever. Later came two severe trials—the
loss of his wife and the consequent loss of his profession. He felt it incumbent upon him to devote
himself to his child. He had risen to the rank of
captain; he was ambitious; a few years more would
make him commodore,—who knows, admiral, perhaps—but what of that? His duty was plain, and
he could not shirk it. He resigned. It hurt him,
but he never winced. There are some men whose
experience does not make them sad, and Captain
Bromfield was the best in this kind. He had saved
something, had inherited something. Helena would
have her mother's ample fortune—his, too, some

day. They were comfortable. He laughed, spun his yarns, grew red in the face and round as an apple, and was happy.

When Helena had grown to be seventeen it occurred to him that he ought to show her the world. He laughed at the thought. He was only too ready himself to see it over again. They made the grand tour, and in the course of it encountered Marvin at a *table d'hôte* in one of the great Geneva hotels, overlooking the Quai des Pâquis. For two days Marvin and the captain sat side by side at table, smoked their cigars together on the terrace, together saw the Mont Blanc extinguished without exchanging a word. To be sure, they were fellow citizens and had never been introduced; Marvin was not one to make advances, and the captain, jealous of his daughter's affection, saw in every new man under forty the son-in-law he dreaded. But chance conducted thither a third American who knew them both, and who called Marvin lightly in the captain's hearing "the man who would never marry." At the very next meal the old sea watch-dog begged Marvin for the salt and the ice was broken. They became friends, of course. Marvin's dry, unemotional habit of thought, his laziness, his apparent freedom from conceit, pleased the captain immensely; his manners, too, were agreeable; the skeleton of selfishness was there, no doubt, but it was well padded with easy good-nature; his sturdy figure formed a pleasant object for the mariner's sensitive eye to

rest upon; above all, he was *safe !* So they had
their morning leap together into the clear, blue
Rhone, as it swept through the huge swimming-
bath moored in the rapids, and they strolled in
company along the quais to study the lockets in
the jewelers' windows, or to lean upon the parapet
over the swirling water, while the eagles of Geneva
glared at them from their iron cage, and the washer-
women stopped pounding their snowy linen to stare
in wonder at this lounging elegance overhead.   In
the afternoon, there was the ride to Coppet or to
Ferney under the wall of the Jura; and, for the
evening, music in the open air, on Rousseau's little
island, round which the river in the moonlight
swept like a sheet of quicksilver, without a ripple.
And always at morning, noon and night, they had
before them the glistening lake, ever the same, and
ever changing, now dotted with the lateen sails in
vogue upon the sea of Galilee in the first of these
short years we reckon, and now stirred frantically
by the waspish little Villeneuve steamer with its
rich lading of American dusters and English bath-
ing-tubs.   The gate of Gaul.   Through it the
hurrying present seems always to elbow its way on
to oblivion; only the remote past has waited long
enough to be remembered.

Helena, of course, often made a third in these
little expeditions. Marvin, at first, thought her
rather a nuisance, but, becoming used to her presence, soon found it tolerable for a portion of each
day.   Her wilfulness amused him ; so did the skill

with which she always contrived to win her own
way, when her father's opinion differed from hers.
She had a pleasant voice, certainly; she was decidedly pretty; on the whole, a very nice little
girl. He summed her up thus to himself one
morning in the Musée Rath, whither they had
strolled through the crooked streets of the old town.
Among the blackened canvases and staring white-
plaster goddesses his eye found no more agreeable
figure than hers to contemplate. It was their last day
in Geneva. On the next he let them go their way.
He had no thought of changing his own plans.
The acquaintance was a ten days' episode of travel,
nothing more. He found their places in the train,
and saw it whisk away without a pang. But Love's
quiver was an arrow short for all that.

Two arrows, in fact! Why else did Helena's eye-
sight grow dim as they drew out of the dark station
into the glare of noonday? Not in tribute to the
sunlight surely! Nor to the slope of the Mont-
Salève, nor to the gilded spires of the Chapelle
Russe, nor to the memories of Calvin and Jean-
Jacques, sad as it was to leave all these behind.
Why else, later on at night, when her father had
fallen asleep in his corner of the coupé, did she
remain awake and cry her eyes out nearly, never
breathing to herself the reason? Ah, Love is a
sad dog, with sly tricks and manners under that
bandage of his, and it may be that the single gentlemen are right when they say that the less one has
to do with him the better.

The brain records some trivial thing, turns the leaf and we think its record is effaced; but years afterward it stands out, freshly written, with an importance that is unaccountable. To Marvin, now, that moment in the Musée Rath came back as clearly as though it were a mote in the dusty beam of sunlight streaming through his window-pane. "On the whole, a very nice little girl." He was standing under a bas-relief—Pradier's master-piece; he had forgotten the subject, but he remembered distinctly the place, his attitude and hers—even their sharply defined shadows on the polished floor. And all because to-day he had received this scrap of paper— this, that he was folding over and over and over in his hands! He dropped it, and pulled out his watch absently. He had been there an hour. An hour in the Musée Rath—deplorable waste of time!

The visit must be paid, of course, and the sooner the better. Up the next morning long before the appointed nautical hour, he was soon tempted out into the streets that looked at this time of day strangely unlike themselves. It might have been a Dutch town, with such a persistent washing of sidewalks and scrubbing of door-posts everywhere going on in it; and not a familiar face was to be seen. By a somewhat indirect course he made his way to that quiet walk along the bank of the river where the city "shows a fair Venetian side;" the water was smooth as glass, and a mile away toward the farther shore a wheezy little tug was towing in a schooner round which there circled a flock of hungry gulls.

Close in under the wall, almost at his feet, came by a solitary oarsman taking his morning pull up the river in the lightest and sharpest of shells. Man and boat were gone in an instant, and Marvin pursued his way undisturbed along the rough and dusty road that in those days was known only to morose single gentlemen and to lovers. So, almost before he knew it, he found himself in one of the shady suburbs, three miles at the least from his breakfast, and with an appetite as keen as any gull's. He wheeled about and walked in briskly by another road, which brought him at last into the double avenue—Boston's Champs Elysées in little— reclaimed from marsh-land and river-bed not so very long ago. Here he crossed into the park and came down under the elms and lindens that were fragrant with their fresh green leaves. The trees grow larger and thicker as one enters the older part of the avenue, and it was where their shade is deepest that Marvin saw approaching him a familiar figure—one that of late had hovered persistently about him like an evil spirit,—none other than that of Maitland Ambrose himself! Ambrose saw him, too, and hesitated for an instant, as if he wished to avoid a meeting ; then he came striding on with coat-collar turned up about his throat, though the morning was anything but cold. Marvin, as Othello to Iago, "looked down towards his feet" and saw, not a cloven hoof, but trousers that could only belong to a suit of sables ; and he gave himself no anxiety about the other's health.

7

" Good morning," said Ambrose. He evidently wished to stop, so Marvin came to a halt and saluted him.

"Up rather early, aren't you?" Ambrose continued.

" Yes ; and you ? "

"Oh, I—" Ambrose glanced at his own costume uneasily and tucked away the end of his white cravat that had revealed itself inopportunely. The man does not live who can be unconscious of a dress suit at eight in the morning.

" And you ? " repeated Marvin, icily, with a quiet enjoyment of his confusion.

" The fact is, you know," Ambrose answered, "that I've been up all night—in town for a kind of lark, just the tip end of the wing of one—a little supper, cards, *et cetera,* don't you see; a bit of a bird with the boys."

"I'll take your word for it," said Marvin, moving off, "don't mind me." As has been before remarked, despite his ancestry, he was no Puritan; but he could not help reflecting that the man was but just engaged, and this meeting jarred upon him most unpleasantly.

"Hold up!" said Ambrose, catching him by the sleeve. "You needn't happen to mention it, that's all. I telegraphed home that I was detained to work up a case—Addison *vs.* Coes. Do you see?"

" Clearly."

" *Verb. sap.* then," said Ambrose, releasing him.

"*Pax vobiscum!*" replied Marvin; and they parted.

Where now were blue sky and morning sunshine? Marvin shivered and saw them no more;
he saw only with eyes that looked a little space
before him into the future a vision of the woman
he loved married to the man that had just left him;
one growing daily coarse, indifferent, brutal; the
other, unhappy and prematurely old, chafing under
the yoke but for the world's sake seeming to enjoy
it. Not a pleasant composition, this, to stand in a
vista of arching elm trees. But it is a group that
has been reproduced often enough in all cities the
world over.

"She will be wretched in a month," said Marvin
to himself. "What is to be done about it?" What,
indeed?

Captain Bromfield's house stood in one of the
older streets of the fashionable quarter. It had a
sunny look of welcome in its white porch and
shining door-knobs that were kept always in man-
of-war order. The snow-drops and crocuses in his
little front grass-plot were invariably the first to
come up in the spring; but this may have been
merely a bit of good luck. Marvin was shown at
once through the drawing-room into a queer little
box of a place behind it called the captain's cabin;
here was a table set for breakfast upon which the
well-trained servant immediately laid a second
cover. The room seemed certainly not large
enough to swing a cat in and had an odor of
the sea. It contained a barometer, chronometer
and sextant, with other denotements of a sailor.

The inkstand was a coil of rope; the mantel-clock a capstan and the thermometer an anchor; all three in French gilt appropriately inscribed from brother-officers. Presently the clock struck nine, and in a moment all the other clocks in the house had taken it up. Then there came a tramping upon the stairs and the captain burst into the room. He greeted Marvin very warmly; then he drew back and passed his hand rapidly over the back of his head in a way that was peculiar to him when he was the least bit annoyed or excited.

"That clock is fast," he said; "I was sure of it." And he set it back a full minute. "There, that's better—you've not been here long?"

"No," said Marvin, "three minutes, thirty-five seconds, accurately speaking."

"Good," replied the captain, "accuracy—nothing like it. At sea it means salvation." And he rang the bell for breakfast.

During the meal he made no allusion to his letter, but it was evident that something weighed upon his mind. He showed more than his usual nervousness, leaving the table now and then to adjust a window-shade or to look at the thermometer, and always with the queer application of his hand to his head that seemed to have a soothing tendency. When they had finished and the table had been whisked out of the way by his orders, he produced cigars, and buttoning his coat about him put both hands in his pockets and began to pace up and down as though he were on the quarter-deck.

This was a favorite habit, to which Marvin was well accustomed. Presently he stood still and sighed.

"I want some information," he began, looking at Marvin sharply, "and you are one of the few men whom I would ask for it. My daughter——"

He paused as if waiting for some sign from the other. But Marvin did not move a muscle. He had half expected that this was coming.

"My daughter is engaged to a man whom I have hardly seen. I hope he is a good fellow—she says he is. Tell me what you think of him." He resumed his walk, and without waiting for an answer went on:

"You are about his age and better able to judge him than if you were an older man. Between ourselves, I don't like his looks; but I should perhaps say the same of any son-in-law; I hoped to die without one. What do you think of him?"

"I hardly know the man," said Marvin.

"You meet him very often at your club."

"Yes, there and nowhere else."

"Well, then, what does your club think of him?"

"They call him there a rattling good fellow."

"Come," said the captain, "that's encouraging." He strode off through the door down the entire length of the drawing-room and came back with an expression of relief upon his face. He was not a club man, and he did not know exactly what "a rattling good fellow" meant, but it sounded well. Moreover, he was in that state of mind that makes one glad to put the best construction upon what he hears.

"Easily out of it," thought Marvin; "it can do no good to tell him my opinion. The thing has gone too far; and I am prejudiced; my judgment is worth nothing." Thus do we juggle with our consciences and persuade ourselves that what is, is not, when it proves convenient to have it so.

"I am very much obliged to you," said the captain. "You have cheered me up immensely. 'A good fellow,'—if I thought he were not—"

Here Marvin caught at a straw.

"In that case," he said, "what would you do?"

"Do? Turn the fellow out of doors, of course. The engagement should be broken at once."

Marvin shook his head, but said nothing.

"What do you mean?" the captain asked.

"I fear that would only make matters worse," Marvin answered.

"Worse? How worse?"

"My opinion is worthless," protested Marvin.

"That may or may not be. I want it."

"I only mean that to oppose the match seems to me the surest way to bring it about. Violent measures might make a Romeo and Juliet affair of it. If he's a bad fellow give her a little time and she may find it out. There are some women that won't be driven and—"

"Miss Helena is one of them!" he was on the point of saying, but the captain stopped him with a sharp whistle.

"Upon my word, Marvin," he said, "you seem to have worked this out pretty well already."

Marvin bit his lip. " By no means," he said; "it is a very hasty judgment—a bachelor's, too."

" Some bachelors have long heads," returned the captain. " It is very odd ; I came to the same conclusion. I have not dared to speak to her. But the man makes me shiver. Who knows what his motives may be ? He has nothing, and she—but then he's a rattling good fellow ! "

" Let us hope so," said Marvin. " At any rate, to wait is best. But I must apologize for giving you advice."

The captain laid his hand tenderly upon Marvin's shoulder.

" My dear boy," he said, " you have made me forget the difference in our ages. I like you. If you had been the man—"

Poor Marvin ! He shook himself free and made no answer.

" But let me pay you back," continued the captain; " advice for advice. Take none of these burdens upon you. You are contented, and married life is full of care. Never marry ! "

" Thanks," said Marvin, " I shall remember."

Then they smoked and talked of other things. The captain's genial spirits came back, and he spun a yarn in his best vein. Then Marvin thought it time to go. His host followed him to the door, and solemnly repeated his word of advice; and again Marvin said, " I shall remember."

The very next day it was that Helena's visit at Winton came to an end, and she returned to town.

Her father had not expected her so soon, and it chanced that they did not meet till late in the day, when Helena, coming in from a walk, stole into the little cabin on tiptoe, in the dusk, flung her arms about his neck and kissed him before he knew that she was there.

"Why, papa," she said, " you have been crying!"

"No, Ellie, darling," he answered. "Look out for my cigar—you drove the smoke into my eyes."

"Oh, poor papa!" she said, and kissed away another of those unbidden tears.

"Sit down by me, Ellie, and tell me about your visit. Was it a pleasant one?"

She knelt at his side, and put her head upon his knee, as though she were still a child. She was very fond of him; but she did not dream how fond he was of her.

"Yes, papa, a delightful visit; only Maitland just now is very busy. He had to stay in town and sit up all night over a horrid lawsuit. I can't bear to have him work so hard."

Her father's hand had fallen lightly upon her hair with a caressing motion; but now the movement stopped. She noticed it at once.

"And that reminds me, papa, that Maitland has taken a strange fancy into his head. He thinks that you don't like him. What do you suppose he means?"

"My dear, you must remember that I hardly know him —"

"But you like him, don't you, papa?"

"And you must remember, too, that he is taking you away from me." He saw that she had lifted her head and was looking at him with a grieved expression, and he went on hurriedly, " But that was to be expected, of course. I will do my very best to like him, darling. Marvin tells me he is a capital fellow."

" Mr. Marvin?" Helena spoke the name very coldly.

" Yes, he breakfasted with me yesterday. You see he did you a good turn."

" I am extremely obliged to him."

" Thank you for nothing, I suppose you mean ; it sounds like it. What has Marvin been doing ? I thought you were good friends."

" So we are ; but he is worse than ever. He is horribly selfish."

" All men are selfish, Ellie, I am afraid."

" All—except one ! "

" Oh, yes, of course, every goose thinks her gander is a swan !"

" Oh, papa, then there are two unselfish men, for I meant you." And she leaned over and kissed him once more.

He held her hand a moment without speaking ; then he said, softly, " I am very selfish ; I want you all to myself."

" Do you, papa, really and truly ?"

" At my worst, yes—at my best, I only want to be sure that you are happy."

She gave a laugh like the merry note of a bird.

" Oh, if that's all ! " she said, in a tone that was an echo of the laugh.

" You are happy—very happy ? "

" Very happy! Sleep in peace, as the Frenchmen say."

" I will, darling," he answered, lightly; " but after dinner. Ring the bell, dear, it is time." And while she crossed the room, he sighed.

VI.

MOTHS OF A FEATHER.

JACK ELLISTON, in telling Marvin that professional anxiety must keep him a little longer
in the country, told the truth, but with a mental
reservation. Who is there that will not, at times,
hold back something from his dearest friend? The
builders worried Jack; but not half so much as did
another affair that lay nearer his heart. In this he
felt that there was a crisis coming; and it was really
to round that turning-point that he stayed on at
Winton watching for a favorable moment. The
moment came, and it passed with marvelous swift-
ness. Like an untrained swimmer, he had shivered
an endless time upon the brink to find the plunge a
matter of a second only.

It was one of the last days in May—warm as a
summer day; and it was the day of Miss Gérard's
recovery. Jack had been busy all the afternoon with
his mechanics, and, tired and hungry, he had taken
the shortest cut toward home, through the fields; the
sun beat down upon him fiercely for fully half the
way; then he came into the woods that skirted the
river, and finding the shade refreshing, he strolled
leisurely along the bank, switching off the leaves to

the right and left of him with his stick, absently, as
one that has a weight upon his mind. Suddenly,
at a turn in the path, he came to a stand-still, with
a low whistle. There, a few yards in front of him,
was Miss Gérard, in search of wild flowers, as it
seemed, for she carried a small basket upon her
arm, and as he stopped, she knelt down to brush
away the leaves. Dressed in the becoming suit of
dark blue that she wore so often, she made now the
prettiest of pictures, as Jack could not help remark-
ing. Yet he hesitated for a moment and seemed
half-inclined to turn back; then he went on and
joined her.

"Oh," she said, "is that you? See! Isn't that
moss lovely? I wish I had some of it."

He plunged off into the woods and came back
with a handful of the gray shroud that covered the
dead fir at which she had pointed.

"You oughtn't to be here," he said. "It is too
damp in the woods for an invalid."

She laughed. "Oh, I am reckless. It is pleasant
to be out again. And so Mr. Marvin is gone," she
said, putting the moss tenderly away in her basket.

"Yes. He stayed longer than I dreamed he
would. You know he does not care for the
country."

"Nor for anything else very much, does he?"
asked Miss Gérard. Jack shrugged his shoulders.
"Pray what does he do with himself?" she continued.

"He is an ornament to our leisure class," said

Jack. "Then he has his property to look after—
he is fairly well off, you know—"

"I see," said Miss Gérard.

"Then, too, he is a bit of a philosopher—"

"Philosopher!" she exclaimed, indignantly. "A
selfish old woman-hater, I should call him."

"I don't think it," said Jack. "He is not so
very old, and he may be caught yet. He will be!"
he added, with conviction.

"Some women are such fools!" said Miss Gérard.

"He's a good fellow," Jack replied. And then it
was Miss Gérard's turn to shrug her shoulders and
be silent.

They walked on, and the silence continued till it
became awkward. It seemed to Jack as if nature
were holding its breath to listen for the next word.
The house was hardly a mile away, but they might
have been walking in a primeval forest; the sunshine was intermittent, the underbrush was dense
and almost impenetrable on either side of the
narrow woodland path they followed. It led them
now back again to the river, and through the
branches Jack caught a glimpse of the canoe at its
mooring some distance down the stream. They
were nearing home then. His pace slackened
involuntarily.

"A penny for your thoughts," said Miss Gérard.

"You shall have them for nothing," he answered.
"They are, perhaps, worth less than that."

"Oh, indeed," said Miss Gérard. "I advise you
then to keep them to yourself."

Jack looked at her intently. "Do you say so because you have guessed my thoughts already?" he asked.

"Pray how should I know of what you are thinking?" she returned, in a tone of indifference that chilled him; but he had gone too far now to retreat.

"You ought to know—you ought to understand. There are some things that explain themselves without words. Haven't I been following you about like a dog for the last three months? Why? Because I love you! That's the whole story, and if you haven't guessed it the fault is not mine."

"I am very sorry," said Miss Gérard. She had not changed color, and there was no tenderness now in her voice.

"Sorry!" repeated Jack.

"I like you very much—" she continued.

"Stop!" he said. "You needn't go on. You want to tell me that you will always be my friend. That's no answer for a man who would die for you, or sell his soul for you. You do not care a button for me—say it if you mean it."

"It is very unfortunate," she replied with the respect that Jack's earnestness commanded, "but I have no other answer to give. It is all a dreadful mistake. I did not mean to encourage you—"

"No," said Jack, "no more does the flame mean to encourage the moth. But somehow he gets into it and burns his wings. The more fool he. The more fool I for loving you more than ever at this moment. Imbecility is incurable."

"No," said Miss Gérard, "it may be cured—it must be."

"How?"

"By putting out the light; it misleads—it blinds you. You do not know me at all. I am the most selfish, the least amiable of creatures. I should make you the worst of wives. See how fortunate it is that I do not care for you—in—in that way."

"No," replied Jack, resolutely; "it won't do. I am not to be cured so. You must let me go on hoping against hope that some time—"

"For not another moment," she answered, almost angrily; "you force me to be unkind rather than unjust. I do not love you; I cannot love you. What you ask is impossible; to continue to talk of this is equally so."

They went on in silence, with steps that had quickened nervously. Presently they came to a little clearing where the path took another turn; at a point very near the river-bank under an old oak tree was a wooden bench—the same upon which Marvin had discovered Miss Gérard in his early morning stroll. She went up to it now and threw her basket down there.

Jack took another step and stood still in the path before her. "Is this your final word?" he asked.

"Yes," she said, "except to beg you to be reasonable and not ridiculous—or you will drive me away."

"I am a fool," he replied, "but not fool enough for that. I give you my word not to annoy you in any way. Shake hands and forget."

She took his hand. "Very good," she said, quietly,—" friends."

He gave a little gesture of disgust. "No, not friendship! Indifference is better—much better!" said he.

She did not even look at him. "I am tired," she said, seating herself in a graceful attitude of mild fatigue. "I shall wait here and rest a little. Please go on; I'll come presently."

"Good-bye, then," said Jack, gloomily; and turning he strode down the path alone.

"Till dinner!" she called after him, in tones that were provokingly cheerful. She watched him pass out of sight behind a great white pine tree, and gave a little sigh of relief when he was gone. "It is a pity!" she said; "I did not believe he would do it." And she laughed a little at the remembrance of Jack's woe-begone face. "But he will recover," she added, drawing out her watch, "and I sent him away none too soon—that is, if—"

The sound of approaching footsteps interrupted her meditations. She listened as if to assure herself that the intrusion was not to be dreaded; then as the step drew nearer along the path behind her, she shook out the folds of her dress a little, caught up the tiny basket and busied her hands with it, deliberately making a picture of herself. A good one, it must be confessed. So thought Mr. Musgrave, for it was he whose solemn presence now looked down upon her. He was faultlessly dressed for an afternoon stroll and carried a huge white umbrella; no doubt he, too, had taken that short cut across the fields.

"Ah!" he said in his usual expansive way. Miss Gérard did not seem awed in the smallest degree.

"I thought you were not coming," she said, "you did not write." And she made room for him upon the bench.

He sat down and looked at her with admiration in his eyes. The tables were turned; it was the idol now that worshipped—and the girl evidently knew her power over him.

"I could not write," he said; "I had not the means—not a single cover left for hidden fire!" And he laughed at the little joke that he had made his own.

"These, you mean," she returned, drawing from the basket a little package of envelopes and handing them to him. They bore her own address in her own hand, like the one that Mr. Elliston had let fall the day of Marvin's arrival. "You may use them all if you choose—but I shall write no more letters to you."

"Ah—and why?"

"Because you lost the last one—dropped it upon the lawn in plain sight; do you remember the night you rode by in the dark and stopped under my window? Fortunately, it was I who found it in the morning!" she added, unblushingly.

8

"It is your own fault. You make me go about at midnight like a thief. If you would let the world know, instead of persisting in this strange, unconventional whim of yours——"

"It is not a whim at all! If you let them know, if you call it an engagement, I shall have no peace until you have married me—I think we shall never be married."

"Absurd! Who is to prevent——"

"Everybody. The whole family would turn against me. Your sister would drive me out of doors. She would find a way to break it off. She would tell you it is a *mésalliance*. She would tell you lies—lies!"

Mr. Musgrave straightened himself up. "You forget," he said; "it is of my sister you are speaking."

"I can't help it; why will you make me wretched? She is sure to hate me always for this. You cannot pretend not to know that."

Mr. Musgrave ploughed up the ground with the tip of his umbrella. "And if she does," he asked, "what will it matter?"

"Not a sou, when we are married. Oh, I shall like it! But before—no! It is too much—you must not ask it of me."

She laid her hand upon his gently. He shook it off. "Can't you trust me?" she asked, very softly; and when she put the hand back he did not resist again. In a moment he spoke and his voice trembled a little.

" Well," he said, " you will have it so. There must be a private marriage—a scandal—a damnable story for the newspapers ! "

" It will be forgotten in a week," she replied. " What is it to a man in your position ? You can laugh at the scandal, and I shall not disgrace you. You are not going to be ashamed of me."

" When are we to be married ? " was his answer. " What is the matter ? " he asked, for she had withdrawn her hand, and looked at him now with an air of displeasure.

" I do not like to have you yield in that way. ' When are we to be married ? '—as though it were the drawing of a tooth, or any other bitterly disagreeable thing. If you really loved me —"

" But I agree to anything ! " he protested. " Is not that enough ? You don't expect me to make a nine days' wonder of myself and like it, do you ? "

" I see we shall never understand each other," said Miss Gérard in a tone of the deepest melancholy.

But Mr. Musgrave declared that his one desire was to please her in all things, and that he was ready to kneel then and there on the damp ground at her feet, if she chose to exact that proof of his devotion. So, little by little, she allowed herself to be pacified, and then their talk took a practical turn. It was agreed that they should be married privately some time in the course of the month following ; that the marriage should be published at the time, and that after the honeymoon they should return to town and receive their friends. "Every one will be away," said Mr. Musgrave; "it will make less talk at mid-summer than at any other season."

"Precisely," said Miss Gérard, though she realized the fallacy perfectly well. The one thing that could not be determined was the positive date of the wedding. Mr. Musgrave had important business calling him from home that must be settled first; all would depend upon that; but to the scheme, and to the irregular manner of it, he gave his consent; indeed, it was clear that he had come there for no other purpose.

Thus this strange pair of lovers talked and trifled as the shadows lengthened round them, until Miss Gérard suddenly realized that the daylight was almost gone.

"It is very late," she said, springing up. "They will think I am lost."

He caught her by the hand, and drawing her to him, held her in his arms and kissed her. She submitted to his caress without returning it, and it left her pale and cold. "*L'un baise et l'autre tend la joue,*" says the bitter French proverb. One gives the love, and one receives it! Had Mr. Musgrave been other than he was, he must have doubted her at that moment. But self-esteem, like a subtle narcotic, had long dulled his senses, and he wore now Love's thickest blinder. He loved her, that was enough.

He stood still, watching her as she hurried away, and he longed to be young again. At the pine tree,

where the path turned off into the woods, she looked
back and threw him a kiss with the sweetest grace
imaginable. He had waited, hoping she would do
it. The night dews were upon him; he shivered a
little, drew on his gloves, rolled up his umbrella, and
went his own solemn way.

One star gleamed in the pale sky when Miss
Gérard came out of the thicket upon the farther
edge of the lawn, and she recalled a line of poetry
that in turn reminded her of Jack's reproaches.

" ' The desire of the moth for the star,' " she said.
" The star shines no brighter for it, and I am like
the star. All the moths in the world could not make
me happy. But if there were a man who loved me
—whom I loved—*Bêtises* ! I might as well hope
for Heaven !"

VII.

THERE is a certain noisy thoroughfare that, starting at one of the sunniest spots in Boston, follows the river shore for a mile or so, and finally loses itself in a *terra incognita* of wharves, coalsheds and freight-houses ; as in some man's life we see a fair beginning with nothing meaner nor poorer than the end. Undoubtedly, this should have been a fine street ; trees were planted in it ; it has handsome houses still. But it threw open a level course across the city for the teamster and his laboring horses ; all his heaviest loads were naturally drawn that way. Then the horse-car, that symbol of progress, was invented to come tinkling and clattering through it at all times, seasonable and unseasonable ; till now hardly an hour of the day or night passes when a tired soul may find peace there. Distracting noise has driven out the old inhabitants ; and within their gates has sprung up an unpleasant fungous growth of stables and bar-rooms ; or the butcher and baker throw open the shutters of the basement, while overhead swarms of single gentlemen set up their household gods as bees store honey, each in his own little cell. English travelers often say that Boston reminds them of London ; and this street, certainly, does bear a faint resemblance to a dull and commonplace side of London—the London of Baker Street, for instance, or the Edgeware Road. The ugliness is there, and only the fog and the soot are wanting.

Like other and better bits of London are the queer little nooks that lie between all this restlessness and the river. Quaint, irregular, quiet places, that bear to Charles Street something of the relation that the Adelphi Terrace does to the Strand ; except that these picturesque spots in Boston lie very near the fashionable quarter, and are rebuilt year by year with splendid modern houses. Where this has been done, good taste has left them something of their picturesqueness; and they still have to be discovered, no stranger knows them; their repose is truly grateful, and the wind and the water are their only disturbing elements ; for sometimes in winter the river breaks over stone wall and iron railing and whitens the pavement with its salt spray.

Prowling about one day in search of the unattainable, Bruni found in one of these by-ways an old wooden house that had escaped the destroyer's hand. It stood very near the river and had a north window with plenty of unreflected light. Sagely keeping his own counsel, he went and hired it at a low rent for a term of years. When the lease was signed in duplicate, he put one copy of it in his pocket and invited his wife to look at the premises; and when she had been dragged up the rickety

stairs to his much-coveted north window he quietly
asked her how she would like to live there. She
informed him that the place was "a rattle-trap!"
Thereupon there was a scene. Bruni dramatically
produced the lease, and his weaker half, with that
splendid, pure, north light streaming over her,
all but had a fit of hysterics. Bruni bore her away
dissolved in tears, that did not move him in the
least. He remained brutal almost to laughter, firm
and unrelenting. In the end, of course, he gained
his point, with certain concessions that were inevitable from the first. The objectionable staircase
was given a new turn; partitions were pulled down
and put up; the house was repainted within and
without in colors of Mrs. Bruni's own choosing.
Even the shingled roof had a coat of what Bruni
called "a soft green." So that by the time the house
was ready, "she of the strong mind" (thus Bruni
designated his wife among his cronies) had grown
almost cheerful about it. "It is the shopping," he
said, with a chuckle, "a day's shopping—real shopping, where things must be 'matched' and bar-
gained for—will bring a smile to the face of the
saddest American woman."

The bloom of novelty worn off, the house became
like any other house to Mrs. Bruni. As soon as
there was nothing more to buy for it, she resumed
her wonted round of lectures and committee meet-
ings. She had no children, and Bruni was certainly trying at times. What more natural, her
friends asked, than that she should identify herself

with the cause of Woman? Her reappearance at their solemn councils was hailed with delight; especially as she now came out with all the strength of her New England nature in favor of Dress Reform. In an anonymous paper on "Vestured Vanities" she denounced the corset, and maintained that no thought should be taken of the morrow, and that the garb of her sex should be sad-colored and angular, of one severe and formal cut, unto the end of time. Above all, the garment of the future, the despair of tyrannous tradesmen, must "hang from the shoulder." "Hard upon those that are sloping," Bruni suggested, and was silenced with a look. But with that delightful inconsequence which is not the least of woman's charms, Mrs. Bruni, in her own dress, still followed perilously close upon the prevailing fashion. She was not a plain woman, and it may be that she feared to make herself conspicuous ere the new day had dawned.

So, in that quiet corner by the river wall, it was a house that the north light flooded—not a home. But Bruni was Italian, and the true meaning of the latter word was unknown to him. Though his wife grew daily more and more like the invisible Madame Benoiton in the French comedy, he made no direct remonstrance; he shut himself up in the studio that was wife and child to him, and when there was no light left he locked the door and went off to his club, more a bachelor than the bachelors themselves. Fortunately for an artist, his work, with the brush at least, must stop at sundown.

Of course this unconventional order of things made the household fair game for the gossips. Mrs. Bruni's friends (chiefly women—men rarely liked her) shook their heads and said that Cesare Bruni neglected his wife shamefully. Other watchful and kindly persons asserted that the fault lay all with her. While a third faction stood always ready to maintain that no fault whatever existed upon either side, and that Casa Bruni was an Eden-bower of bliss. However it may have been, Bruni, inconsistent, unpractical and selfish as he often was, had a personal charm that attracted even those who disapproved of him. He was not a true Bohemian; he preferred high life; but he went anywhere, was welcome everywhere; men, women, children and dogs liked him.

The studio was more a work-shop than a museum. Bruni had always been too poor to collect rare tapestries and antique gems. But it was by no means a barrack-room. One wall was well covered with the work of various hands—sketches, studies and finished pictures of brother-artists. Another vast space was masked by the ivy that grew over it from a great jar in a corner. The slip from which this splendid leafy screen had sprung brought tears to Bruni's eyes when he first looked upon it, merely because it came from Tuscany, and his birthplace was Arezzo. Like him, it had been transplanted, and had gained and lost something in the process. He pruned and trained it tenderly, and its living green delighted his heart. Near by, quite in shadow, hung a faint pencil drawing yellow with age. No one ever spoke of it, perhaps no one ever noticed it at all ; it had little merit as a work of art, but was merely Bruni's portrait of his first wife, who had been dead and buried over there in Tuscany so many years.

Into this gentle atmosphere, so unlike the nipping one of Boston that most of us know, came Helena Bromfield two or three times a week to pose for the portrait of which she had told Marvin in an unguarded moment. A little maid tripped in behind her, silently arranging Helena's dress in the ante-chamber, and as silently stowing herself away afterward in a remote part of the studio, where she worked demurely upon something woollen with long wooden needles. Sometimes the captain or Ambrose would look in for a moment, glance at the unfinished picture critically, with an ill-considered suggestion, and go away again. Of these visits Bruni had come to have a nervous dread that was very unusual in him. The fact was, that he found Helena a difficult subject. Either her best expression was desperately hard to catch, or he had blundered fatally to begin with in attempting to paint her half in shadow. Exactly what was wrong he could not tell. So he painted in and painted out ; one day the likeness would seem to him nearly perfect, and the next the face would look insipid as any in an antiquated " Book of Beauty." Then, groaning in spirit he would smilingly declare the sitting ended, and gnash his teeth in despair the moment Helena had gone. This was invariably the case when Ambrose had

been with them.   He did not like Ambrose.   "Why
is it?" he would ask himself.   "What earthly reason
is there?"   Then his eyes would wander away to a
canvas that stood on the floor in a corner with its
face to the wall, and he would smile sadly and leave
the question without an answer.

And now one afternoon he walked away from his
easel with an air of weariness, and threw his palette
and brushes down.

"That will do," he said to her almost savagely.
It was with himself that he was angry.

Helena stepped down from the little platform
surprised and pleased.   The hour had seemed very
short.

"Do you mean that it is finished?" she asked,
drawing away into the proper light, and looking
askance at the picture with half-closed eyes.

"By no means!   We have only done for to-day."

Helena went up to the easel.   "Tell me," she said
presently, "do you work at this when I am not
here?"

Bruni laughed.   "Why?" he asked.

"Because it never looks to me twice the same —"

"Are you dissatisfied?"

"Oh, no—no indeed.   Pray don't think that!"

"I know," said Bruni, "it is like the web of
Penelope—an endless task.   Perhaps it would be
better to end it so!"   And he caught up his palette-
knife.

"Oh, no!" she said, coming between him and the
picture.   "Is all my time to be wasted?"

"Ah, we will try again with better luck."

"And give up the day like cowards? No! We will finish this, or I will never sit to you again."

Bruni shrugged his shoulders, and tossed the knife away. The little maid rose and detached herself from her clinging mass of sky-blue worsted.

"How beautiful that ivy is!" said Helena, by way of changing the subject. She walked over to the wall and touched the vine overhead. "What splendid shining leaves! May I have one—just one?"

She stood with her arm outstretched against the dark-green background, and turned toward him smiling. "What a pose that would have been!" he said to himself. Then aloud: "Oh, as many as you please!"

She picked two leaves by mistake, and one of them fluttered down to the floor. A draught of air caught it and carried it into the corner, where there was a canvas leaning with its face to the wall.

"What's this?" asked Helena, as she stooped for the leaf.

"That?" said Bruni. "That?" he repeated in a queer, embarrassed tone. "What do you mean?"

"Why, this!" she replied, putting her hand upon the picture. "May I see?" Then, as he did not answer immediately, she looked at him sharply, and added, with a little toss of her head, "Oh, a mystery!" But she did not withdraw her hand.

"Not a bit of it," said he; "the picture is unfinished, that's all—but I shall be glad to show it to you."

So he wheeled up an easel to fasten the canvas upon it. And, this done, he trundled the picture about the studio, carefully keeping it turned away from Helena until he could be sure of just the light he wanted. "It needs a frame—I have none large enough," he said; "but there—you can see it now."

She crossed the room and stood beside him with her back to the great north window. The picture was of a landscape—one thrice familiar to her—and the first look was enough to make her wish that she had been less hasty or that Bruni had been more disobliging. In the foreground rose a splendid oak tree, gnarled and twisted and old; like that famous one in the forest of Arden,

> "Whose antique root peeps out
> Upon the brook that brawls along this wood."

There, too, the brook swept away in shadow, foaming first round some huge stepping-stones over which two figures seemed passing with uncertain feet. In the background was a wide, green meadow, full of sunshine; and away to the right another oak, with another and still another beyond. It would have passed for a finished picture but for the figures which were hardly indicated.

This charming subject was certainly the very last one that Helena had expected to see. She felt her cheeks burn, and she could not help fearing that Bruni was a very deep person and that he had tried to startle her. She dared not meet his eye;

she could not run away; she must say something,
she knew. To wander from the truth a little—a
very little—seemed best. A mistake that an older
woman would not have made.

"Lovely!" she stammered; "what trees are
those?"

"The Waverley Oaks," said Bruni simply. "I
thought you knew them."

"Oh, of course," she replied, repentant and more
and more disturbed. "Now I see!"

"Spring-time!" said Bruni, apparently absorbed
in the picture. "An old subject—overdone enormously—but I want to try it once. The figures
trouble me. Shall I make a shepherd and a shepherdess—shall they wear colonial dress, or shall
they be quite modern—of our day?"

"Shepherd and shepherdess," said Helena, gain-
ing courage. "After all," she thought, "how
should he know I ever crossed that brook?"

"I knew you would say that!" Bruni answered,
"but I want to do the impossible—to paint the
lovers—of course they are lovers—of the nine-
teenth century, yet with nothing commonplace
about them. Do you see? As if they had strayed
away into Arcadia and grown suddenly poetical."

"For half an hour," said Helena, bending forward
to look more closely at the picture. There was a
queer dimness in her eyes. The light was very trying.

"Oh," said Bruni, carelessly, "ten minutes!
Long enough to catch them there!"

He started at his own words. He had not meant

to say exactly that.   There was a moment of silence; then Helena beckoned to the maid who brought her cloak; and, as she put it on, Miss Bromfield said:

"I would paint the figures out if I were you.   I think they spoil it."

"But then—my idea?   What becomes of it?"

"I don't know.   It is your problem, after all, and not mine.   I can't advise you.   Good-bye!" And she was gone, with the maid following, like a pet dog, at her heels.

Bruni, left alone, thrust his hands deep into his pockets and stood staring at nothing like a caged owl.   "Who knows most, believes least," he said, oracularly, "and it's no affair of mine.   But knowing so much I wish I knew a little more."   Then he paced up and down the room, scratching his head and knitting his brows.   Finally he stopped again before the picture.   "There, just there!" he thought, laying his finger emphatically upon the stepping-stones.   "Now I wonder if he really made her an offer in Arcadia that day.   Who can tell? But I know he loves her, and it was well done to cut that little pig short in his story the other night. Why, in the names of all the saints did she look so strangely just now?   Ah, she has taken the wrong man—there are times when any girl will do that. And now it is too late.   Ambrose!   Bah!"   Thereupon, he bustled about the studio, setting it to rights in an angry fashion that gave a kind of Latin accentuation to a dislike that was entirely unwarrantable, since Ambrose had never hurt a hair of his head. But he liked Marvin; and, lying under the shadow of the oak on that memorable afternoon in Waverley, he had drawn his own discreet conclusions, and had settled the match in his own mind to his entire satisfaction. There was a warm spot that would betray itself now and then in Bruni's heart, though he tried to think it was all dust and ashes. He had been born for the joys of domestic life and they had been denied him. He railed against marriage; yet could he have married Marvin and Miss Bromfield, by main force, on the spot, nothing for the moment would have pleased him better.

He put away the landscape and the portrait, too, over the latter shaking his head sombrely. As he went down the stairs he looked in at the open door of his little drawing-room. Perhaps he hoped to find his wife, but she was not there. In the hall hung a porcelain tablet, upon which he read, scrawled in pencil, "Educational Tea at seven." "Of course!" he said, with a shrug of the shoulders; then he lighted a cigarette, and strolled off toward the club, where, upon reflection, it seemed best to him to dine; and there, dining alone, was Marvin, who, though he liked to sit apart, now threw down his newspaper and joined Bruni unbidden. And Bruni joked and laughed, and his white teeth glistened, and his leathern cheek was all in wrinkles. Then, over the coffee and the cognac he begged Marvin to smoke a cigar in his studio. So this he did two or three times over, and they sat together in the dark at a deeply-recessed window, that was always screened off in the daytime, through which they now looked out upon the wide blackness of the river and the rows of light shining into it from the distant bridges. And Mrs. Bruni never disturbed them even for a moment; and Bruni told of his early life: how he had fought for Italian liberty; how he had been wounded and imprisoned, and had seen Mazzini once, and Garibaldi. Then he would burst out with some bit of his own philosophy, startling in its extravagance, and would end by laughing himself at his too advanced ideas. And, now and then, his mind would dwell for a moment upon Marvin's love affair, and he would wonder if Marvin had any remote suspicion of the sympathy that was latent in him. He did not mention the Waverley Oaks; nor did he offer to show Miss Bromfield's portrait; nor did Marvin, for his part, ask to see it, though he must have remembered that it was there.

But when the time came for breaking up, there was a very friendly note in Marvin's voice, as he thanked Bruni for his hospitality. The grip of his hand, too, was warmer than it need have been for a couple of dried tobacco leaves. " He knows,—he knows," said Bruni to himself, locking the hall door behind his guest. " There is a time to crack jokes and a time to keep silence,—but he would rather die than tell me so. That's because he is American. But I don't want his thanks. No! It is enough that he knows and is grateful."

VIII.

FACES IN THE CROWD.

IT was just at this time that Surbiton, the favorite actor, died suddenly, leaving a widow and one small child. with hardly a dollar in the world. For the moment the city talked of nothing else. The poor fellow, after a struggle for existence, just as the future seemed to promise everything, was knocked senseless by a falling scene at rehearsal, and never spoke again. Exeunt Touchstone and Falstaff, Goldfinch, Ollapod, and all the rest, to be seen no more! The great actor has his years of toil, his intoxicating triumph surpassing any that the poet or the painter knows ; and when all is said and done, he leaves but the faintest of scores on the world's calendar. Already we begin to wonder if Garrick had mastered the rudiments of his calling. Who knows if Talma in our time would have been counted really great ? And as for poor Tom Surbiton, who thinks of him now ?

But for a few hours he was sincerely mourned. The great public spoke his name, sighed, and was sorry. Verses were made in his honor, his obituary notices were half a column long. It is a pity that we never say our kindest things about a man until after he is dead and gone. Here was one whose heart would have been far lighter could he have foreseen that his dear public, often indifferent and chilling, would not only heap laurels upon his grave, but would even consider it a duty to bestir itself in behalf of his family. He had his successes, it is true, but nothing in his life like the memorial benefit that brought his widow in what seemed to her a fortune ; and indeed it was a very pretty sum for those days. The whole affair, from first to last, was all that Surbiton himself could have desired. Many good actors offered their services—it was late in the season, and their engagements were over— and professed themselves ready to play anything from *Hamlet* to the *Second Grave Digger* for his sake. The play finally chosen was " The Tempest ;" it had been revived within the year, and the scenery needed no preparation. As for the cast, it beggared all description of the gentlemen who write the hand-bills and posters. They printed the list without comment, and in uniform type down to the very sprites and mariners. What an array of noble names it was! And the next day the blue-faced monkey of a circus blotted it out. Take comfort, ye obscure ones that write for the stage and act upon it, only to miss the mark! Nothing is so soon forgotten as theatrical failure—nothing except theatrical success.

They made of it what is called a morning per-formance, because it occurs always in the afternoon. " You must go," said little Hunter to Marvin one night at the club, "all the crust will be there!"

And Marvin thereupon perversely decided to stay
away. But when the time came, he thought better
of it, and at vast expense procured a seat—a very
poor one, remote from the stage. When the curtain
fell upon the first act, Hunter's speech recurred to
him. " Let me see which of us are crust !" he said
to himself, and struggled out of his seat to survey
the house. The theatre was very full; and there
was an unwonted hum and bustle about it, as if
every one were saying to his neighbor: " We are
safe, these are our friends." Marvin found a vacant
place near the stage, and looked about him. All
the world was there, undoubtedly. It was not long
before he discovered Hunter, with a yellow rose in
his button-hole, whispering amiably in the ear of a
chalky and angular young woman, in whom Marvin
recognized Miss Jewsbury; but he looked another
way when he found that Miss Bromfield and her
lover sat directly behind them. Far away on the
other side of the house Captain Bromfield had discreetly placed himself, alone. And directly opposite, leaning against the wall, stood Jack Elliston.

Marvin was at once reminded that he had not
seen Jack for days; not since his return from the
country, in fact. He would go round through the
lobby and join him. He pushed open the little
door at his side, took one more look at the crowded
theatre, and then—

The door swung back into its place, that was all.
He did not go. And why?

Merely because, for the past few seconds, some

one down there in the crowd had been trying an
experiment which needs nothing more than a pair
of sharp eyes.   These should be fixed upon a face
in a crowd—a distant face, the farther away the
better, so long as the eyes in it are discernible.   In
a few moments, more or less, as the case may be,
those eyes will turn to meet yours, if it is you who
make the experiment.   It will be a coincidence, or
it will be due to magnetic influence, according to
your faith in the occult sciences, or otherwise.   Try
it the next time you are at the play, and decide the
question for yourself.

No thought of this problem crossed Marvin's
mind when he let go the door.   He saw that the
eyes were fixed on him, that there was recognition
in them, that they were the eyes of Miss Gérard.
She was alone; there was a vacant place beside
her; she sat but a few rows in front of Miss Bromfield.   All these things he saw too in a flash.
Which one of them made it seem his duty to pay
his respects to her ?   Who shall say ?   It is by no
means certain that he could have answered that
question himself.

Miss Gérard knew perfectly well that he would
come; yet when he appeared she affected a pleased
surprise, and at once moved into the vacant place,
begging him to take hers.   As he did so, he
chanced to catch Miss Bromfield's eye for an
instant, and he observed that she was watching him.
But one cannot bow and smirk across a crowded
theatre.   She made no sign ; and he seemed not to

see her, but began at once to smile upon his neighbor with an air of mingled devotion and contentment, as if this place at her side were the only one on earth he had ever coveted. And Miss Gérard was radiant.

"Are you alone?" he asked, when they had compared notes about the play.

"Oh, yes," she replied. "This seat was for Annette; but she is ill, and so I came alone. I hope you are not sorry."

"Quite the reverse. This is a great piece of good luck."

"Then stay and keep me company. That is, unless you leave better company behind."

"No; I had only my own thoughts."

"And they are dangerous, I am sure. You will stay?" she asked.

"With pleasure," answered Marvin. And then the bell tinkled, the great drop scene rattled up out of sight, and the second act began.

Meanwhile, as has been said already, this little scene had not passed unnoticed. Two of the spectators, in fact, had been so absorbed in it as to find stage illusion for the time impossible; Prospero's enchanted island might have been Nova Zembla, for aught they knew or cared. Jack Elliston still leaned against the wall, twisting and pulling his moustache, while his blood rose to fever heat, and his face contracted with a vicious scowl. All through the first act he had been watching Miss Gérard with a hopeless longing, that yet carried with it a vague kind of comfort. Suddenly Marvin stepped in between them—by a preconcerted plan, too, for of course that vacant seat was his. This conclusion was natural enough, for Jack had returned to town the day after his discomfiture; and since then he had passed most of his time in repeating Miss Gérard's crushing words. They were signs that pointed all one way. She loved another man. Well, here the man was! Marvin! Marvin, whom he had fancied a blighted being—whom he had treated with tender consideration. Now all was clear. Marvin's delight in the country; his fondness for early morning walks; his curious questions about Miss Gérard; these latter, mere subterfuges, of course; no doubt he had known her for years. So, as "jealousy shapes faults that are not," Jack went on from one suspicion to another, and began inwardly to accuse Marvin of treachery, and to call him viper and various other hard names. What were Ariel and Caliban to him? The stage thunder roared and rumbled, but he hardly heard it.

Upon Helena Bromfield almost at the same moment a sudden chill had fallen. From the brightest sunshine to the deepest shadow is always but a step. And even that step need not be taken. Wait, and the shadow will surely come. Out of her father's anxiety a vague fear had grown to haunt her. What was it? She would not permit herself to think. She put the question out of her mind. But in Bruni's studio it came again in clearer shape and she was forced to answer it. Was she, indeed, making a mistake to be repented bitterly in after years? No! She assured herself with tears in her eyes. No! She repeated bravely in the watches of the night, and once more the ghost was laid. To-day she sat beside the man whom she had promised to love, whom, as she tried to think, she could love better than any other in the world. And before her eyes there passed another man who turned his back upon her to smile upon another woman. The man whom she had called selfish, of whom she had no right to think. Had she not willed it so herself? Woman's will is Heaven's will he had told her. This time it was no phantom doubt to be dismissed with a single word. The truth stared her in the face and it appalled her. *There* was the man she— No! She could not say the word even to herself! But she hated that woman with her cat-like ways decoying him away. And it was she who had brought them together. That photograph—that unlucky photograph had been the means. Had she not begged him to ply Miss Gérard with questions? And he had not even found time to return it—had forgotten it now, perhaps. But she had no more the right to blame him than to think of him in that way. What were they doing on the stage? How bright the colors were in all their dresses! What were they saying? She heard the words, but they were like words in a dream—she could not put them together. She was very miserable! It seemed as if she had grown old in an instant,

as if all her senses were oppressed and dulled. A
mist seemed to hang between her and the actors.
Through it their figures flitted away, afar off. Was
she going to faint and make a scene? She opened
her fan and flourished it about. Ambrose turned
and whispered to her. "Are you ill?" he asked.
The color came rushing up into her face. She
breathed more freely. She could hear and see.
The people were laughing and applauding. But
why Caliban should caper about so strangely she
could not remember, she did not know.

After the third act, with its solemn and strange
music and the "high charms" by which the conspiring princes "are all knit up in their distractions,"
Miss Gérard drew a long breath.

"Ah," she said, "it is enchanting."

"Yes," said Marvin, smiling, "that is the word."

"You know what I meant to express," she retorted, with a shade of annoyance in her tone.

"Yes," he answered, "and I envy you."

"Why?"

"Because you thoroughly enjoy it. I can not."

"Do you mean that this bores you?" she
asked.

"No, not that. But I can not feel about it as
you do. It is all very well; but there is no enchantment in it for me."

She drew another long breath. "You must have
a very dreary time of it," said she.

"Oh, I do!" he answered, laughing.

"And yet," she went on, "I envy you decidedly.

I pay for all my emotions. I enjoy a little—then I am very wretched. For you there is neither heat nor cold. You live in the temperate zone. Your equanimity is delicious; it would make you a wise counselor—a good friend. You are a very safe person."

How well she knew her man already! This insidious flattery touched him at a vulnerable point. It was like the scratch of a venomed stiletto; and the poison at once began to work.

"A kind of social anchor," he said, benignantly. "Yes, I am heavy enough for that perhaps."

She gave one of the quiet little laughs that he liked to hear. Rather too soft and musical it was for honest laughter. She was congratulating herself upon her success with him.

"You are too modest," she said. "I would come to you with a problem to be solved, with a secret if I had one." Here she opened her eyes very wide and looked at him ingenuously. "I would trust you as I would a father confessor."

"With anything?" he asked, looking straight into the eyes and admiring them.

"With anything!" she repeated. Then she lowered her eyelids a little in a becoming way. Her lashes were fine; and beside, just then over Marvin's shoulder she caught a glimpse of Jack Elliston's distant face, and even in the distance it bored her. In a moment more the bell tinkled again and the play went on.

Too soon, as it must always come, the time

arrived for Prospero to break his staff and drown his book. The green curtain fell upon his insubstantial pageant; the epilogue was spoken—the great performance was over. The audience shouted, stamped, applauded, recalling the players again and again; then it began to disperse reluctantly, slowly. Miss Gérard moved toward one of the side doors of the theatre and Marvin followed her, after one restless glance behind him toward the place where Miss Bromfield should have been; but she was already gone. Neither he nor his companion spoke as the crowd carried them along with it under the flaring lamps of the corridors. A fine play often leaves one in a dazed condition much as a pleasant dream does. The first thought is rather a sad one: "This is only I after all—here is the world again!" and it takes a moment or two to recover one's balance. But when they came into broad daylight at the theatre doors Miss Gérard looked at Marvin anxiously and asked the time.

He pulled out his watch and started. "After five!" said he. "We have been almost four hours in the place."

"So late!" she cried, looking more and more disturbed "Oh, what shall I do?" and she clasped her hands in picturesque despair.

"What is it?" he asked, with a look of amusement.

"I have missed the train—the time never occurred to me. What will they think?"

"Is that all? They will think that you have

missed it, and you will take the next. There is another, of course ? "

" Yes ; but not for two or three hours. I am not sure of the time. How utterly stupid of me ! "

Marvin laughed. " You look as if you were alone among cannibals. Reassure yourself. I will protect you. As for the train—just wait here a moment."

He dashed across the street, bought an evening paper at a news-stand and was back again in an instant. " There is your train," he said ; "seven-forty-five ! " and he pointed at the figures in the time-table. " This is the most delightful of adventures," he continued. " We shall have time for a walk and something to eat into the bargain. I am at your service and glad of the chance."

As they walked on Miss Gérard protested against the sacrifice which she felt he must be making for her sake. He replied that nothing could suit him better, that he was ready to go when she was tired of him, and that until then there was no more to be said. And she discreetly said no more.

" You are saving me from myself," Marvin went on, as they turned into one of the broad, trim walks of the Common. " Think what it must be to dine every night in the same corner of your club with the same bottle of claret and the same review, or with your own particular *bête noire* if the fancy suits him. Any change is a relief, and to-night I gain enormously."

" Which is your club ? " asked Miss Gérard.

"The Ægean : there it is ;" and he pointed with his stick toward the stone balcony that seemed to frown upon them through the trees.

She looked at it curiously. "There is one of the creatures now on the balcony," she said.

"It is Jack Elliston. Shall I signal him to join us ?" asked Marvin, mischievously.

"As you please," she replied. But she was ready to catch his arm if he really meant to carry out the threat. He did not mean it, however, and just then· Jack turned back into the house.

"So that is where you live," said the girl as they walked on. "I see why you are dreary. Tell me, are you alone in the world ?"

"Yes," replied Marvin, gravely. "Quite alone."

"I understand," she said, in a gentle voice. "My life has been a very lonely one—like yours."

"Tell me about it," Marvin returned.

"Not now,—another time ; you promised me a walk ; let us go on and enjoy it."

So they went on rather soberly to the end of the path and then through one of the huge gateways out into the sunny garden that lies beyond. Here all was light and color ; the flowers on all sides were grown in great masses of red, purple and yellow, triumphs of art and splendid to behold ; they seemed to take a sort of peacock pride in their own beauty, and to bask in the sunshine like animate things. Miss Gérard lingered long over a vast bed of pansies that had been carefully shaded from the faintest violet to the deepest purple.

"It is like a painter's work," she said ; "I did not know there were so many colors in existence."

"Yes," said Marvin, "but see ; that is finer still."

He pointed to the clear expanse of western sky that was all aglow with a light indescribably beautiful and serene. A distant spire loomed up against it, and through the pointed windows the same sunset gold was shining.

"The colors of another world," said Marvin.

"You are right," she answered. "This is all forced and artificial. I doubt that water even ; it is unreal. Let us go to the river," she added, abruptly.

They crossed the garden through the admiring throng that at this hour and season is always to be found there, and in a few moments came out upon that neglected walk along the river wall in which Marvin delighted. Here they found themselves absolutely alone.

Miss Gérard leaned upon the rough wooden railing to look at the water. A breeze was springing up and the waves came dashing in against the granite blocks at her feet.

"I call this the city of wasted opportunities," said she; "you tear down your best relics of the past, spend your money for a thing like that—" and she pointed to the distant obelisk of Bunker Hill, " leaving a place like this to tramps and vagabonds!"

"And to us," Marvin replied. "Bless the city fathers! It is still possible to enjoy this unmolested."

" I am never tired of watching a river," said Miss Gérard, "but this is too tame. I know one that

leaps and rushes and laughs and roars. Ah! That
is a great river; there is some life in it. I have
looked at it for hours."

" Where ? "

" At the convent. Do you know the convent of
Notre Dame de Lorette ? " she asked.

" No," said Marvin.

"Of course. How should you ? It is on the shore
of the Niagara river just above the Falls. From my
window I could look straight down into the
wildest part of the great rapid. It was glorious—
like an evil spirit all unchained. I used to sit there
and read ' Undine,' till I believed in Kühleborn."

" I think I remember the place. It is on the
Canadian side—"

" Oh, yes," said Miss Gérard. " In Canada, of
course. I am a Canadian."

" Ah," said Marvin, struck with a sudden thought,
"that reminds me of a question I must ask you."

" A question ! " she repeated, looking at him with
a faint smile.

Marvin took out his letter-case and produced the
photograph of Miss Bromfield's *protégée*.

"Do you know this face ? " he asked, watching
her expression as he handed her the little picture.

She was silent a moment, and then met his gaze
without flinching.

" No," she said simply, without constraint of look
or tone. Her attitude was merely one of surprise.
" Whose is it ? I have never seen it to my knowledge."

"We—that is I—fancied you might know; of course it was only a fancy; she is a Canadian; I have seen her somewhere—"

"You have seen her? Where?"

"The curious part of it is that I can't remember. I think that I have seen her; and there is a certain likeness —"

"A likeness?"

"Yes, to you."

She blushed a little, and looked at the photograph again with evident amusement. Then she gave it back.

"It is a compliment," she said, "but I do not see the resemblance. I am sorry that I can not help you, unless she is in need of charity." And in a moment her purse was in her hands.

"No," said Marvin, annoyed, "it was not that."

She blushed again, and put away the purse.

"How lovely the river is!" she said, leaning over the rail, as though she longed to be within reach of the waves. "Water is my element. After all, it is well there are no rapids."

"Why?"

"Because though I love them, I fear them, too." And she drew back, laughing and shivering at the same moment.

"You are cold," said Marvin. "We ought not to stay here longer. The sunset is glorious, but it is time to think of dining."

"I am not hungry."

"You will dine with me all the same," said he.

10

So they walked back for some time in silence.   It was Miss Gérard who spoke first, as they passed through the garden, where the same idle throng was soberly taking its ease.

"All these people," she said, "and not a familiar face—not one, since we left the theatre!"

"Yes, one."

"Whose?" she asked.

"Jack's, on the club balcony.   Don't you remember?"

She did remember perfectly, but she had not counted Jack, who was but a superfluous cipher in any calculation of hers; less than that even, for with the least displacement of figures a cipher may count immensely.

They dined at a great, showy restaurant that went long ago the way of all things good, bad, or indifferent, and is now almost forgotten.   It fronted the elm-trees of the Common in the ground floor of a huge corner building, whose outward aspect is still unchanged, and before whose doors still passes nightly the same sad procession that Marvin and Miss Gérard looked out upon from their table in the window.   It was the hour when work is over, when the chains are slackened, not removed, and those who wear them get their breath of pure air and their glimpse of such sunshine as may be left.   The joy of release rarely shows itself in these worn and nervous faces that are all set one way.   "To be rich —to be rich!" they are all saying to themselves. This one desire consumes them—"To be rich!"

It is the fatal passion the envious fairy left in young America's cradle as her gift to the newly-born.

Miss Gérard still protested that she was not in the least hungry, and though Marvin tried to tempt her with elaborate dishes, it was a very simple dinner that he ordered at her suggestion. While they waited for it, she watched the people hurrying by in the twilight and he watched her. In her manner to-day he had found nothing repellent. He felt that she liked him, and he was more than ever interested in her—of course, as a study simply. His afternoon had been very short; this was a pleasant ending to it. There was a kind of sympathetic melancholy about her that suited his case precisely. She must have a history worth knowing. He wished he knew it. Just then all the lights in the place were turned up, and the sudden glare drew Miss Gérard's attention in-doors.

"Is it at all like your club?" she asked, looking up at the plaster cornice, of which the prevailing tints were red and yellow, aggressive in their tone.

"Not in the least," said he. "I like it better."

She sighed, softly; "I don't believe you. You men have much the best of it in this life."

"Has your life been so very sad thus far?" he asked.

"It has been wretched—miserable—and is likely to be worse. No matter, I laugh at it!" And she did laugh bitterly as she spoke. "After all," she added, "I have been spared your trouble."

" Mine ! And what may that be ? "

" I see you think I can't read signs."

" I see you think I am afraid of you. Pray what is my trouble?"

" Shall I tell you ? "

" By all means."

" Well, then," said Miss Gérard, lightly, as she played with the morsel of chicken she had accepted, " you are in love—with a woman—and she has rejected you."

"Good!" said Marvin; "An admirable guess! Try again."

" I am glad you don't deny it."

" But I do—it is not true."

Miss Gérard dropped her knife and fork. "Say that again, please," said she.

" It is not true."

" Would you admit it, if it were true?" she asked.

Marvin burst into a laugh. "Probably not," he answered; and Miss Gérard shrugged her shoulders as if to say her case was fully proved.

"Admitting for argument's sake," said Marvin, "that your random shot hit the gold, you have made me forget my troubles; allow me to do you the same good turn, if possible. Remember, I am a social anchor."

" I do not understand you," she replied.

" I did not like the way you spoke just now," he explained; "about yourself, I mean. Are you really alone in the world? Have you no family to help you—to advise you ?"

" No," she said ; " my mother died when I was very young.   I can but just remember her."

" And your father ?   He is dead, too ? "

" Yes."

" There is no one, then ? "

" No one.   I had a rich friend—an American woman much older than I—she made a pet of me ; she took me abroad; it was with her that I came to this part of the world.   We are not friends now ; I do not even know where she is.   So I am left alone with my own way to make.   It is not easy."

" No," said Marvin ; " it is hard enough for a man to fight the world.   Will you do me a favor ? Count me as your friend—one who will gladly help you if he can."

She had really eaten very little and he had observed that she looked worn and tired.   But now a flush of pleasure stole up into her pale cheeks.

" You are very kind," she murmured; "it may be that I shall come to you with a problem.   One has so many."

" Good," he answered ; " it is a bargain !   I drink to your complete happiness !   Long life and few problems ! "   And he filled his glass with the Sauterne he had ordered for her and drank the toast.

" Complete happiness ! " she responded, touching her lips with her own glass and setting it down again.

As Marvin drank, his eyes wandered a little, and it chanced that they fell upon a face that passed across the window-pane. It came and went in an instant; there was no recognition in it—the eyes were not even turned his way; but the sight gave him a violent fit of coughing. The empty glass had almost fallen from his hand.

"Did you see that?" he asked, as soon as he could speak.

"What?" asked his companion who had seen nothing.

It was the face of Marvin's photograph that had startled him; he knew the girl at once; and he also knew where he had seen her before. It was she whom he and Jack Elliston had watched one night from the club balcony, she whom the reckless jockey had barely escaped killing. He did not care to tease Miss Gérard about her any more; so he laughed the matter off with a joke about his awkwardness;—said that if his hand were unsteady it came from being cooped up in a theatre —he never could bear "the smell of the tan." Then he hastened to add that all other experiences of the afternoon had proved most exhilarating; as for the walk, he wished they might take one oftener. Was Miss Gérard never in town?

Again the changing color in that astute person's cheeks betrayed her inward satisfaction. And she not only explained that each week entitled her to a day of liberty, but she also took pains to state what particular day of the week it was. She came to town often, had often an hour to spare; in which case she always walked one way. He had been very, very kind; her afternoon had been one that she could never forget; and finishing these remarks and her cup of *café noir* at the same moment, she looked up at the clock and said it was time to go.

They walked through a dozen dreary streets to the drearier station; past shabby shops with half-closed shutters, a musty hotel or two, the great red and blue eyes of an apothecary's window. Hideousness unredeemed attended them for every foot of the way, conspiring with the night to give Marvin a comfortable sense of responsibility. He could not remember when he had last performed such escort duty. It amused him; and even though the light pressure upon his arm did not come from the hand he would have liked to find there, he could have borne it very well for a few minutes longer. So it was entirely natural that he should privately determine not to leave Miss Gérard until she was safe at home. Knowing that she would protest against this, he said nothing about it. He would quietly take the train with her at the proper time; then argument would be useless.

They found the station oppressively warm; and, rather than to wait in the train, Miss Gérard preferred to walk up and down the dusty platform till the last moment. When that came, Marvin followed her to the steps of the car. She turned, offering her hand, as if to take leave of him; and before he could speak, Jack Elliston jumped down from the car as if by magic, and stood between them.

"You here?" said Marvin; "I did not know—"

"Yes," said Jack, inwardly noting and enjoying his friend's disappointment.

"I was on the point of offering my services," continued Marvin, "as escort."

"There is no need," said Jack, "I will take care of Miss Gérard."

"Oh, no; there is no need," she repeated, giving Marvin her hand. Jack went up the steps, and she had a moment to whisper in Marvin's ear, "Remember, Saturday is my day in town." The car began to move, and Marvin, following it a little way, saw Jack find her a seat, then take a cigar from his pocket and walk on toward the front of the train, leaving her behind alone.

"Deuced civil, I call that!" Marvin growled, as he came out into the street, that was now doubly depressing. "He might as well have taken another train!"

He could not, of course, understand why Jack preferred to sit alone. He had no suspicion of his friend's newly-awakened jealousy, and attributed his slight abruptness of manner to the hurry of the moment. None so blind to suffering as those who suffer.

And Marvin, reviewing the day's adventures, as he took up his lonely life again, allowed his thoughts to drift in a new direction. Desperate ills required desperate remedies, and his troubles, perhaps, were desperate. But he could not become a Trappist, nor could he stop at the apothecary's and demand poison for rats. Such bitter forms of con-

solation were entirely out of date. Why not console and revenge himself at the same time? Why
not find another woman, marry her and prove to
all whom it might concern how utterly cold-
blooded and reckless he had grown? Here was a
girl now! Why not?

It needed but another turn of the imagination to
figure himself already at the altar, swearing eternal
fidelity to Miss Gérard. She was amiable enough;
presentable enough. He dared swear they could
live together as happily as most married people.
Why not? It was not to be false to one's ideal to
discover that there was another woman in the world.

When he reached his lodgings he sat down immediately and wrote a formal note to Miss Bromfield, returning the photograph, with the statement,
that the fancied resemblance was a chance one and
nothing more. He did not tell her that he had been
startled again by it an hour before. That was a
coincidence of value only to himself.

IX.

"QUIS CUSTODIET IPSOS CUSTODES?"

IN a few hours after her evil fifteen minutes at the theatre, Miss Bromfield's scruples had brought her almost to the point of breaking her engagement with Maitland Ambrose. Since marriage was not to give her supreme happiness, it seemed best to her to live a single sister all her life, supremely miserable. With the morning came a kind of reaction, which Marvin's indifferent note perhaps helped in some slight degree to bring about. Why should she mope in a corner for a man who from the first had done little more than to civilly acknowledge her existence? Why break her word to one who was and would be always her devoted slave? Without her, as she liked to think, his life would be a blank. How could she throw him over? He might do some awful, desperate thing. No, it was too late now; she had chosen and must abide by her choice. It was always so, she supposed; and then she hummed to herself a little song of Heine that she had once learned by heart. "The other loved another," she said.

> "The maid out of spite was married
> To the first convenient man;"

She wondered if he ever guessed his wife's secret. The song did not go so far as that.

All this, as she sat alone at the breakfast table over the fragments of Marvin's letter. She allowed herself few such idle moments. American life is a hurry and a scramble; and most of us, men and women, do our thinking as we go along. Helena was a general favorite; her engagement book had no vacant pages. And beside the never ending duties of society there were various charities to which she devoted much time and money. This, her last week in town, was unusually full. Moreover, she was now trying under Bruni's guidance to devise some practical help for the sculptor Ruel and his daughter. She had planned a conference with the Italian for that very morning; and Miss Feathering, who was subject to spasmodic attacks of the charitable fever, had volunteered to come to town by an early train and help them out.

It must be time for her now, Helena thought. There was sure to be a list of trains in the morning paper, for which she searched the room in vain; then she rang for a servant.

"Where is the paper?" she asked.

"Indeed, Miss, I don't know; perhaps it's the captain's took it out with him—he was up and away in a great hurry."

"What do you mean?" asked Helena, looking for the first time at her father's vacant place. "Why, he has had no breakfast!"

"No, Miss, not the first mouthful! He said I

wasn't to tell you—and I ain't." Whereupon, the little maid, having discharged her small petard, moved noiselessly about the performance of her duties.

Unwilling to betray uneasiness, Helena left the room and went into the little cabin where her father usually shut himself up for his morning cigar. There was no tobacco smoke, no other sign that the place had been disturbed.

Wondering what strange current was running counter to all the captain's methodical habits, Helena, in vague alarm, went through the house that seemed to have grown unnaturally still. Silence and mystery everywhere; the clue must lie in the missing morning paper, and she was on point of sending for another copy of it, when a carriage rattled up; then, with a great slamming of doors, Miss Flossie Feathering rushed into the room, her face glowing with excitement.

"Oh, my dear," she cried, kissing Helena on both cheeks violently, "how do you do, and isn't it queer and horrid?"

"What?" asked Helena, gravely.

"What? You haven't seen? Why, it's all in the paper!"

"What is in the paper?" Helena demanded, now thoroughly out of patience.

"Mr. Hutchinson, the lawyer. He has gone away."

"Gone away!" repeated Helena, trying not to understand.

"Yes—with enormous sums of money. They say his accounts are all wrong and have been so for years. You know he was everybody's trustee. It's just a chance that we lose nothing, as pa said in the train. Look!" And Miss Feathering produced a crumpled newspaper, wherein the sudden disappearance of Mr. Jerome Hutchinson was duly chronicled and his misdeeds becomingly emphasized with a luxury of space and a profusion of capital letters.

"Just think of the wicked old thing!" Miss Feathering continued, lightly. "Fifty, if he's a day! I had such a nice talk with him at the Whateleys' garden party. And it has been going on for ages. So handsome, too! The loveliest white hair, and pa says that yesterday he would have trusted him with millions!"

Helena tried to read, but the letters danced before her eyes. She knew that much of her own property had been left in this man's care, and she at once understood her father's absence. He was at this moment trying to learn the truth, and he had carried away the paper in order to spare her the pain of it as long as possible. In spite of her trouble, her mind dwelt upon this little act of kindness, and her first thought was of sympathy for him.

"It may not be so bad, after all," was the only thing that seemed possible for her to say.

"It's sure to be worse when everything is known," replied Miss Feathering. "I only hope they will catch him, that's all! Where do you suppose he is?" Then she noticed Helena's preoccupied look,

and an alarming contingency occurred to her for the
first time. "I do hope *you* have nothing in his
hands."

" I hope so," said Helena, controlling herself and
putting aside the paper.   The true state of her affairs
would of course be common gossip in a day or two,
but she preferred to have nothing to do with the
announcement.   So the subject was changed, and
they talked of indifferent things until Bruni burst
in upon them with his thin face wreathed in smiles.
Whereupon he was called to account for his unwonted gayety.

" Heaven   helps   the   light-hearted," he   said,
becoming suddenly grave again, " and it is easier to
be cheerful than not.   But I have sold a bit of our
poor sculptor's work.   Oh, it won't bring him a
fortune—only a little bread and butter.   That's
something.   I believe Ruel would die of starvation
rather than ask a favor.   He's as proud as an exiled
emperor."

This was excellent news, for the sale, beside pro-
viding the ready money upon which their courageous
friend depended, would inevitably act as a spur to
incite him to redoubled effort.   There ensued much
discussion and much writing down of names among
the three conspirators.   Such and such people must
be made to take an interest in him.   An exhibition
of his work must be arranged ; the apathetic public
must be stirred into recognition of his genius.   His
daughter, too, must be rescued from the milliner's
shop, where she was now forced to lead the life of

a galley-slave; for her some gentler employment must be found. The morning was gone before their schemes had assumed definite shape, and the discussion was prolonged over the luncheon-table, where Miss Bromfield, though a shade more silent than usual, was still a perfect hostess. No shadow of impending misfortune was permitted to cast itself between her and her social duties. Her father was still absent, and therefore she secretly rejoiced. His presence might have made all this repose impossible. Luncheon being over, and Bruni having taken himself off, she had a momentary longing to confide her fears to Miss Feathering. But her friend was just then taking the utmost delight in her own talk, which seemed more frivolous than ever, and Helena reflected that her sympathy could only be oppressive. So she wisely said nothing; and before long Miss Feathering likewise took her leave. Then Helena caught up the newspaper, fled to her chamber and locked herself in to read and re-read the evil tidings. A flood of tears naturally followed, and naturally proved an immense relief to her. She had wanted a good cry all day, and now that it was over, she could look at the matter more calmly. She dressed for dinner as usual, and when the time came, she was able to meet her father with dry eyes and in some degree of composure. The moment his step was heard, she gave one last look at the glass and then went down and faced the captain in the drawing-room. He was pacing back and forth with his hands in his pockets, but as she came in he stopped in his walk and looked at her gravely. She did not give him time to speak.

"I know," she said, simply, showing the tell-tale newspaper in her hand.

The captain gave a sigh of relief and resumed his walk without speaking.

"Is there any news of him?" Helena asked.

"No," replied her father, quickening his pace as he spoke; "we shall never hear of him. He has a three days' start—for Patagonia, I suppose."

"It is all true, then?"

"Yes; his accounts are in disorder—nothing can be made of them. There is no money; much of it was lost, they say, in speculation months ago. At all events, he has made off with everything, except a trifle of yours that chanced to be in my hands. You see how much I am to blame."

"To blame? You?"

The captain stood still and looked at her with a strange, anxious expression. Then he laid his hand gently upon her shoulder.

"My child, your money was left in his care and mine jointly. If you lose a fortune, it is through my neglect; of course, I am to blame."

For answer, Helena flung her arm around his neck.

"Papa, papa, you shall not say such things. He was a man whom everybody trusted as you trusted him. As for the money, it is nothing. If you ever speak so again I can't forgive you."

"You are very brave, darling."

" That is nonsense. Surely, we have something left ? "

" Oh yes ; there is my money—we shall not be absolute paupers, but—"

" You are not to say another unkind word ;—you are not to think unkind thoughts ; you are not to make me unhappy—I forbid you ! "

Then the captain bent down and kissed her.

"Where is Maitland?" he asked.

" I have not seen him all day," replied Helena, recalled at once to life and its responsibilities; for she had been since the morning in a kind of waking dream. She observed with some surprise an unusual friendliness in the form of her father's question ; he had never before failed to speak of her lover as Mr. Ambrose.

"I have seen him," said the captain : "he will be here presently. He promised to dine with us to-day."

" You have seen him," said Helena. " Then of course he understands—"

"Of course; I told him in so many words. He behaved admirably."

Thereupon Helena was seized with a desire to know exactly what had taken place between them. She insisted that every syllable of the conversation should be repeated to her. The captain made heroic efforts to recall it, but in vain. He had found enough to confuse him, that day, poor man ! Then, in spite of his troubles, he became amused at her persistency and actually laughed at it.

11

And Helena, only too glad to change the current of his thoughts, laughed with him. And so Ambrose found them when he came into the drawing-room.

"Poor Ellie!" he cried. "Is this the way you lose a fortune?"

Helena drew herself up proudly. "I am not to be pitied, sir. I mean to bear it as well as either of you;" and she laid one hand upon her father's arm, and gave the other to Ambrose. So they stood for a moment silently, looking at each other with sober faces.

"Is there any news?" the captain asked. Ambrose shook his head.

"She is very brave," continued the captain. "She does not realize it."

"I realize it so well," said Helena, "that I will not hear another word upon the subject. If I must go into hysterics, let us keep them for to-morrow— Hush!" she added, as the maid announced dinner. "Remember the servants!"

In the dining-room she did at first a great deal of talking in order to raise her father's spirits. Ambrose saw her motive and helped her out, making a very good second. Under this treatment the patient revived; he lost his look of fatigue and pronounced the dinner excellent; in short, he seemed quite himself again. Helena led the two men into a political discussion, and then watched them quietly, ready with a leading question in case of a fatal pause. "So he behaved admirably!" she said to herself, repeating the captain's words as she looked at Ambrose. He was certainly doing his best now to win her whole heart. And when he turned her way her eyes assured him that she was grateful.

After dinner, in the little cabin, she pointed with her fan to the backgammon-board and Ambrose challenged the captain to a rubber. They talked and laughed and wrangled. Helena brought some work and sat down between their table and the open window through which there came a low murmur of the city. There, the great mystery of the night with all its shining worlds beyond it. Here, her own little world—her home. Perhaps it was not to be her home any longer; they would be poor, they must retrench. The thought made her heart ache, while the men moved their checkers and rattled their dice, really believing all the while that she "did not realize it." She hoped they would continue to think so.

They played three games of backgammon and then a fourth and a fifth before Ambrose took his leave. Helena followed him out into the hall, as usual.

"You have been very good to papa," she whispered.

"Well, he seems rather cut up. It is hard luck—hard all round."

"After all, it is only money—nothing to what we might have lost."

"What, for instance?" Ambrose asked, with a laugh that had a note of sarcasm in it.

Helena's eyes filled with tears. She turned her back upon the light so that he should not see.

" Does it make so much difference to you ? " she asked.

" To me ? No, of course not. I was thinking of you."

" You may be sure that I shall not complain. It is only giving up curry and caviare. A little economy, with papa and you to help me ! "

" Good ! " said Ambrose. " I admire your pluck. I don't half deserve to have you. Good-night ! " Then they had a last word or two at the open door, and he went out smiling.

But the smile did not wear very well ; in fact it was quite worn out before he had carried it a dozen yards. Then he drew a long breath and scowled and muttered something that was meant for no ears but his own. As he turned the street corner, a little fluffy terrier that had lost his master came toward him sniffing and hoping against hope to find a friend.

" Curse you ! " said Ambrose, fiercely ; and he kicked the dog into the gutter. The poor brute howled with pain. His latest enemy strode away, but a huge policeman looming up out of a distant shadow crossed the quiet street and spoke to the dog kindly. The frightened animal gave him one look and then shot off into the darkness.

" Miserable hound ! " said the man, roughly ; but it was not the dog he meant.

X.

"LES AFFAIRES AVANT TOUT!"

FROM the scandal-monger's point of view it need hardly be said that Mr. Jerome Hutchinson's little escapade proved triumphantly successful. At first, the wildest rumors were eagerly caught up and believed. In a small way, many people were "interested" as commercial courtesy euphemistically puts it; and these petty losers, being loudest and fiercest in their denunciations of the missing trustee, lent a certain air of probability to the fabulous sum total at which his ill-gotten wealth was set down. But the greatest sufferers wisely held their peace; and to this day no one really knows upon what cash capital the false steward established himself anew at his villa in Para. For to that sunny South American port he was supposed to have sailed; perhaps, because no hotter place is known to be habitable in any but a supernatural world.

Let us leave him simmering there forever, and return to his victims. At first it was said that the Bromfields were left without so much as a dollar to their names; but this was soon contradicted by the knowing ones, who hinted that the captain was a shrewd old boy and had a very pretty property of his own to fall back upon.   Then it was proved by the best authority that they had given up their country home and were to pass the summer in town ; over which the club men shook their heads sympathetically.   Finally, it was whispered about that their town house was actually in the market.   There had been no bill in the window, but so-and-so knew that it could be bought for such a price.   And then the club men shook their heads still more solemnly and said it was a bad lookout for Ambrose.   Meanwhile Miss Bromfield and her lover seemed to behave very much as if nothing extraordinary had happened.   The captain, too, deprecated sympathy by every look and gesture, skilfully declining to be led by any leading questions and keeping up his spirits, as everybody said, amazingly well.

Marvin sat about the club, saying little as was his habit, but listening attentively to all these rumors.   Before many days he became convinced that the loss to his friends, if not so great as was at first imagined, must at least be serious.   Then he absented himself for a day or two from the club house, but turned up down town, as some of the busy men remarked, rather oftener than usual. During this time as it happened, he did not meet the Bromfields.   He knew that he ought to go to the house, he felt that the captain would expect it ; he meant to call, in fact, but kept postponing the visit ; and when a fortnight had slipped away it was still unpaid.

One day the captain came home very late for luncheon,—so late that Helena had given him up, and he found her alone at the table.

" I am sorry," he said, penitently; " but a very strange thing has happened—"

"If it's a disagreeable thing, let it wait," said Helena, with a gayety that seemed a little unreal like that of the stage.

" I said strange, my dear, not disagreeable. I have had an offer for this house, that's all."

"Oh ! " replied Helena, soberly. "Is that strange ? "

"Yes, for it comes in a curious way. More is offered me than I could possibly ask, and I am not to know the buyer's name."

"How can that be, papa? "

"A lawyer called upon me at the club—said he was acting as attorney for some person or persons to remain unknown. Moreover, he made a condition—to wit, namely, viz:—that we are to stay here for the present at a nominal rent, with the privilege of buying back the house when the lease expires."

"What a very kind thing! Oh, papa, what did you say? "

" I asked him if his client—or clients—was—or were insane."

" How brutal of you ! " said Helena, laughing. " Well ? "

"Well, a discussion followed on the yea and nay principle. I declined and he insisted. Finally, I gave him a flat refusal ; but he would not take his 'No' so abruptly and left me with three days leeway to consider it."

"Ought we to refuse?" Helena asked. To her the plan seemed very enticing and she could see no harm in it.

"To accept a gift of money from the Lord knows whom? Most assuredly. I think so."

"It is not the same thing," Helena argued.

"Isn't it? To me it seems precisely that. However, I have brought home the three days and am willing to leave them with you. Think the matter over and give me my answer. But don't consult anybody—don't tell Ambrose."

"Do you think it was he then—"

"No, he has not the wherewithal," returned the captain, bluntly. "But he may have suggested the thing to some one else—or, at least, he may be in the secret. In that case he could hardly give an unprejudiced opinion."

"I see," said Helena, thoughtfully; and then they talked of other things.

The next day it was that Marvin, overcoming his natural indolence, forced himself to ring at the Bromfields' door. He asked first for Miss Helena. The maid was not sure that he could be received; nevertheless, she showed him into the drawing-room. He waited a long time, pounding the floor with his stick, and staring out of the window. Then he heard a light step behind him, and turned about to face a slight, hesitating figure, that was not Miss Bromfield's. He saw, instead, a woman whom he had never met, but whose face he immediately recognized.

"I am Miss Ruel," said the intruder, softly. Marvin bowed, and in a moment had compared her mentally with Miss Gérard. Younger, shorter, prettier, not so very like her, but carrying herself much in the same way.

"Miss Bromfield asked me to say," the girl continued, timidly, "that she is very sorry not to see you."

"I am sorry, too," said Marvin. "And Captain Bromfield? Is he at home?"

"Yes," she replied. "You will find him in the smoking-room."

Marvin thanked her, and took up his hat and stick again. But he waited a moment, for the girl stood still, as if there were something more to be said.

"You came to Belmont, didn't you?" she asked. And the question stirred Marvin's thoughts with a twinge of pain like that of a bodily wound that has healed.

"Yes," said he. "You are the patient!"

"I was," she answered, with a smile, that was the smile of Miss Gérard, "until Miss Bromfield cured me. I remember seeing you with her that day. I watched you from the window when you were not looking."

"Just my case," said Marvin. "I have seen you in the same way—twice."

"Where?" she asked, with a look of great surprise.

"In the street," he returned, amused at her be-

wilderment. "I thought we should meet some
day. You are staying here?"

"Only for to-day. I am to have a place in one
of the libraries. Miss Bromfield found it for me.
She has been so very kind."

"She could not be otherwise," said he. "Tell
her—" and he would have sent a kindly message,
but that the captain, just then, threw open the
cabin-door with a shout of welcome. Miss Ruel
disappeared; and Marvin went into the cabin, where
the two men sat for a long time, talking earnestly,
with closed doors. What took place there between
them can never be accurately known. We are
none the worse off, however, for their talk was of
business, and the details of business are proverbially
dull. From the way in which they parted in the
hall, an hour or two afterward, it was clear that the
discussion had been a friendly one.

The captain dined alone that night, for Ambrose
did not come in, and Helena kept her own room.
When she appeared the next morning, her father
thought she looked pale, and said so.

"No sleep, I suppose. I see—you had a white
night, as the Frenchmen say. Wherefore ' white,'
I wonder?"

"No," she said, with a woman's readiness for
small deception. She had really counted all the
hours. But the captain was not so easily deceived.

"It will not do," he replied. "You have been
lying awake to reflect upon your answer."

" Must it be to-day?" she asked,

" Yes, to-day. And what have you decided ? "

" Nothing. I cannot decide."

The captain laughed. " So I must do all the work. Very well; let me speak for you. We are to accept the offer of our unknown friend. I have changed my mind. I think it will be best."

" Oh, papa ! " cried Helena, overjoyed.

" Yes," he returned, " that is my conclusion. Some day, perhaps, he will discover himself, and allow us to repay him. Until then, let us put our pride to sleep."

" I am not sure,—" began Helena, inclining to doubt if this were proper, after all.

" But I am," replied her father; " and that settles the question."

" Then I may tell Maitland," she said, " since it is all settled."

" Yes," said the captain, after a moment's thought; " he might hear of it. The news had better come from you."

She told Ambrose the story the next time they met. He betrayed no delicate scruples like those her father had at first expressed so clearly. In fact, he was inclined to treat the matter rather lightly. And at this she was annoyed and grieved. It would have pleased her better to find him over scrupulous. Then it suddenly occurred to her that his indifference might be assumed. She was only too ready for such an explanation, and grasped eagerly at the thought, following it up as though she had found a clue.

" I believe," she said, " that you knew of this."

" If you think so," he replied, " it will do no good to swear the contrary."

" You did know of it !" she cried.

He only answered her then with a tormenting laugh. But, afterward, pushed into a corner, as it were, he was forced to say something for the sake of peace; and he said "No!" But there are fifty ways in which this word may be spoken, each with its own peculiar shade of expression. His way did not quite clear up the matter. If he was willing to remain, when all was said and done, an object of suspicion, he had perhaps taken the very best means to that end.

The days went on, and the hot weather came, bringing with it social desolation. The brood of fashion took its flight to the mountains and the seaside, or nestled in the shadows of neighboring country houses. One half the city shut its eyes and took a long siesta while the sun kept a fierce watch over it. Little tufts of grass forced their way up between the bricks of the pavement, and the trees in the squares and gardens grew yellow before their time, and began to shed their leaves. But the Bromfields stayed on in town ; and Helena, who had feared that this new experience would prove unbearable, soon declared that she enjoyed it, and wished that the quiet summer might be prolonged. What if the familiar streets were grass-grown and deserted ? Their very solitude had its charm ; she was free as the air, and could walk in them or not, as she pleased. At almost any time she might have escaped, for her invitations were many and urgent; but she would not leave her father, and declined them all. Now and then some friend would appear in town, for an hour or two, upon one pretext or another, and it became the fashion to lunch with her. The house at mid-day was a place of rendezvous. Ambrose would come in to help her entertain the chance visitors; there would be laughter and gossip; a little music sometimes; then the butterflies would spread their wings and flutter away in the sunshine; and the sleepy, afternoon life would go on again.

Lightest and shallowest of these summer morning guests, Miss Flossie Feathering was often to be found among them. For her friendship, Helena, in her heart of hearts, did not care two straws. Miss Feathering, on the contrary, adored Helena, or said so; and Helena, amused, perhaps a little flattered, for she was three years the younger, allowed herself to be adored. Moreover, Miss Feathering, though flighty and uncertain, was always amiable, and never dull; with her in the room, all was sure to go smoothly; she had the small talk of society at her tongue's end, and when Ambrose met her, these two were always chaffing each other across the table to the great diversion of the company. Then, too, Miss Feathering had now definitely taken up charity, as she said, and having plenty of money, was only too eager to be generous. Nothing daunted her; and she was always ready to

push her way through swarming streets and up
unlighted stairways where Miss Biomfield would
never have ventured alone.   Helena, since her
reverses of fortune, had busied herself more than
ever with the poor, and in certain dingy quarters of
the city she was almost worshipped.   When she
came the children smiled, clinging to her dress by
way of welcome, and staring wistfully after her
when she went away.   Summer homes and excur-
sions were then little known, and Helena had helped
many of these small wretches to a holiday in the
open air.   To them she seemed an angel, and Miss
Feathering was a mere attendant spirit.

The mind had wrestled with the heart, and gained
the mastery.   She never permitted herself now to
think of Marvin, who, having paid her his visit of
duty, did not come again.   She was all gratitude
to Ambrose for his manly way of facing their misfortune, for it was his as well as hers.   She was
proud of him, too; proud of his good looks and
his good manners; of his success in the law, for
she knew that he was successful.   She had been in
his office.   It had seemed to her a very untidy
place; even the floor was ankle deep, as she said,
with books and papers.   But all that meant success,
and he was busier than ever; so busy that sometimes for days she had no more than a glimpse of
him.   And thereby crept in a thought of bitterness.
She could not help fearing that he cared more for
making money than for anything else in the world;
more even than for her.   But, of course, they needed

money. They were to be married in the autumn; that had been settled; all but the day was fixed. She must make her sacrifices with the rest. She must help him and not hinder him. It would never do to be jealous of a man's profession.

She found more time to herself now than she had ever known before; but time never could stand still with her. She had her music and her books; of the latter she knew very much more than the outside. But she was skilful in avoiding a display of knowledge, and people interested her so much that she pleased all sorts of people. Her little *protégée*, Miss Ruel, for instance, showed a regard for her that was almost pathetic. The girl was now an assistant in the library where Helena sometimes went to have a word with her. It was a cool, shadowy place of refuge from the glaring street; so that Miss Bromfield was often tempted to linger there. She would retreat with a book into a certain quiet alcove that overlooked one of the old city grave-yards,—a place of sunken head-stones and worn-out epitaphs, with now and then a marble tomb of an old-fashioned design—for there is a fashion even in such things. The place was almost disused; even the dead passed it by, and it was given over to grass and flowers. Just under the alcove window, in an angle of the wall, was a great bed of holly-hocks, erect and stately like a group of pompous courtiers. These flowers, with their trim stalks and splendid colors, delighted Helena; and at times in looking at them she would forget her book, and let her hands fall upon its open pages. So she wasted many minutes, or seemed to waste them. And the girl she had befriended would notice this, and wonder what sorrow weighed upon her. For quite unconsciously Helena always looked at the flowers with a sad expression.

One afternoon she heard voices out there under the trees. Marvin and Miss Gérard were loitering about among the graves and had stopped to read an old inscription. The color came into Helena's cheeks and went away again. The sight had annoyed her, but only for one instant; she smiled to think she had been annoyed at all. " Let him walk with her all day, if he likes her," she said to herself, with a toss of the head. But it would never do to be seen there. He might think she was watching them. So she dropped her book and left the window.

" Do what we will," Miss Gérard was saying, " Death's hand is upon us all! I can never realize it."

" Why should you," Marvin asked, " if you still believe that Death ends everything? This would not be so bad a place to sleep in forever."

" I know the place that I would choose," she returned; " it is in the Basque country near Biarritz —a patch of long grass under a castle wall where a few English soldiers fell in battle and were buried. The sea breaks upon the rocks close under it. If we must wake, as you think, I would like to wake there in the sound of the waves."

"We are growing desperately gloomy," said Marvin. "Let us change the subject. Where is Jack? I haven't seen him for a dog's age."

"Oh, didn't I tell you? He is in the West—telegraphed for by his uncle, who has been seriously ill and is now better, but still too weak to travel. It will be some time before they can think of coming home."

"His uncle? You mean Mr. Musgrave."

"Yes," said Miss Gérard, turning away her face lest some guilty change should be noted in it. Mr. Musgrave's illness had given her a respite that was not altogether unwelcome. She was even beginning to dread the day of his return.

"Mr. Musgrave," continued Marvin, "is too ornate a person for the prairies. What on earth took him there?"

"Business," she replied. "He has given it up, but one never conquers a ruling passion. 'Les affaires avant tout,' you know! Please to remember that you are one of the few Americans who do not make business the absorbing thing in life."

"And even I," said Marvin, "have become a true American. I am going to take to the law and work like a coal-heaver."

"Are you serious?" she asked, with a look of amazement.

"Yes—entirely serious," he replied.

"You, of all men! And why?"

"Because the life I lead is a poor and selfish thing—unprofitable, even to myself. I have no hope of a brilliant future, no distinct ambitions.

But I am here in the world and must make my mark in the world, however slight the mark may be."

Miss Gérard sighed. " Yes," she said; "I begin to understand."

"Then, too, I need money. I am not exactly poor—nor am I likely to become rich. But money gives one an immense advantage, and I have but . just learned its real value. I am willing to wrestle with my fellow-men for a little more of it. If I make a fortune, so much the better for me, so long as I neither hoard it nor spend it unwisely."

" It will be in good hands ! " said Miss Gérard, and her eyes shone now not in wonder but in admiration. " You are doing the right thing, I am sure, and I wish you all possible success."

"Amen ! " he answered.

They had walked entirely round the small enclosure and were at the gate again.

" It is time to think of my train," said Miss Gérard. " No ! Do not come with me ! Goodnight. Success to you—and another wish ! "

" What one ? " he asked, taking the hand she offered him.

" You enter upon this new life single-handed ; it is a pity that there will be no one to share its trials —its successes. My wish is that, if such a one exists, you may find her."

" Amen to that, too ! " said Marvin ; "but I can't say that I think her lot would be enviable."

" You are trying to force a compliment," she replied ; "but you shall get none from me."

That was her last word.   He laughed and went his way—she, hers.   But as she walked alone, " I think that he will ask me ! " was her thought.   And at almost the same moment he was saying to himself: " Why not ask her? "

XI

MACHIAVELLI AND HIS WIFE.

"*MADONNA MIA*," said Bruni to his wife one morning, as he looked up from his coffee and crushed an open letter in his hand, "*Madonna mia*, are the Featherings very rich?"

"Why do you ask?" she replied, rousing herself from a reverie of her own at the other end of the table.

"'But for a satisfaction of my thought; no further harm.' Shakespeare, my dear; 'Othello,' act the third!"

"I wish you wouldn't always fling the poets at me; I detest it," said his wife, impatiently. The fact was that he knew more of them than she did and the circumstance annoyed her.

Bruni laughed. "Excellent lady," he said. "Poetry to you—owls to Athens! But you provoked me to it. I do not find you *cinquecento* at all this morning. On the contrary, you are new, very new, oh, enormously American!"

"What do you mean by that?" she asked, sharply.

"To answer one question with another is not nice; and whatever is nice I call *cinquecento*," he replied.

The "excellent lady" laughed in spite of herself. "I did not mean to do it," she explained. "I am perfectly willing to answer your question. The Featherings are rich. Mrs. Feathering was a Robinson and had a fortune from her mother who was a niece of old Martin, the grocer. And they are all in some way connected with the Whateleys, I believe."

"That explains it," said Bruni, reflectively, smoothing out his crumpled letter. Perhaps he hoped that his wife would repeat her question, but she wisely held her tongue. So in a moment he went on: "You see, they wanted me to paint Miss Flossie's portrait. She doesn't interest me, but I preferred not to refuse; so, instead, I put an outrageous price upon my work. Her father writes me a letter and sends me his cheque for all I asked, before the canvas is stretched or the picture even thought of."

"I suppose that is not *cinquecento*," said Mrs. Bruni, viciously.

"Decidedly modern. However dollars are dollars, even in this degenerate day. I shall make the best of it.. The girl has no coloring, but she was very good in that affair of the sculptor Ruel. So we will admit her within our four walls—home, as you call them."

"He meant well, I am sure," Mrs. Bruni replied, "and it is certainly a great compliment that he pays you."

"Compliment? Bah!" growled Bruni; and he rose abruptly and walked away to the window.

His wife kept her place at the breakfast table, which was singularly typical of this ill-assorted household. Before her was set the substantial fare indispensable to every morning meal of the luxurious and dyspeptic American; while at Bruni's place there stood only the frugal coffee-cup of Italy. He had never learned to begin his day fiercely with an appetite. She, at first, had tried to conform to all his little ways, this early coffee habit among the rest; but in vain. So that now, making dinner their one meal in common, they had grown to be rather like Mr. and Mrs. Jack Sprat in the fable.

"I can't understand you at all," she said, going on with her breakfast leisurely. Bruni merely shrugged his shoulders without looking at her; she was in the habit of telling him this a dozen times a week.

"You are always incomprehensible," she continued, turning her threadbare statement tenderly. "I say it is a compliment and a great one!"

"Because she is a millionaire's daughter! Bah! That for her!" he said, snapping his fingers. "I would rather paint Miss Bromfield ten times over— and she is to be poor, they say."

"Miss Bromfield is a sweet girl," replied his wife. "I don't like that man she is going to marry."

Bruni looked at her sharply. "What has turned you against him?" he asked.

"I never fancied the fellow," she answered, vaguely. "And then he refused to subscribe to my 'Higher Light for Women' fund; but I had my revenge!" she added, in a tone of triumph.

"Revenge? How?"

"I sent a collector to his office for six days in succession—a new man each time. I made his life wretched, and he paid me a dollar at last!"

Bruni chuckled with delight and came back to the table jingling some coins together in his pocket. Then he threw down a gold piece into an empty plate where it tinkled merrily.

"Put that into the fund," said he, "from a lesser light!"

His wife betrayed no emotion, but drew out her purse and put away the coin with business-like rapidity.

"Thank you," she said. "I will send you a receipt."

Bruni stared at her for a moment and then burst into a roar of laughter. "You are delicious!" he cried, and thereupon stalked out of the room without another word; while his wife finished her breakfast with a sigh, and wondered why she could never understand him.

So Bruni stretched a canvas and Miss Feathering began to give him occasional restless sittings. After each visit the usual strong distaste for his work would overcome the artist, and his pent-up displeasure would find relief after the Italian fashion in exaggerated speech. "Dollars!" he would say. "That is all she says to me—dollars! That is all I can see, all I can express! and when it is done I shall paint the dollar sign in the upper corner like a coat-of-arms ! "

Meanwhile, he worked a little now and then upon Miss Bromfield's picture, which still oppressed him with a sense of incompleteness. He would have been glad to paint it out altogether and let his wasted time and color go for nothing. In fact, he had prayed devoutly that the loss of Miss Bromfield's money might lead to that very thing. She had given him no sittings for some time. But lately, a note from the captain had left him no choice in the matter; the sittings must be resumed and the picture finished at whatever cost to his reputation as a skilful conveyer of likenesses. He passed many unhappy quarters of an hour studying the composition and picking flaws in it. His critical spirit, once roused, was merciless—above all, to himself.

One afternoon his wife came into the studio and found him in one of these gloomy moods, standing before the Bromfield portrait and looking askance at it with muttered imprecations. His face cleared at once, however; he was only too glad to be interrupted.

" Are you going out ? " he asked, for she was in street dress.

" No, I have just come in.   I lunched to-day with the Bromfields.   Helena is looking thin and pale, I think.   That is very like her."

" Don't look at it ! " he said, taking the picture down from his easel and turning its face to the wall. " It is detestable ! "

" That man was there ! " his wife went on.

" Ambrose ? Well, why shouldn't he be there ? "

" Because I hate him. He flirted to-day outrageously with that Feathering girl. Helena seemed not to notice it, but I think she really did and that it troubled her. I have made up my mind that the brute neglects her purposely."

" *Cospetto !* " cried Bruni. " Here's a drawing of conclusions ! What's the matter ? Has he refused another subscription ? "

" Nonsense. You know I am entirely unprejudiced. But women see things that men never notice, and I saw that to-day—I know it."

" I thought all women were match-makers."

" Not American women. They have higher aims, I hope. The future of our women—"

She would have gone on breathlessly for half an hour, but he cut in adroitly.

" American women are all angels ; and I say they are match-makers, for it is Heaven's work. But what they do, they can undo. Match-maker— match-breaker ! Break this one for me and I will be more a slave to you than ever—if that is possible."

" Why, Cesare, what are you saying ? " she cried, in dismay.

" She must not marry him. It will give me the heart-ache ! " And he pressed his hand to his heart as if he already felt a physical pain there. " Think of some way to prevent it ! " he continued.

" I ? To meddle—interfere—with what does not

concern me? No indeed!" And she moved toward the door as if to fly from a thought so criminal.

But Bruni intercepted her upon the threshold, planting himself there firmly between her and escape.

"Would you wish that sweet little child to be eternally unhappy?" he asked in English that was very like Italian.

"No; but we may be all wrong. And to part a pair of lovers! Why, it would be improper—immoral! Besides, it could not be done!"

"We are not wrong. If you do nothing worse, you are sure of Heaven. There is a way—what way I don't know, but there must be one—not by direct interference, of course not. She must be made to see him as we see him—as he really is."

"It is no affair of ours."

Bruni strode back into the room impatiently.

"It is impossible to argue with a woman!" said he.

"Really, Cesare, I can not see that this is my duty."

"How deal with the beam if you overlook the mote? You want to help all women and you will not save one!"

Mrs. Bruni colored and bit her lip. "That is not true!" she said. "If I were sure—"

"Why so you were just now!"

"How disagreeable you are and all for nothing. Miss Bromfield is quite able to take care of herself without your help or mine."

"Ah, indeed? We shall see."

"If I can see the way to anything consistent with

my duty—" She paused reflectively, without finishing the sentence. "What time is it, Cesare?"

"Half past four."

"What! And I have a new circular to write about the Emancipation Gàrment! Do you dine at home to-night?"

"No; at the club."

"Then I shall take tea with the Charity Class—and—about the other matter—if my duty—"

"Good! Your duty, come what may. For me, I shall do mine."

And so they parted.

Bruni worked on until the twilight came, "I am a fool," he thought; "what is it, after all, to her, or to me." But it weighed upon his mind, nevertheless. He woke in the night and was thinking of it still. "I shall explore a little in undiscovered countries—it will do no harm," said he.

The next time Miss Feathering posed for her portrait she found him in a very talkative mood. He rattled on about books and pictures and ideas in a way that was quite disheartening to her; she would have preferred to listen to herself a little. Then he began to talk of people, and at last abruptly but not unnaturally he introduced the name of Ambrose.

He was holding up his brush, at the moment, to measure her face with the handle of it, his head being comically cocked upon one side like a bird's. One of his eyes was closed; and with the other, sharp as it was, he could only detect the faintest possible flush overspreading the face he had called colorless. The next minute the color was gone and they were discussing the approaching marriage.

" Miss Bromfield is lovely; don't you think so ? " said Miss Feathering. " She looks better in black than in anything else. I wish she would wear it always." Then she saw her chance and discoursed upon the art of dress for the next half hour, during which Bruni became absorbed in his work and agreed with her in everything. He had devised for the portrait a gold background of innumerable dollar-signs like arabesques in tapestry, interwoven artfully,—so artfully, indeed, that the scheme of the design might easily escape detection. This idea pleased him immensely and he chuckled over it; while for the rest of the sitting, Miss Feathering was permitted to do all the talking.

A few nights afterward he found Ambrose dining alone at the club, and joined him with a suggestion of champagne, which they accordingly ordered. But it was a wine that Bruni disliked; so that he drank little more than his first glass, while Ambrose finished the bottle. They had brandy with their coffee; and more brandy later on, in Bruni's studio, where they went to smoke their cigars. They wheeled chairs into the wide recessed window, and sat there in the dark, looking out at the river, with the great, black, empty room behind them. The night was cool and still, and, though the window was open, the city was out of hearing and even out of sight. Time, place and atmosphere were very

soothing to the spirit. Ambrose found it all
delightful, and said so. He always talked easily,
and in this unguarded hour he exhausted every
subject that came up, with a reckless fluency. From
clubs and club life he dashed into politics, to state
his views at great length upon the important questions of the day. Bruni listened till he could bear
it no longer, and then took the conversation into
his own hands.

"How is the law?" he asked.

"The law? Only so so; no money in it, I am
afraid. I begin to think a man ought to die if he
can't control plenty of money. There's Hunter,
now—he's done it. Just his infernal luck."

"Miss Jewsbury, you mean; I hear they are
engaged. That means another portrait for me, I
hope."

"Lucky devil!" said Ambrose. "You get them
all, sooner or later, don't you? I wish I were a
painter. By the way, how is that portrait of Miss
Bromfield?"

"Getting on."

"Where is it?"

"Here—but you can't see it. Don't alarm yourself. It shall be done before your wedding-day."

"Yes, be sure of that," said Ambrose. Then a
light wind springing up from the water blew a puff
of smoke into his face, and he coughed a little.

There was a moment of silence, in which the two
men effaced themselves behind the glowing tips of
their cigars. Then Bruni jumped up.

"That reminds me," he said, "that I have another picture almost finished. Oh, a *capolavoro!* I must show it to you. Wait a bit." And he groped his way into a corner to light up the room.

"Is it a portrait?" inquired Ambrose out of the darkness.

"Yes. The portrait of a lady. See!"

A blinding glare followed. The gas jets were high overhead, and as Bruni turned them down a little it seemed to Ambrose that all the light had come from the splendid white and gold likeness of Miss Feathering.

"The devil!" he cried. "That is amazing!"

Bruni laughed. "I told you it was a *capolavoro*," said he.

Ambrose came out into the room and gave a long low whistle. "What a background!" he continued.

"Yes," said Bruni. "I like the background myself. I think it suits her. But the likeness—"

"Perfect! Don't change a line; it is a most interesting picture."

"She is a type," said Bruni; "I wanted to do her justice."

"By Heaven, you have done it! And you didn't spare paint nor canvas, did you?"

"No. That was the way to do it. Besides—" and here Bruni, with certain reservations, told the story of his order for the picture and the cheque he had received.

Ambrose expressed his admiration with sparkling eyes. "The old man is an immense fellow," said he; "only a month or two ago he settled a fortune upon her."

"Ah, indeed? Then there's a chance for some-body," Bruni replied. "I wonder she doesn't marry."

"Oh, she won't marry," said Ambrose, carelessly. "She has been out three seasons, you know; and she has had a disappointment, I believe. We lawyers, you understand, are like doctors; we hear these things indirectly."

"Ah, is that possible?" said Bruni, in a tone of the greatest interest.

"Certainly. Why not?"

"Because I had almost fancied—no matter—"

"Go on. What do you mean?"

"Well, it is hardly fair to speak of it—but I almost fancied that she was—how do you say it—attracted, caught, I mean. I have seen Dr. Dudley making her his devotions—and the other day, when I mentioned his name— The painters, you know, like the lawyers and the doctors, have their oppor-tunities."

Ambrose never dreamed how closely he was watched while Bruni made these reflections with the utmost deliberation; but had he been on trial for his life he could hardly have held himself in better shape; he never turned a hair, and his face was like a painted mask, devoid of all expression.

"Dr. Dudley," he said; "it may be—it may be. I never thought of him. And the other—Miss

Bromfield's portrait, I mean, of course—show me that too."

" No," said Bruni, "not to-night." And he was off like a flash to put out the lights. "Sit down here and smoke again."

" It is too late—I must be off."

" At least another glass," urged his host, finding the brandy in spite of the sudden darkness.

" Just one—and then I'll go."

They shook hands at the door, and Bruni stood there a moment looking after him. As the footsteps died away, the Italian blew a great puff of smoke into his open palm, as if to disinfect it from the grasp of Ambrose. "*Canaglia!* Oh, but I could wring your neck for you!" he muttered. Then he went in-doors, and found his wife sitting alone with inky fingers over a great pile of freshly-printed circulars.

" *Madonna!*" he cried. "It must be done!"

" What must be done?" she asked, with a blank look.

" Bah! Why, anything. *Polenda* for to-morrow's dinner—what you will!"

" I shall never understand you," she murmured, absently, and went on folding circulars.

XII.

LETTERS OF GREAT MOMENT.

THE long, stifling summer waned at last, and after one fierce effort it suddenly went out like a sputtering flame. The nights grew longer and cooler, the afternoon breeze came up oftener and was less grateful, the streets were filled with flying leaves. One by one the houses reopened their barricaded doors to the painter and his myrmidons. The city lost its look of languor; every soul one met in it seemed alert and cheerful. In town, at latitude 42°, the first day of autumn is like the signal of hope to a beleaguered fortress, and with it the drooping spirit stirs and revives.

Marvin's first act after taking upon himself new duties had been to face about and neglect them. He had opened his office merely to turn the key upon it. The heat had become intolerable; and, to escape it, he went off alone for a fortnight's tour of the mountains. He had often taken such solitary journeys. He liked to make his own reflections and to travel leisurely in his own way. But this time he was bored; the heat pursued him everywhere; the people he met were dull beyond expression. He returned to town in the early days of September and almost the first man he saw at the club was Jack Elliston, with whom he undertook to have a long chat. He learned the particulars of Mr. Musgrave's illness, and was also informed that the great man might return any day; that Jack meanwhile was installed in his uncle's house to remain there for some time—at least, until Mr. Musgrave came entirely round again. After this, the conversation flagged a little. Jack seemed cold or abstracted, he could not quite determine what was the matter. But, presently, much to Marvin's surprise, his friend walked off and left him sitting there alone. Precisely the same thing happened the next time they met. Then Marvin drew back and made no more advances. It was not in his nature to get up a scene, and he did not choose to ask for an explanation. If Jack had taken offence where none was intended, Jack must set it right; time, no doubt, would bring him to his senses.

So Marvin opened his office door again, this time in earnest, and for the moment gave himself wholly to the law. Under this pressure of affairs he saw nothing of Miss Gérard and was even without news of her. Then, too, he carefully avoided further complication with the Bromfields; so carefully, in fact, as to cross the street when he passed their windows. One day, however, he met Helena on her way to Bruni's studio. She made a movement as if to detain him, but he would not notice it. For what had they to stand chattering in the street about? There was more than one excellent

reason for the discouragement of any such pro-
ceeding.

That morning Bruni found Miss Bromfield by
no means at her best. She looked pale and tired,
almost ill; and her thoughts were evidently a
thousand miles away. He tried very hard to
entertain her, but she answered him in monosyl-
lables, with hardly a smile for all his pains. He
complained of this afterward to his wife.

" Well," she said; " I told you so! Poor child!
She has engaged herself to that man—of course she
is unhappy!"

" And you will not interfere," said Bruni.

" If I could, it would not mend the matter. Can't
you see that she is too conscientious ever to break
with him?"

" I begin to think you are right," he sighed.

A day or two after this, it happened that Bruni
took his mid-day meal, which he called breakfast,
at the St. George, the great, gilded restaurant where
Miss Gérard and Marvin had once dined together.
After one or two light dishes the Italian ordered
macaroni served in a peculiar form that could not
be prepared in a moment; but time so wasted was
no loss to Bruni. The waiter, who was an old
friend, took a professional interest in the foreign
gentleman whose tastes in cookery were always
imaginative, and he set down the macaroni tenderly and lifted the cover with an air of triumph.

" It's done just perfect, sir," said he.

But Bruni pushed his plate away impatiently

and called for his account. Something had thrown
him into a state of strange excitement, for he
bustled off in a moment leaving behind him a fee
that was enormous from the foreign point of view;
while the waiter stared, shook his head at the un-
tasted dish, and then accepted his earnings with a sigh.

Through the crowded streets Bruni hurried
toward home, his lips moving all the while in
angry communion with himself. As he drew near
his own door, he saw his wife walking in the same
direction just in front of him. He hesitated for a
moment; then he went on and joined her with all
his usual calmness of manner.

"Ah, Cesare," said Mrs. Bruni, "I have been
lunching with Helena again to-day." And she
sighed.

"Alone?" he asked.

"Yes; I was so thankful! That fellow was
to be there, but he sent a note at the last minute, to
say he should be detained in court."

"What?" cried Bruni; "say that again!"

"Certainly—'detained in court.'"

"Did he say so?"

"Yes. What then?"

"Are you sure?" he persisted.

"Why, of course I am! Helena handed me the
note."

"*Santo Nome!*" shouted Bruni, overcome with
rage and joy together. They had reached their
own door-steps, up which he now rushed like a
whirlwind, almost dragging his wife after him over

the threshold, through the hall and into their little drawing-room.

"Sit down and write," said he.

"But—"

"Don't stop to talk," he went on, in a pleading tone; "do as I say—trust all to me—there is not an instant to be lost. Write!"

His wife took up the pen without a word.

"'Come at once to the St. George restaurant,'" dictated Bruni, "'where I am waiting for you. It is a matter of immense importance—come immediately!' Underscore that last word, and sign," he continued.

She obeyed, then folded the note and addressed it to Miss Bromfield at his command.

"Now give it to me," he said; "and go there, yourself, at once."

"Go where?" she asked.

"*To'!*" he cried, angrily; "why, of course, to the St. George! Wait there till she comes. There is a small room on the left—from it you can watch the door."

"But what am I to do or say?"

"Invent some excuse, if she asks you—no matter what—anything. Don't delay! Go! You will know the reason soon enough."

"And you?"

"I shall see that this note is put at once into Miss Bromfield's hands. I do my part—you will do yours—promise!"

"It is the strangest thing —" she protested.

" Promise ! " he repeated, throwing open the hall-
door. " Only promise ! "

" Yes ; I will go," she said ; and so they hurried
away in opposite directions.

Miss Bromfield, as it chanced, was dressed for a
walk that she had planned to take with Ambrose.
There had been some talk of a charitable expedi-
tion which they were to make together and which
had been more than once postponed. She had decided that it would be best to carry out the plan to-
day alone. On her way down stairs, she waited a
moment on the landing for there were voices at the
door below. Then the maid came up and handed
her a letter.

" It is very important," said the girl.

" What can it mean ? " thought Helena as she
read the blotted lines of Bruni's dictation. " She
was here just now—but it is certainly her hand."
Then she trembled at the only possible conclusion.
" Some accident ! I am losing time ! " And
throwing down the letter she hurried into the street.
There almost at the first step she found herself
growing faint with alarm at the unknown danger
that seemed to threaten her. " A carriage," she
thought; " it may be needed." She turned back,
passed the house again and went to the nearest
livery-stable, where she was known. Her look was
quite enough ; every man in the place was at her
service instantly. " Drive quickly," she said.
The man lashed his horses, and in five minutes drew
them up at the St. George.

This breathing-time, short as it was, had given her courage. She was ready now to meet the worst that could be dreaded. As she went slowly up the steps a boy in livery threw open the great, swinging doors that fell back behind her with a muffled sound. The huge dining-room was full of people. She waited for an instant just upon the threshold with a strange, confused impression, that haunted her for years, of light and color, of ringing glasses and the hum of voices. Then, directly opposite, far off across the marble floor at a small table in a window, she saw Maitland Ambrose and her friend, Miss Flossie Feathering.

It seemed as if her heart stopped beating. She drew back; they had not seen her; he was leaning forward and laughing with a champagne-glass in his hand. She turned to go out; then she changed her mind, wondered if she could walk, and did walk as steadily as possible to the door of a smaller room close by where Mrs. Bruni was standing.

Of course that dear, absent-minded, philanthropic woman had not seen her; she had been looking another way. But now she put out both her hands to Helena.

" My dear, you look like death ! " she said. " Do sit down."

" It is nothing—I want a glass of water—that is all."

Everything whirled. Helena tried to look about

her and to think why she was there and where she was. But it was all bewildering.

Mrs. Bruni found a smelling-bottle and put it into her hand. " Take this, my dear; I will call a carriage."

" No," said Helena, " I have one here; it is nothing—I am better, but I think I will go home."

" Of course; of course; come out into the air— it will do you good. I shall go with you." This, as Helena stepped into the carriage.

" No, indeed! On no account. Indeed, I would much rather not!" said Helena, while her friend insisted. "I am perfectly well now,—drive on!" she added to the coachman. And she leaned out of the carriage window smiling and nodding her thanks to Mrs. Bruni, who was left behind in spite of herself. " All my invention wasted!" she explained to her husband afterward. "With a perfect fib all ready to be told!"

In her bewilderment Helena quite forgot to ask the meaning of her strange summons—forgot, even, her surprise at it. All faintness had passed; her face burned with indignation, as if she had been struck, and were still smarting from the blow. She could think of nothing else.

But when she reached home there was the letter lying just where she had left it on the table in the hall. She read it once more and read between the lines. The mental numbness left her, and the message no longer needed explanation.

She sat down at her desk in the drawing-room

and looked over her engagement-book. Yes—
there was one that she did not care to keep. Then
she rang the bell and wrote a formal note in the
third person :

" Miss Bromfield regrets that she finds it impossible to keep her
appointment for to-morrow with Miss Feathering."

" Post this immediately," she said to the maid.

When the girl had left the room, she opened a
little drawer in the desk and took out all that it
contained—some letters, one or two withered
flowers and a tiny velvet case made to hold a ring
that was there upon her hand and that she now
drew off. She looked at it thoughtfully for a
moment, read the date engraved upon the inner
side and put it away in the box. Then she wrote
another letter—this time an informal one, without
date or signature or any of the usual convention-
alities :

"I have learned why and with whom you were detained to-day
at court—no matter how, I know it. There is no need of any explanation. These things I send you will explain themselves.
Please return mine to me—send all at your convenience. I can
think of no reason why we should be forced to meet."

She sealed these recollections up together, putting this last letter with the others. Then she
called the maid again, and ordered her to send the
package by a messenger.

" Will there be an answer, Miss Helena ?

"I am not sure. Tell the man to wait and see."

He waited long, and so did she. The afternoon

passed, night came. She went to her room, dressed for dinner, and admired her own self-control. She came back to the drawing-room, cut the last number of " Punch," and tried to find it amusing. At last the door opened, and a package very like her own, but not her own, was put into her hand. When she broke the seals, two or three trinkets fell out of it—a watch-charm, a pencil case, a little gold pansy, made into a scarf-pin. With these she found her letters and one from him :

" You leave me no choice, and I take you at your word, of course. I might defend myself, but why should I? You would not listen. I thought you cared for me a little, but that, it seems, was a mistake—and if you have no excuse to offer for a course so heartless and unfeeling, why let it go. All things considered, we are both well out of it."

She read this twice; then she tore it up, and threw the pieces into the fire; her letters, too. They blazed up gloriously. At that moment in came her father.

" Ellie! Why—what is the matter? "

" I have broken my engagement," she replied.

The captain had tried hard to like Ambrose. Indeed, a moment before, he would have assured himself that there was nothing to dislike in the man. But now he gave a cry of something more than mere astonishment—of exultation. Then she broke down, leaning there upon the mantel-piece, and crying like a child. And he was all kindness and sympathy for her, and soothed her in the tenderest and gentlest way. Only afterward, as he lay awake in the watches of the night, he told himself that he was, without doubt, the happiest father in the world.

XIII.

PROBLEM AND SOLUTION.

ONCE more Mr. Musgrave waited at the old place on the river bank, and watched the great white pine tree. His long illness had left its mark upon him; he looked thinner and paler for those dreary days and nights in the West. His step had grown more cautious; but he carried himself with the old precision, a model of elegance, even to the finger-tips. That very afternoon, before his glass at the Waterside Hotel, he had smiled complacently to think how remarkably well-preserved he was. What were a few years, more or less, in him, when his heart still beat wildly with one absorbing passion, like a boy's? He had often heard that women were flattered by the attention of older men—men who might reasonably be supposed to have outlived love-making, but who were yet unable to resist its charm. The idea was so clever that it must be true.

Still, that shade of uneasiness that seems inseparable from all courtship would steal over him at times. Her letters had not been all that he had hoped to find them. There was not sentiment enough—or rather, there was not variety enough in

the sentiment. It was as if her complete letter-
writer had opened at the word Love, and then had
lost all its remaining pages. To be sure, letter-
writing was a gift; few, perhaps, could write so
faultlessly as he. Yet he had been at home now
four days. He had seen her once at dinner with
the family, had exchanged a few hurried words
with her in the dark, afterward. But she had made
no definite movement toward him. Even this
appointment he was keeping had been granted at
his demand. It would not do. They must be
married, and at once. He was determined to insist
upon it. If she hesitated, it could only be that she
had grown less fond of her bargain. She would
not hesitate, of course, in the face of all his sacrifices—this clandestine marriage, for instance, to
which he had pledged himself, and which must
surely set everybody on to say disagreeable things.
But when they were fast married, what could it
matter? His social position was absolute; on all
sides he was respected and feared. He need only
present his wife to have her accepted everywhere.
What could it matter then? Let the gossips enjoy
their nine days' wonder while it lasted; he could
afford to snap his fingers at them. She had gone
too far to hesitate. No, she would not do it. But
why should she keep him waiting now this chill
September afternoon, even ten minutes after the
appointed time?

He strained his eyes in vain and sighed impatiently. He heard a light, mocking laugh close

behind him and felt a gentle touch upon his sleeve ;
then turning quickly he caught her in his arms and
kissed her.

"Don't!" she said, struggling to free herself;
but he still held her by the hand. "See how you
have crushed these flowers," she went on, pointing
to some wild asters in her dress. "They were
lovely!"

"Yes—lovely," he repeated; but it was of her
that he spoke, as he took her other hand in his.

"How cold you are!" said he.

"Yes; it is cold. I have been for a walk and I
came back slowly through the woods. Have I
kept you waiting?"

"No," he said, his impatience all forgotten. She
had brought him back from September into June.
"Let us walk here up and down; it is so long since
I have seen you."

"Yes; forty-eight hours nearly."

"But that was only a glimpse. I have been
without you four months.—I want you all to myself
—always. Don't you understand?"

"Yes," she answered, feeling that his eyes were
fixed upon her and not daring to lift her own; "yes,
I understand."

"It is time to end all this—to make our scandal
and have done with it. Now, before this week is
over!"

"So soon?" she asked, trembling. "So—suddenly, I mean?"

"Suddenly?" he cried, angrily; "suddenly?

When we have considered it from spring to autumn! Is that the way to make a sudden resolution?"

"No, no; I was thinking only of you,—of your illness. You have been ill so long—you are hardly well again."

"Absurd! Look at me! I was never better—never in my life—look at me, I say!" She obeyed, but only to perplex him. "I don't understand you," he went on; "or rather I begin to think that I do understand you perfectly. What is it? What does it mean? Are you tired of me? Are you playing fast and loose with me, Denise?"

"You have no right to ask that," she cried, indignantly. "I have watched and prayed for you. I have had no other thought. What else have I told you in my letters? You do not love me, then, since you can doubt me. Well, we will make no scandal. We will part here and go our separate ways."

"Denise, are you blind? It is my love that makes me doubt. I am jealous of everything—of the flowers you wear, the time that keeps us apart. Your way is my way—there can be no other. Are you not ready to take my hand and go with me?"

"Yes," she answered; "I have said so a thousand times. Whenever you like—to-morrow, if it pleases you."

He caught at the word. "To-morrow it shall be then! Listen! To-morrow at this time you will

take the afternoon train to town. Leave a letter
behind you explaining your absence in any way
you choose. Tell the truth, if you think best. I
will meet you at the station when the train arrives
and to-morrow night we will be married. My sister
shall have a letter from me to confirm yours, and
the family may fight it out among themselves. We
can return to face them when we see fit. Do you
approve of this?"

"Yes."

"And you will do it?"

"Yes—to-morrow."

"To-morrow," he repeated, bending down to kiss
her. At that moment they were startled by a
sound in the woods—a shrill war-whoop followed
by a shout of Miss Gérard's name.

"It is only Annette," she said. "Go!"

He hurried away and she followed him with her
eyes. "He has grown very old," she thought.
"He is gone, and it is done. But I have one little
chance left—one little chance, that is all!" Her
eyes fell upon a glove lying at her feet where he had
dropped it. She caught it up just in time, for
Annette came out upon her, struggling through the
underbrush.

"Why didn't you answer me?" she asked.

"I was thinking," said Miss Gérard.

"Thinking!" returned the child. "I wouldn't
be always thinking! What makes grown-up people
think so much?"

And again Miss Gérard could not answer.

When she was safe in her own room she wrote a few lines to Marvin asking him to meet her in town the next morning—Saturday, her free day. " Don't fail me—" she added, in a postscript. " I am going away for a long time."

" That will bring him," she said to herself as she came down stairs to despatch the note. There were several letters lying in the box on the hall-table ; she put them all together and sent them to the village in time for the night mail.

After dinner Mrs. Elliston called for music. She played a while and then took an early leave of the family. " I am going to town to-morrow morning," she said, carelessly, " about that plum-colored skirt of mine." This, to account for any possible piece of luggage she might take with her.

" Oh, then, my dear, will you get one or two things for me ? " asked Mrs. Elliston. " It is too bad to trouble you, but Mr. Elliston forgets everything on principle and Jack is never here, you know. I will hand you a list in the morning."

She smiled to think how little they dreamed of the thunderbolt in hand and ready to be hurled. Upstairs she moved quietly about, putting all her possessions into the exquisite order that her methodical mind suggested. She reflected that all would be sent to her some day, and she wished to leave nothing out of place. Then she packed a small portmanteau for her journey. And last of all, she composed her note to Mrs. Elliston. This was a hard task that it took long to accomplish. Finally,

14

her statement of the case was condensed into a few
words pleasantly vague in their nature. She
mentioned no names, but hinted at a new relation-
ship that was soon to exist between them ; and she
begged forgiveness for all her little failings, especially
for the ungrateful manner of her departure. She
locked this up in the empty drawer of her dressing-
table, leaving the key where it could be found
readily. Then she put out her candle that was
flaring low in the socket, and soon slept the sleep
of gentleness.

Up betimes in the morning, she sent her portmanteau away by the first train, that it might escape
Mrs. Elliston's wandering eyes. She did all that
was expected of her, giving the servants their orders
for the day and making plans for the next. And
when the hour came she went away without casting
any tell-tale look behind. In town, she found
Marvin waiting at the station. They passed at once
into the streets, that were filled at this mid-day hour
with all sorts of people drawn out of doors by the
splendid autumn weather. Miss Gérard looked
about her uneasily.

" Let us get out of the crowd as soon as possible,"
she suggested. " I have something to say to you."

" We will go to our old retreat—the graveyard,"
said Marvin. " There no one will disturb us."

They hurried on in silence, till suddenly she
plucked him by the sleeve. " Quick !" she whispered.
" Let us wait here a moment—here in this doorway.
Look there !"

"Jack!" said Marvin, peering out of the shadow. "He has crossed the street—he did not see us."

"Are you sure?"

"Yes; but if he had? What then?"

"Nothing, of course. I did not want him to join us—that was all."

They found the sexton unlocking the iron grate, to throw his picturesque little breathing-place open to the afternoon public. They were first upon the ground, which for the moment was all theirs. "It is a dear place," she said, as they began to lose themselves under the elm trees. "I shall always remember it, wherever I may be."

"You are really going away?" he asked.

"Yes—unless—"

"Unless?"

"Unless some miracle should prevent it. You promised once to help me, in time of need. Do you remember?"

"Yes. In case you had a problem."

"That is it," she sighed. "A problem. I want you to advise me—if you will."

"Of course I will. What is it?"

They had come to a remote corner close under the library walls. She left the path and went up to a low tomb, covered by a broad slab of marble, with names and dates that were almost worn away. She tried to read them absently.

"Dead and gone these hundred years," she said. "Let us rest here and I will tell you."

"It will be hard to make you understand," she

continued, seating herself upon the stone while he stood by attentively. "How can you put yourself in my place? Remember I am a woman and poor, finding work detestable, asking myself why I endure it longer. And to me there comes a way out of it—not the best way, perhaps—but one to make life easier for me."

"Go on," said Marvin.

"Well, there comes to me some one older than I am—much older, but who is very rich and very presentable, to save me with a single word from all this wretchedness. Some one who says : 'I am at your feet—make me happy—be my wife !'"

"And you have answered him, 'Yes.'"

"I am deciding what to do; that is my problem."

"One question," said Marvin. "Do you love him ?"

"I respect him," she answered.

"Do you love him ?"

> "Que ne suis-je sans vie
> Ou sans amour ?"

she murmured, softly. "You remember the song. Love proves sometimes an infliction."

"You are begging my question—not answering it," he returned.

Miss Gérard shrugged her shoulders impatiently. "No, then," she replied, "I do not love him."

There was a moment's pause. She traced out one or two of the worn letters with the tip of her parasol, and he paced up and down thoughtfully.

The hum of the street rose and fell; a cricket chirped in the long grass; some one in the library closed a window gently. But they were still alone and these sounds passed unnoticed.

Marvin stopped in his walk and met her look gravely. "You want an answer," he said, "and I think there is but one. Stop while there is time. To go on is to do him wrong, and you would escape from slavery only to sell yourself to a master. What could you gain by it?"

"A home," she said, quietly. "How much that means? Think of my life, its daily drudgery, the loneliness of it! Only to look forward is to be unhappy. But how can you judge of this? I knew you would not understand."

"A home, without love! Why not without light and air? In a month you would hate him and all the rest of it. You would despise yourself. It is a great temptation that he offers you. Yield, and you will make a terrible mistake."

"You are horribly severe. I exchange one form of misery for another that seems to me less miserable. Well, why not? Why not take the one chance that falls to me?"

"And the man?"

"The man? If it comes to that, I can pretend a little. He need never know."

"You are unjust to yourself. At least, do nothing rashly. Wait and think it over."

"I have waited. I must decide now—to-day. Why did I ask your advice?" she added. "I have decided."

"No, you must not—you shall not do it. I will not permit it. I will prevent you."

"Prevent me? You? By what right—why?"

"Why?" he repeated. "For the best of reasons! Because I—"

"Because I love you," he was on the point of saying. "Why shouldn't I say it?" he thought; and the very thought at such a moment was its own answer. He hesitated.

She had done what she had hoped to do, and now she looked at him with tender eyes. "Why?" she asked again.

He saw the look and understood it. "She loves me," he said to himself. "She loves me." Yet still he hesitated.

"Denise!" said a sweet, trembling voice close beside them. "Denise!"

Absorbed in their discussion, neither had noticed that a door in the wall behind them had opened, and that they were no longer alone.

Marvin looked up, startled at the interruption, and stood face to face with Miss Bromfield's poor little *protégée*, Amy Ruel.

"Denise!" said the girl again. Then she added, by way of apology to Marvin, "It is my sister. Don't you know me, Denise?"

Marvin turned back in surprise to Miss Gérard, who had risen and now stood adjusting a ribbon of her dress. "There is some mistake," she said, indifferently, without looking up.

The girl drew back and her eyes filled with tears.

"Oh!" she cried, in a tone of indescribable sadness. Then, recovering herself, she continued: "I know why you say that. But the mistake is yours, not mine. Mr. Marvin will believe me, for I am speaking the truth; it is so easily proved. See!" And from a shabby leathern purse, worn and shrunken with its years of emptiness, she took a small picture and put it into Marvin's hands.

It was an old photograph not unlike that which Helena had once given him; but this time the likeness was Miss Gérard's; and upon it was written in the scrawling, foreign hand that he knew perfectly,

Denise Laurence Valérie Ruel.

Marvin glanced at this, read the name and returned the picture to its owner. Then he looked again at Miss Gérard, who had seen it too, and whose confusion was most evident.

"I thought you had no relatives," said he.

There was nothing in the words themselves; but in the tone with which he spoke them there was everything. She stood before him convicted of deliberate falsehood, feeling that in one instant all his respect for her, his friendship even, had passed out of her reach and could never be regained. What should she do or say? She spoke in desperation and the words choked her.

"They were dead to me," she stammered.

But the sister she had denied interrupted her with scathing words.

"You did your best to kill them!" she cried. "Shall I tell him what it was and let him judge you?" Then the tears would not be kept back longer; she hid her face in her hands and sobbed bitterly.

All that was worst in the older woman's nature rose into her face and distorted it with rage. She looked malignant as a fiend.

"Tell him what you please!" she retorted; and, brushing by them angrily, she swept out into the path and away.

"I have lost him," she thought as she hurried on. "Well, what does it matter? It might have come to nothing, after all."

At the gate she stopped and looked back. Through the trees she could see Marvin bending over her sister, who had fallen like a flower broken in a storm. On her knees, with her hands clasped over one of the old gray head-stones, she was still sobbing as if she would sob her heart away.

"She will tell him!" said Miss Gérard, as she went on through the streets. "She will tell him, and what is it to me?" She tried to laugh away the thought that haunted her.

The man was lost irrecoverably; she had loved him honestly, she loved him still; but her love had come too late.

There were other things that she must think of. If the story from which she had fled to-day, like a guilty thing, were to be known everywhere to-morrow, it could do her little harm. To-morrow, her position would be unassailable; she could defy the world's contempt and its reproaches, with the world indeed at her feet as Mr. Musgrave's wife. For, of course, she had no idea of withdrawing from this bargain now. That name was her safeguard, her cherished amulet always in reserve. Mrs. John Musgrave! How well it sounded! How Mrs. Elliston would hate her for it! But she, to-morrow, would be only a poor relation—her envy would add lustre to the triumph.

Near the station was a quiet, old-fashioned hotel, that had been a tavern with a grass-plot and swinging sign-board before it in stage-coach days. Now many times enlarged and rebuilt out of all recognition, yet still hampered by some of its homely traditions, it was a sober, respectable place enough, much frequented by plain country people and by commercial travelers of the steadier sort. Here Miss Gérard secluded herself for the few hours of single life remaining to her. As she watched them out in a corner of the haircloth sofa that meagrely furnished one side of the dingy "Ladies' Parlor," it occurred to her that this wedding-day had been a strange one. The novel in her lap lay open at its first page; she could not distract her mind with it; nor could she delude herself unto the belief that she was altogether happy. She had been too near real happiness for that. She knew that Marvin had stated her case justly, so far as he could judge of it; and she knew, better than he did, how utterly false, mean and cruel her course had been throughout. But she admitted this only to declare that there was no help for it; that the blame lay not with her, but rather with the unknown quantity—the fate that had shaped this future she was now accepting. She was a victim; she must endure her martyrdom bravely, and make a virtue of it. The trial could not last forever. Some day, perhaps no very distant one, would bring release. To a widow with a fortune many of the world's joys were possible. Perhaps even the love she longed for and had dreamed of stood aloof there among them, only waiting to be realized.

So she went on building ghostly castles in the air until her hour came. In ten minutes the train would be due at the station where, perhaps, Mr. Musgrave was already waiting. He had once given her a ring, a splendid, antique gem that she had never dared to wear before the Ellistons. She put it on now, and it recalled to her a great picture that she had seen years before in some foreign gallery, —a picture of a youth, laurel-crowned, in a purple garment, with treasures heaped around him—with jewels and golden vessels scattered at his feet, and on his face a look of profound melancholy, of weariness and distrust of all things; for everywhere, round his wrists and round his ankles, through the embroidered robe and through the gifts spread out before him, ran the links of a heavy, iron chain. She remembered it well, and thought it the saddest picture she had ever seen; and now a chain like his was forged for her, and she had just placed its first link upon her hand.

Mr. Musgrave was not upon the platform, and she withdrew from the crowd into a narrow waiting-room with huge windows that commanded an interior view of all the fierce activity of the place. The trains came and went, the hackmen shouted, the porters and truckmen rushed hither and thither through a horde of restless passengers. Another train came in—her train. Other people met their friends, clasped hands with them and were gone; she, only, was left unprovided for. But she was not uneasy. There was a second train due a little later in the afternoon. She had misunderstood Mr. Musgrave, of course; it was a matter of another half hour, that was all. But when this, too, arrived, and she was left alone once more, her face length-ened with an anxious look. He had been detained. Something must have happened. What? It was idle to conjecture. She could only wait—wait and hope. Who has not at some time waited out a dreary hour at a railway station? Who can not easily imagine the misery of waiting when the hours of suspense are multiplied? She grew faint and pale under it; the jarring of the trains gave her a racking headache; it was torture. The shadows fell under the dim, smoky arches. Night drew on, the lamps were lighted; the officials eyed her sus-piciously; why should this woman linger there so long alone? For no good, surely. For no good, indeed!. Yet still she waited—and still he did not come.

XIV.

"SHADOWS WE ARE, SHADOWS WE PURSUE!"

UNFORTUNATELY for his peace of mind—a mind none too tranquil now at best—Jack Elliston had seen Marvin and Miss Gérard while they were waiting in the doorway. Moreover, with that inward eye, which, the poet to the contrary notwithstanding, is not always "the bliss of solitude," he had seen very clearly that they were waiting there to avoid him. Now he had taken his little affair of the heart by no means philosophically. The discovery of its utter hopelessness had lashed him into a fury, all the fiercer because suppressed by the remnant of common sense in him. He had chosen to think himself wronged, and neither time nor absence had availed to cure him of this false impression. On the contrary, he had nursed it tenderly, taking a positive delight in telling himself how completely miserable he had become. The hidden fire smouldered sometimes, but it was always there; meanwhile his attitude toward the rest of mankind grew vaguely misanthropic. His friends shook their heads over him and feared that Jack was "losing his grip." Western architecture had soured him, one said out of respect to his profession;

the doctors hinted at malaria, and wondered which of them he would call in; of course, until he said the word, a closer diagnosis was no business of theirs.

On this autumn afternoon, without betraying his consciousness of Miss Gérard's manœuvres, he kept on his course until he felt sure that she must have forgotten him. Then without asking himself why he did so, he turned and followed her. Marvin's tall figure easily detached itself from the surroundings; he soon caught up with them, and at a perfectly safe distance could perceive that they had dismissed him from their thoughts, and that they were walking leisurely absorbed in talk which it maddened Jack to think was the talk of lovers. All at once, he found that they had disappeared as suddenly as if some rose-colored cloud had intervened between them and the things of earth. He rushed on, stopped at the open gate of the graveyard, and caught a glimpse of her dress making its bit of color between the gray trunks of the trees. To intrude upon them there was out of the question, and he was on the point of giving up his unworthy pursuit when he remembered the library. "It was made for me," he thought; and, by taking a short cut at breakneck speed up one blind alley and down another, he was actually on the ground before them. He went into one of the lower rooms where two or three gray-beards sat dozing over their newspapers; and, catching up a review, he planted himself at a window that overlooked the vines and hollyhocks,

the verbenas and petunias, every foot in fact of the
familiar ground that for half the year seems to
smile at its own solemnity, as if it would divert our
thoughts from death to life. "Ostriches!" he said,
as he watched the pair come slowly up and stop at
the old tomb. How graceful she was! He knew
all her pretty poses by heart and that day she was
at her best. He was just too far away to catch their
talk, but he could imagine it. All his lingering
doubts as to their relations were now removed.
They loved each other, it was clear. "He will kiss
her next!" he thought; and then he could endure
the sight no longer. He threw down his crumpled
paper, and went away with one last look at her that
he remembered all his life. She was half reclining
on the great slab of marble to trace out thoughtfully
its worn letters—like some sweet, monumental
figure of antiquity, for ever gentle and for ever
young! She was at her best that day!

Only to get away from people—that was his one
thought! And he plunged into the back streets to
avoid an encounter with any of his friends. His
home was now at his uncle's house; and at this
hour of the day his uncle was either riding or gos-
siping at his club. He would go home then, and
have the house to himself for an hour or two at least.

It was a sober little house in a retired place,
where every footfall echoed back from the sur-
rounding walls. He let himself in quietly, and
rejoiced to find that he was alone. His uncle's
rooms were on the first floor, behind a library that

opened directly from the entrance hall; this latter
was a gloomy, ill-lighted place, heavily wainscoted
in walnut, after a former fashion; and its tone of
depression was admirably seconded in the library
itself, where the great black bookcases seemed to
support the cornice, and the furniture was covered
with dark leather, like the hangings. The careful
servants, old retainers of Mr. Musgrave, had drawn
down the shades in this room, lest any stray sunbeams should venture to frolic on the carpet there;
but Jack did not pull them up. All this sombreness
was grateful to him. He sat down in the nearest
chair, leaned forward upon the writing-table, and
buried his face in his hands. So he remained for
some time, silent as the house itself, till he was
roused a little by a certain slight sound that seemed
to come from the next room. His uncle was at
home then. He listened; yes, he knew the step;
he could hear it crossing and recrossing the
chamber. Then, to Jack's surprise, his uncle, unconscious of any listener, began to sing softly to
himself the air that intoxicated all men in the days
of Mr. Musgrave's youth—the Duke's song in
" Rigoletto "—"*La donna è mobile.*" And before Jack
could take himself off with his despair to his own
quarters overhead, the chamber doors were flung
open, and Mr. Musgrave burst into the room with
all the afternoon sunlight behind him and the light
music on his lips.

He stopped in some confusion, breaking down in
the song.

"Why, Jack!" he cried.

He was in his shirt sleeves, and held a dressing-case in his hand. The chamber was in disorder; papers and clothes were scattered about, and a portmanteau was lying open on the floor.

Jack, too, was somewhat confused. In the half-light of the room he looked paler than he really was. His uncle stared at him for a moment. "What's the matter?" he asked. "Are you ill?"

"Ill? No!" said Jack, trying to laugh. "I didn't know you were at home." And he turned away indifferently.

"Don't go," said Mr. Musgrave. "I want to talk to you. Come in here."

It was a large, high chamber, meant for a drawing-room, and in spite of the sunshine, there was a dismal air about it that recalled one of those awful, disused, royal bed-chambers shown to the public in a foreign palace. The chairs and tables were of a florid style that has passed away, never to be revived. The huge bed had heavy, flowered curtains hanging from a rococo garland, in tarnished gilt, that seemed to float in space close under the ceiling. Perched over the door was a wheezy Dutch clock, like an overgrown toad in black and gold; and in the farthest corner, behind the bed, stood a worm-eaten cabinet, suggestive of secret drawers. Jack, exploring it on the sly in his younger days, had been sure of one at least, but had never found the spring.

"You are packing," he said, as he sat down in one of the sunny windows.

"Yes," replied his uncle. "I am going to take a little journey."

"Alone?" Jack asked.

"It is only for two or three days," said Mr. Musgrave, ignoring the question, and kneeling beside his portmanteau. He would have liked to tell Jack everything, but did not know how to begin.

"You are just the least bit shaky, you know," continued the latter. "Are you really going away alone?"

"Yes—that is, no!" returned the other, packing now very busily. "I have an appointment that I must keep—a little appointment, and—but that's not what I want to talk about—it's about you."

"About me?"

"Yes," said Mr. Musgrave, looking at him intently. "You are out of sorts—I have noticed it for a long time. What is the matter with you?"

"Nothing—nothing at all."

"My dear boy, it won't do—I know better. Why not tell me? Are you in any scrape? Is it any money trouble?"

"No—it's not that," said Jack, incautiously.

"Ah, then there is something! I was sure of it. You ought to tell me. I will do everything in the world to help you."

There was an unaccustomed tenderness in Mr. Musgrave's voice, due not only to his fondness for

15

the boy who bore his name, but also to a kind of remorse at withholding his own secret. "I will tell him presently," he thought.

Jack deliberated a moment, and was lost. It would be a comfort, after all, to make a clean breast of it.

"You can't help me," he said, "nobody can help me. The fact is I've made an infernal fool of myself for a woman—there, the murder's out now. I've gone mad over her—and she has rejected me."

Mr. Musgrave's face flushed. Here was a new difficulty; it would be harder to confess his own good fortune now.

"I see," he said, gravely. "It's rather an awkward business. But then, it's a woman's no; don't give up too soon—it may mean yes."

The clock gave a little whirr and struck the hour. How the afternoon was going! But the portmanteau was nearly full.

Jack rose and paced the room despondently. "No," he said, "she has thrown me over. There's another fellow at the bottom of it—my best friend, I thought he was—a regular wolf in sheep's clothing! He has played the devil with me!"

"That's bad!" said Mr. Musgrave, looking about the room thoughtfully. Then he pulled out a key, and going over to the cabinet began to fumble at the lock. "But are you sure about it?" he asked.

"Of course," said Jack. "He is always at her heels. I followed them this very afternoon. They are engaged, I know."

" Who is he ? " called out his uncle from behind the bed-curtains.

" You know him. Marvin,—Gilbert Marvin."

" That clumsy brute—she prefers him to you? What kind of woman can she be ? "

" Well," said Jack, " it can do no harm to tell you—"

" Confound this thing ! " cried his uncle, still at the cabinet. There came a kind of snap, and Jack knew that the secret drawer had opened. He heard a rustle of papers, and Mr. Musgrave shouted back :

" Tell me, of course. I want the whole story— out with it ! Who is she ? "

" Well, you know her too ! My mother's governess, Miss Gérard."

No answer. " Miss Gérard ! " he repeated.

Then a smothered groan, a heavy fall. He crossed the room at a bound, and saw his uncle lying flushed and speechless with distorted features. He made a dash at the bell, and rung it twice or thrice so violently that the cord broke in his hands. The servants came rushing in with frightened faces ; trembling, they helped to lift their master up and lay him gently on the great bed. Jack cut short all their questions and sent them this way and that. He heard the hall door close behind them. He sat down by the bed where his uncle lay under the damask curtains, breathing heavily, with half-closed eyes and face drawn all awry. The house was oppressively still ; the clock slowly ticked

away the minutes; it whirred and struck again dis-
cordantly.   Then his uncle's lips moved in a faint
whisper, indistinct, unintelligible.   What was he
trying to say?   Jack bent down and listened.
The sound came again—one word only, twice repeated:

"Denise—Denise—"

Until that moment, Jack had found no special
significance in Mr. Musgrave's sudden attack.
What connection could there be between it and
his own trifling love affairs?   All at once the truth
began to dawn upon him dimly.   He watched
eagerly, hoping for more light, some clearer sign.
But none came.   The sick man's breathing grew
heavier and more irregular.   There was no further
effort at speech, no gleam of intelligence in his
eyes.   Jack left the bedside, and searched the room
for a clue.   He found the half-open drawer of
the cabinet and in it only a bundle of letters.   He
ran them over; they were all addressed to his uncle
in her hand; one had been taken from the envelope
and had fluttered down to the floor.   Close beside
it something glistened—a plain, gold ring.   He
read three lines of the letter, and knew the secret.

"They were to be married!" he gasped.   Then
he began to blame himself unjustly.   "If I had
only held my tongue!" he cried, bitterly; and
going back to the bed he took his uncle's hand.
His own tears fell upon it, but they brought no
sign of consciousness into the dark face, so sadly
changed that he could not look at it.   "My fault—

it is my fault!" he said, and hid his face in the curtains.

The silent minutes went on. "Will they never come?" he thought. And then he blessed the lucky chance that kept them away, giving him time to perform a duty he had forgotten. He must keep his uncle's secret. No one else must ever know his weakness and her treachery. Very quietly and quickly he destroyed the letters, tossed the ring into the secret drawer, locked the cabinet and replaced the key. Then he watched and waited, with thoughts of her that were more cruel even than she deserved. But a while ago he had seen her at her best; now, he thought the worst of her that any man can think of any woman.

At last his father came; the doctors, too; they did all their skill could do, but so little. The patient never spoke for all their pains. No one slept in the house that night. But long before the morning, there had stolen into that solemn chamber a presence that defied all earthly watchers.

XV.

PROGRESS.

EXHAUSTED in mind and body, and having told herself many times that it would be folly to linger at the station a moment longer, Miss Gérard at last went back to the hotel and passed a sleepless night there. More than once, as the hours went on, she reviewed the events of the last two days, even to the smallest detail, dwelling long upon Mr. Musgrave's suspicion of her at their meeting by the river. Had that suspicion been confirmed in some way at the last moment? Had Annette by chance overheard their talk, and had Mrs. Elliston interfered? Or had Marvin told his tale of her double dealing? This last might well be; yet how could Marvin know whom to take into his confidence? How could he dream that she was anything to Mr. Musgrave? Perhaps the latter had merely repented of his hasty resolution, overcome by his old repugnance to the secret marriage. This was not improbable. And perhaps she had misunderstood his directions, and had kept the appointment in one place, while he had been keeping it in another. Here there was a grain of comfort. They might have a good laugh yet over some such absurd complication.

She would send a line to his house in the morning, and know the worst at all events. Why had she not done this before, instead of waiting all that dreary time? The thing now was to sleep. But then her tormenting doubts would come back, refusing to be quieted until she had been over all the ground again. And so she counted out the hours.

Early in the morning, she wrote a short note in pencil very cautiously worded, and signed only with her initial. She took this down stairs herself to despatch it by some careful hand. It was Sunday, and there was no one stirring in the great hall of the hotel. As she crossed the marble pavement, her eyes fell upon the bulletin of a morning paper— done in huge black letters designed to startle and allure—that stared her in the face. She could read it all at a glance, but she saw in it only one line: *Sudden Death of John Musgrave!* The brutal advertisement gave her an explanation that was simple enough—so simple, in fact, that it had never crossed her mind. She need not send the letter nor any other letter now.

She bought the paper, and went back to her room. A few lines of fine print, after the date of his birth and an estimate of his money-value, stated that he was never married, and that his loss would be sincerely mourned. Above, in larger type, were the meagre details. He had dropped dead in his chamber while packing his trunk for a journey. So he meant to come then! Apoplexy, the doctors called it. They hinted at no underlying cause.

How was she to know of that? She never guessed
that she had killed him.

What to do, what part to play in life, henceforth—
that was the all-important question. She sat down
to face it fairly and squarely, and she considered it
for hours. At first many courses seemed open to
her; but, one by one, she rejected them all. She
could not return to the Ellistons; her letters to Mr.
Musgrave must exist and would be discovered;
there was Marvin, too, who came to the house—she
could never meet him any more. She might seek
out her father and beg his forgiveness; but that, if
granted, meant a life of struggle and privation like
her sister's. No; they were better off without her,
and she had done with them. As for drudgery,
she was tired of it. Why not let all go, cease
contending with the other vipers, no longer gnaw
like the fabled viper at the file of life? Why not
destroy herself? Here was an issue to which all
must come sooner or later in one way or another;
why not choose her own way, her own time? She
contemplated this seriously and calmly, like some
Roman woman with drawn dagger and hornbook
of philosophy; then she put the thought away for
future use, labelled, as it were, "Not yet." There
was another refuge toward which she had been
drawn in times of doubt—the Canadian convent of
Notre Dame de Lorette, at Niagara, where she had
been sent to school. One of the sisters had been
very fond of her. Sister Félicienne! How well
she remembered her gentle face! Smooth and fair,

like Del Sarto's "Charity" in the Louvre! Could
her own face over there in the glass, haggard and
worn as it was, ever grow to look like that? Why
not? There was infinite rest in the old convent
garden, with its high, gray walls. She had tried
the world, and it had played her false at every turn.
She needed rest; she would try that. Surely, no
plan was better, none easier to pursue.

Her mind was made up; there were few preparations to occupy the remnant of the day that seemed
an eternity. She kept her room, dining there alone
and restlessly, eating little, eager to be gone. She
took the night train, slept soundly and woke to find
another day beginning and her journey drawing to
its close. There was a hurried breakfast at a way
station; then miles of dullness under leaden skies;
then a city full of spires and tall chimneys, with
grimy warehouses built along a muddy river. There
were few passengers; no one spoke to her. The
morning passed, the day grew brighter; and at noon,
just as the train stopped at the great suspension
bridge, the sun burst through the clouds, shining
out gloriously upon the gray cliffs against which
the river went roaring and plunging away from the
smoother water under the white smoke of the falls.

She knew the ground here, every inch of it. She
was very tired and hungry, and the convent was a
long way off; she would dine, rest a little, and cross
the river in the ferry afterward. She went straight
to a little German hotel that she knew of, away from
the bustle of the village. It was a quiet inn with a

very home-like air about it. There were flowers in
the windows; the polished floor of the hall shone
like glass, and in the little parlor a rosy maid was
at work sweeping the spotless carpet with tea
leaves. She had come to dinner? It would be
ready in half an hour. The parlor was in disorder;
few guests arrived so late in the season. She could
have a room to herself until dinner-time. Would
she be so good as to step this way? They were
very civil; it was a relief to see their pleasant,
foreign faces; still more of a relief to be left alone.

She sat down at a window that overlooked a
small garden full of scarlet geraniums and mari-
golds. Its paths were carpeted with yellow maple-
leaves, and a great coffee-colored cat had come out
there to bask in the sun. Overhead a spire glistened with the greenish-gold lacquer peculiar to
that region; and between the maples the American
Rapid splashed along in broken ridges. Not a
human creature was in sight, and there were no
sounds but the rushing of the river and the more
distant rumble of the falls. Yes, she had done
wisely. This was the place for her. Only to look
out of that window was to rest. Here, away from
the world of cities, with such surroundings, peace
must come at last.

Some one knocked at the door. Dinner was
ready. And such a dinner! What tempting dishes
were served at it! How clear the glass, how fresh
the linen! She sat near one end of a long table at
which there were many vacant places. A priest

came in, and a young student—both well-known in the house, evidently; and two or three elderly women, who seemed to be traveling alone like herself. These were all the guests, except a queer bridal party that had taken possession of the other end of the room. They were Germans, attended by the bride's sister, and by their pastor and his wife. The bride was a girl of twenty, very slender and graceful, blonde and beautiful.; the groom, a rich brewer from the next town, was a man of fifty, rough, noisy and very red in the face. These people made merry in the manner of their nation, pronouncing strange spells and clinking high in air their yellow glasses; and after dinner, when Miss Gérard had returned to her quiet window, she could watch them as they drove away in their barouche, to the box of which the pastor mounted, taking his place beside the coachman. They laughed and waved the landlord their farewells; and when she saw this, the tears came—the first she had shed for the other life she was leaving. How silly it was! The past was past, no tears could save it. As she drew out her handkerchief something fell from her pocket. A glove! Ah, yes, *his* glove dropped in that hurried leave-taking three days ago. Poor empty glove! She smoothed it out thoughtfully, but it was not altogether of him that she thought. She called for pen and ink, and, instead of a letter, wrote a single line—"Sans vie, sans amour"— addressing it to Marvin. " He will understand that," she thought; " I want him to know that I have failed in everything." It was her only farewell to the world.

She went out into the village to post this message herself, and the splendid sunshine tempted her to go on as far as the river shore, and finally over the bridge to Goat Island. She had but one short stage of her journey left to make, with the whole after-noon before her. The walk was enchanting. The air was clear and fresh with just a touch of frost in it, cool in the shadow, but very warm in the sun. In a little patch of garden before the one house upon the island, the clumps of crimson and yellow dahlias had just reached perfection. A collie dog had stretched himself out in the porch. Near by, stood a middle-aged woman picking grapes from a trellis. She had in her face that same placid, saint-like expression—the look of Sister Félicienne. "It is the place," thought Miss Gérard, and she longed to talk with her. But the woman looked at her shyly and did not speak. She walked on. The sumachs were blood-red, the maples were pink and gold; at her feet the ground was purple with great beds of wild asters. The little wood-paths running off into the wilderness were ankle-deep with fallen leaves, through which the squirrels scurried away at the sound of her step. She met no one. The rush of summer travel was over; the world and his wife had taken themselves off, and the wonderful island in all its tangled beauty was hers to enjoy alone. All around her, through the flickering leaves, the rapids leaped and shone and sung to the eternal drum, drum, drum of the cataract that thrilled her with its invisible presence. All that she could see delighted and exhilarated her. She gave herself up to this mysterious charm, lingering at every turn to draw long breaths, and to study the book that is open to all men, that no man ever learns. There was an old tree cut all over with names and dates,— long-forgotten challenges to Time, some of them already blotted out by his reproving fingers. One name, high above the others, interested her. " Kenyon 1821." A good name, an uncommon one; she remembered it in an old romance of Hawthorne. Perhaps he had first seen it there, and had stopped in that very place to write it down. " 1821." It must have been deeply cut to endure so long. She wondered if Kenyon were still living and who he was.

She wandered down to a reedy spot on the shore, where the rapid, none the less swift for being shallow, went gliding along with hardly a ripple. For some time she watched its glassy surface and the smooth pebbles lying there just out of reach; then, turning away, she stumbled and almost fell over a rock half hidden in the yellow grass. Her eyes caught some lettering upon the stone, and she knelt down to read it. Many winters had dealt rudely with it—it was almost gone. There was no name; no date; but at last she made out these words :

ALL IS CHANGE
ETERNAL PROGRESS
NO DEATH

She pondered long over this strange inscription. She had never heard of it before. Whose work was it? The old story of the hermit of the falls came back to her; if that were true, he had built his rough shelter within a stone's throw; and but a few yards off he had gone to his death in the river, under the American Fall. Had he carved here at his own gravestone? Or had some hermit of a day, like this of hers, devoted himself to this memorial? No; the man who did that knew the ground well, and loved it as one loves a dear relation. The words would not go from her mind. "Eternal Progress!" The whole spirit of the place was there.

She followed the path again to the outer shore of the island, till far off upon the Canadian side the familiar lines of the convent came out against the sky. At last she stood in sight of home, yet parted from it by the wide river at its fiercest point—by that scene which is the despair of all who try to paint it, either in colors or in words. There was the broken verge of the great Horseshoe, along which the water waited, as if in wonder at its own recklessness, with the shining stretch of unbroken green in it, down which nothing seemed to move. There, too, almost in the centre of the fall, and on its very edge, was the flat rock that the water never covers, even for an instant. As a child, she had often longed for the power to stand there and look down. She had known the Horseshoe well, but never well enough. For the greater fall, unlike its American fellow, permits no one to enter upon intimate relations with it, but holds itself aloof, as Jove did from Semele. From many points upon the shore it is possible to get glimpses of its far-off grandeur. At either end one may draw nearer, and lose one half of it in peering over at the other. But no man has ever seen it all and lived.

Leaving behind her all this tumult of the waters, Miss Gérard turned off into the quiet woods, among the startled squirrels, through the thickly-strewn leaves, and over mossy logs that crumbled when she stepped upon them. Here, there were no paths; but she pushed on, until she came out upon another shore, at the southern end of the island. Here, a triangular shoal stretches away for a long distance, to a vanishing point where the river divides into two branches that form the American and Canadian Rapids, between which Goat Island lies. This reach of still water, hardly three feet in depth, is smooth as the water of a lake—so smooth, that on that day it only lapped gently the grassy bank upon which Miss Gérard sat down to rest. There was little here to attract the eye or to divert the mind. It was a quiet nook, where one might easily drowse away an hour in a waking dream. And before long, such a dream began to steal in upon Miss Gérard—a dream of her past life, in which, one by one, came trooping back, unbidden, a host of recollections. Some sad, some bright; all its great events, and others so slight that they had been long forgotten. She recalled the old Canadian city of her birth, with its tall spires and its narrow streets, its busy docks and dingy warehouses; the dismal counting-room, where her father, burdened with a family and with the soul of a sculptor in him, had been forced to add up columns of figures for his daily bread. He could never earn much more, poor man; he was not a good accountant, they told him; no wonder that he was generally gloomy and sometimes ill-tempered. Her mother had died while she was still a child; but she remembered perfectly the weak, pretty woman, who had been an actress of great promise. Cut off from this career by a terrible fever, she had been left to recline through the rest of her short life, and to so pet and spoil Denise, that her husband on this account had been moved to many an angry remonstrance. The moment his back was turned she would kiss the child and tell her that she was growing more beautiful every day, and that she must live to marry a lord, and sit beside him in a coach-and-four. "And shall I have a silk dress then?" Denise had asked, after one of these scenes. "Yes, my darling, and jewels like these. A duke gave them to me." Whereupon, her mother had shown her a sapphire cross that she wore about her neck, always hidden away. "Oh, let me have it!" Denise had cried. And then she had been permitted to keep it and admire it for one whole day. Long after her mother's death, the cross had been shown to her again. Her father had taken it from his desk, and had called her to him. "Denise, look at this;

it belonged to your mother. I will give it to you
on your wedding day, if it is not turned into money
long before that time." How his lips had quivered!

" Are we poor ? " she had asked.

" Yes, child, we are poor—very poor indeed."

After this, fortune had smiled upon her for a
year or two. An old friend of her father stepped
in and sent her to the convent-school. She was
fond of books, learned easily ; and her pretty ways
made her at first a general favorite. But she was
wilful and obstinate ; and as time went on her
vanity and selfishness became ungovernable. She
grew envious of the rich girls who had fine dresses,
and were always getting presents from home.
Nothing ever came for her. This tone of discon-
tent gradually turned them against her ; till Sister
Félicienne was at last her only friend. Even she
lost her patience at times. "You must learn to
conquer yourself," she would say ; "no one else
can do it ; you are your own enemy." And Denise
had her excuse—that ready one of selfishness. "I
can't help it ; I was born so," she always replied.

One day, just before the time for her return
to the home that she dreaded to see again, two
strangers paid a visit to the convent and the school.
Such visitors were not uncommon ; but these people, a man and his wife beyond middle age, strangely
attracted Denise, who as it chanced went about
with them ; perhaps, because she saw at once that
they were rich. The man was over dressed ; the
woman's fingers were covered with rings ; but in

16

her eyes they were types of elegance and ease—
like the high-bred courtier people that she knew in
books. They, too, fancied her, it seemed; for she
heard them whispering about her with the sisters,
when her back was turned. But they went away,
and nothing came of it. Till one day after her return home, when she was moping out a dull morning with hopeless forecastings of her future, they
suddenly flashed in upon her, and carried her off to
lunch with them at their hotel. Then they unfolded
a scheme that amazed and delighted her. They
were going abroad; they had no children; the
languid lady needed a companion; the duties
would be very light; would she accept the place,
travel with them, speak the languages for them—
in short, make their home hers indefinitely? She
lost no time in taking them at their word. If her
father would only consent! Her new friends made
light of this doubt, promised to call upon him, and
did so the next day with much ceremony. To
their surprise and his daughter's sorrow, he hesitated,
took time to consider, and his final answer was a
curt refusal. To Denise, who was heart-broken, he
gave his reasons. He did not like these people, he
could learn no good of them. On the contrary, he
knew they were not of the right sort. He would
never trust his child to their keeping. Moreover,
he had been very ill—he was still far from strong.
There was her sister, too young to be left to herself.
He could not send her to school. Denise must take
care of her and of him. It was her duty. Then

she implored and insisted until he grew very angry. The scene ended, on his part, with a positive command to her never to see the purse-proud schemers again ; and on her part, with a storm of tears.

His command she disobeyed. She saw her discomfited patrons again and again. They comforted and coaxed her treacherously. She was old enough to know her own mind; her father would change his. She wanted to go, she must go ; all would be well in the end. And in the end they enticed her away. She left her father's house secretly in the night, went with her companions on board the nearest steamer, and the next day was far out at sea. Nor was this all. That the finishing touch might not be wanting to her misconduct, before going she broke open her father's desk, and took from it the precious, jewelled cross, wearing it away upon the same faded ribbon that her mother had flung round her neck when she was a child. "He told me I should have it some day," she said to her conscience. "Let me take it now, or he will turn it into money." The explanation of her flight she left to the strangers, who sent in their letter to her father a cheque for so large a sum that it seemed, in itself, all in proof of their goodness of heart that the most exacting parent could demand.

But the cheque followed them out by the next mail in a furious letter to Denise. He ignored her benefactors. "Did you think you were worth so much?" he asked. "You have behaved brutally and I have done with you. You are not my daugh-

ter. Never let me hear of you again." It was a
dreadful letter. She assured herself that she did
not deserve it; but she shook her head when they
told her he had not meant half that was written in
those hasty words.

Later, came a piteous letter from her sister. Their
father had been ill again, and was still unable to
work. It was hard to know how they were to live.
Would she not come home? She was always in
their thoughts. If only she had kept the cross and
would send it back. It was that which had turned
her father so against her. Did she know what he
said of her? That he called her wicked and ungrateful?

Under this last word was something else that had
been erased. Only the faintest lines were left, but
Denise made them out. "A thief." It was that he
really called her. A harsh word, but a true one nevertheless! She admitted it. But she never answered
the letter. "It is too late now," she said; "I am
better off without them, and they can live without
me; some one will take care of that. They will
never starve; nobody starves now-a-days."

So she stifled the spark of conscience that was
left to her, and went on through the picture galleries,
leading that easy, foreign life for which she was so
admirably fitted, happy without responsibilities, cul-
tivating herself and growing every day more selfish
in the process. She resembled in this the soft,
white stone that the French builders cut like clay
after they have placed it in position, and that

before long hardens into flint, growing darker and
darker in the sunlight. She told herself often that
this was a dream too bright to last; and all at once
there came a rude awakening. It was one summer
night on the shore of the Lake of Geneva, in a
garden at Ouchy. The man, old enough to be her
father, who should have been her protector, suddenly turned upon her with insult, catching her by
the wrist, making fierce love to her, swearing that
he was ready to sacrifice wife, reputation, everything,
if she would say the word. Poor and mean as she
had grown, she had still the saving grace to be
overcome with horror. She broke from him,
rushed to the station, and an hour after found herself alone in Geneva, without money, without friends.
At a hotel where she was known, she told a plausi-
ble story and found a lodging. There she made
her plans. She would join a party of Americans,
chance acquaintances of travel, who had been kind
to her; tell them this chapter of her history, and
make a fresh start. But they were a long way off,
traveling for dear life in the Netherlands. To
follow them there she must have money. Well!
Her mother's cross was still about her neck! She
sold it the next morning to one of the jewelers on
the Grand Quai. The man was honest; she was
startled by the sum he paid her, and she remembered then her mother's words—" a duke gave it to
me." Had her father known its value, she wondered?
She, herself, had never realized it.

Her new friends, who were plain, warm-hearted

people, received her kindly and brought her back with them to America. Afterward, they helped to find her a situation as governess. From that time until her coming to the Ellistons, she led a life of routine, dull and commonplace enough. But she assumed its burdens cheerfully, as she would have welcomed any manner of hard work that could lead her to forget certain passages of the past that haunted her. In time she did forget them, or remember them vaguely as misfortunes that had befallen her through no fault of hers. The old formula never failed her. " I could not help it," she said, and remorse fought against it in vain.

To-day, all these forgotten things came back with strange vividness, as she sat alone in sight of the very spot where her career of ingratitude had begun. An hour passed and left her still absorbed, struggling against herself in her own defence, this time with indifferent success. At last she forced herself to think of other things. She looked out over the quiet shoal to the point beyond it, where the rapid changed its course and broke into two streams; beyond that still to the distant river, that looked as calm as the water at her feet. She could see the white sail of a boat there miles away. She wondered how near the rapid it would be safe for the boat to come. What if it should venture too near and be drawn down beyond the reach of help? It would not take long. From that place to the great fall could hardly be a minute's journey—by the river.

The shadows were growing longer. Just one

look at another place close by, and she would turn back to the hotel, and then to the ferry. It was time to go on.

Stretching from the south shore of Goat Island straight out into the heart of the boiling rapid are three wonders of Niagara, that till lately were inaccessible,—three feathery islands, known as the Three Sisters, separated from their huge brother by three chasms, over which light bridges have been thrown. Through these channels, that it is always wearing deeper, the river plunges in three sister torrents, all beautiful, yet resembling each other only faintly as sisters are wont to do. The first stream, that falls over its black rocks like a net-work of jewels, is comparatively shallow, yet it would be unsafe to set foot in it. The first island, like the others, is a jungle of pine and birch and swamp-maple, struggling up between mossy rocks and the decayed stumps of older growth. Miss Gérard did not wait here long, for just at the end of the bridge she found an artist sketching. She remembered his face at the hotel, and perhaps he remembered hers, for he eyed it curiously over his easel. She went on over the second torrent, which breaks into a bar of foam above the bridge and tumbles all in a heap below. Queer little bits of rainbow play about the foaming places, but if looked for twice are not to be found. She watched for them a moment or two, and then followed the path along over the middle isle to its farther shore, where some wooden steps lead down to the rocks below the last bridge. She was well out into the river, and this was the point she wanted. Here she seated herself close upon the brink of the third torrent, which is deeper and wider and wilder than the others. As she looked up at it, the water formed for her its broken horizon line against the sky, and seemed to come tearing down out of the blue distance, as if all the evil spirits of Baron Fouqué were struggling and snarling in it for the mastery. It was of all colors from bottle-green to black; and, at its lowest point, the water was lashed into showers of drops, tossed high into the air and glittering like bits of ice. The gulf is perhaps thirty yards in width, and beyond it lies the narrow strip of the outer island; beyond that, the great Canadian Rapid stretches away like the sea, but more terrible than the sea, because of its reckless onward movement that never slackens, that no human force can stem or resist even for a single instant. Far out in this fearful current, a great, broken globe of foam rises and falls incessantly above the highest waves. This column of water, which has been named the Leaping Rock, seems to nod and beckon with uncouth gestures, as though there were life imprisoned in it. To Miss Gérard, in childhood, it had been the embodiment of Kühle-born, the evil genius of the story of Undine. She had watched it often from her window; it had been a real thing to her then, and she half believed that its frantic motions had some hidden meaning in them that could be learned. To-day, she looked at it again and shuddered.

All around her the noise was deafening. The
water at her feet was of the purest green, so beautiful
that it was hard to believe death lurked in it. Down
the river, a few hundred yards to the north, this
same color repeated itself in a clear, glassy line—
the brink of the Horseshoe—where all this rush
and roar of water seemed to end quietly without a
murmur or a ripple. And the convent had come in
sight again; it made a dark blot there on the western
sky. That was her goal. It looked not unlike a
prison. It was a grim rest, after all, that awaited
her behind those stone walls. Was it worth while
to come so far and gain so little? She shook her
head, and sighed.

Then the past came rushing back with all its
bitter memories, its charges that she knew were
just. They could not be denied, they would not be
forgotten. The cross! Ah, the cross! If she had
only not stolen it; if, having stolen it, she had only
sent it back in answer to her sister's letter! And
her course with Mr. Musgrave—how she had deceived him! She had been false as the water there
—as cold and cruel and heartless as that smiling
rapid. How she had lied over and over again to
him and to Gilbert Marvin! Marvin! Ah, there
was a despairing thought! She had been so near
to real happiness. In another moment she believed
he would have spoken. Then all these wrongs
might have been set right. Her love for him was
so far above all other influences she had ever
known, that in time it must have changed her

nature, and given her the power to make atonement
for every sin she had committed.   How, she did not
know; but in that way peace of mind would have
surely come.   And now she had shut the door
upon the world.   Well, it had treated her harshly.
Why had she been made to suffer and endure so
much ?   She had not asked for life—it was all a
mistake ; and yet, perhaps, she had fifty years to
live.

A white sea-gull soared along overhead.   How
strange to see him there so far from home!   She
watched him as he flew northward toward Lake
Ontario.   " He will drop down there," she thought,
" upon some gentle wave, fold his wings and rest."
And for her there was no rest.   She could never
stay in the convent.   While life lasted, through all
those fifty years, the eternal struggle must go on.
She was like the rapid.

She looked down at it; the spray was flying over
her, the water was within reach of her hand.   She
knew every turn of it well.   It had a dreadful beauty,
like that of Medusa and the Sirens; their danger,
too.   To watch and listen there gave one a longing
to leap into it.   It held her now with an impression
of enchanting loveliness, of power and of cruelty.
It was merciless, irresistible.

"Sans vie, sans amour!"   Yes, she was like the
rapid.   Then, why not one with it ?   Why not yield
to this new impulse, make the plunge, and become
a part of that inexorable force that seemed to draw
her down ?   One little moment would spare her all

the weariness of living. "It is only putting one's foot into cold water," she thought. She caught up a twig and tossed it into the foam. "Just there—it would be just there!" she said aloud; and before she spoke, the twig was out of sight.

An old tree grew on the very edge, throwing one great lower limb out over the water. She leaped up and ran along it, ready to throw herself headlong. She waited a second too long and could not do it. "No, I dare not," she cried; "I am not fit to die so. I must live—live and pray!" She started back along the branch; there came a crash, and she knew that it had broken. Then, with a wild shriek that her own ears hardly caught above the mocking uproar that surrounded her, she fell through the shining water-drops,—and was gone.

They never found her. Hours afterward, when she was missed, the artist remembered that she had passed him on the way to the outer islands, and that he had not noticed her return. A search revealed the broken branch and a footprint or two, from which her death and the manner of it were surmised. The story passed into the folk-lore of the place; and to this day the queer, amphibious guides to the ledge below the Horseshoe whisper of a sunless cavern, where her bones are said to lie with the water dripping over them, turned into stone so hard that not Niagara itself can ever soften it or wear it away. And on through all the years go those foaming ridges, howling like fiends, lashing the dark cliffs, sweeping round the great whirlpool and still pressing forward in eternal progress.

Eternal Progress! Yes. But it leads on through an Eternal Peace in the depths of the great lake, where the white-winged sea-gull settled down. And the waters there are as blue as the wide arch of Heaven.

XVI.

TIME may outrun the swiftest river, or it may drag heavily one foot behind the other, as on leaden shoes. It ambles, trots, gallops or stands still here with us to-day, as of old in the forest of Arden. And so, in divers paces, with the divers persons of the story, there traveled on more than six months of which but the briefest chronicle needs to be set down. With Marvin it did not trot, but went, nevertheless, at " a fine easy amble." This, thanks to many things. First of all, work ; which may be said to rank, as a consoler, second only to sovereign Time himself. His mistress, the Law, proved exacting, and he did his best to please her. Of course, he was among the first to know that Ambrose and Miss Bromfield had broken their engagement. That subject was discussed freely in quiet corners at the " Ægean" for nearly a week. The very day he heard of it came the unsigned message from Niagara. But Miss Gérard had taken far too much for granted in believing that he would at once grasp its meaning. On the contrary, a glance at the post-mark led him to a strange misinterpretation. " I see," he said ; " she is on her wedding journey. 'Sans vie, sans amour;' it means that she has sold herself to old Crœsus, whoever he may be. Well, I am sorry for him." And he destroyed the letter, contemptuously. He heard nothing of her death, as it happened, until long afterward. Then, believing that she had voluntarily withdrawn from the marriage and had taken her own life, he bestowed upon her more pity than her case, sad as it was, demanded. It was written that he should misunderstand her hopelessly. And she had erred again in supposing that he knew the story of her youth. After the flight of Denise, her sister loyally refused to throw any more light upon it; and neither she nor her father ever betrayed it to the world.

As to the broken engagement, that made a very bright spot in Marvin's heart. Nevertheless, he pretended to believe that this satisfaction was wholly on Miss Bromfield's account. "She has had her little experience," he argued; "she will be in no hurry to repeat it. I pity the poor devil who asks her next. As for me—well, there are three gray hairs in my moustache, and I shall probably never marry." He did not trouble himself to wonder how the engagement had been broken; it was an escape for her, that was enough. The world, however, lent its ear readily to every idle whisper that came and went upon the wind. One day, Helena had broken the match for good cause; the next, Ambrose had cast her off most unreasonably. They had settled the business by mutual consent, as the phrase goes ; they had quarreled, ostensibly over a dinner at a restaurant ; but jealousy, the green-eyed monster, was really more to blame than any terrapin or turtle. Here was introduced a shadowy third person, whose name and sex depended upon the story-teller ; and so the tale fell to pieces of its own weight. Mrs. Bruni had her failings, but tale-bearing was not among them. She never hinted at what she knew ; while Bruni eagerly questioned everybody and knew nothing.

All the old stories were revived three months later, when Ambrose became engaged to Miss Feathering ; and those, who had blamed him most, were the first to take his part. That he should turn to her for consolation was pronounced entirely natural, after the shameful way in which he had been treated. "Such a nice thing for Flossie ! " said her intimate friends. "What a handsome couple ! They are to be married at Easter, and she has sent to Paris for her wedding-dress ! " and they were married with the utmost splendor of which the rite permits ; with six bridesmaids, and Dr. Dudley, who was dead in love with the bride himself, standing quietly by as best man. The newspapers said the wedding gifts were numerous and costly. And Miss Bromfield, that no shadow, however faint, might cast itself upon these festal proceedings, took the opportunity to make a long visit upon some distant friends.

She had seen little of Marvin that winter. Not that she shunned society and his in particular. It was entirely his fault that they met but once or twice and talked of commonplaces. Having no desire to pose as a martyr, she went out a great deal where Ambrose was not; sometimes, indeed, where he was, when she knew it would be easy to avoid him ; at some great ball, for instance, where all the small party factions rallied under one standard. He often brushed by her at these reunions; and whether she saw him or not, she always knew when he was near ; if not instinctively, by reading it in other eyes.

One thing troubled her immensely in the early days of her freedom. This was the thought that perhaps she owed the house in which she lived to Ambrose, directly or indirectly. She resolved to consult her father about that, and accordingly did so.

"What an absurd notion!" said he. "Do you imagine that I would ever have lent myself to that? Don't you know that he has no money to waste upon such trifles ? "

"I thought he might have borrowed the money, papa," she explained; "or else have arranged it in some other way.   I felt sure that he knew about it."

"Not he!"

"Who can it be then?"

"I think you might guess, my dear, if you tried. But don't try; for I am pledged to secrecy and could hardly lie with a straight face, if you should happen to hit upon the right man."

To his disappointment, she took him at his word

and let him alone. Nothing would have pleased him better than to betray the secret by a look when driven to the wall; nothing, that is, except one other thing. He was only half happy in the loss of his prospective son-in-law. He wanted her to marry now, as earnestly as he had formerly hoped she would remain single all his days. But she must marry the right man—none other would do.

Being a woman, she by no means dropped the subject, merely because she ceased to talk about it. For her inward satisfaction she made many guesses, any one of which was probable enough; but all were wide of the mark. She never guessed Marvin, strange to say. But all her thoughts of him were of the bitterest kind, to be dismissed as soon as formed. She could only associate him in her mind with Miss Gérard, of whose disappearance and tragic end no news had reached her. She felt sure that he loved that most distasteful person, and she was prepared to hear of their engagement at any moment. When they met, Marvin was formal and distant enough to strengthen her in this false impression. She never spoke of him to her father, and, if the captain ventured to pronounce his name, her manner of greeting it was so reserved and chilling that he drew back in alarm. For Marvin was his man, though he had the tact not to let her dream of it. "Better to wait, old boy," he would say to himself. "You can manage a ship, but not a woman. She used to like him, though; I would give a month's pay to know what it means."

17

One night when they were dining alone, he said suddenly: " Why in the devil doesn't that leathery Italian send your portrait home? Does he think it belongs to him?"

" Suppose I write and ask him," she suggested.

" Do so, this very night. I won't have it on his wall any longer. Some of his cronies will say she's as handsome as her father, and fall in love with it next. It's my property, I want it." Helena laughed, and wrote the letter. Word came back from Mrs. Bruni that, though the portrait was really finished, her husband desired to retouch·it, and would be very grateful for just one more sitting. It need not be long—half·an hour, at most. Would she not lunch with them the next day, and sit afterward?

Mrs. Bruni, during the last few months, had caused her eccentric worser half to knit his brows more than once in silent wonder. Her ways had never been his ways, and he had long ago accepted the fact that their married life must be, at the best, one of harmonious disagreement. If he had a pet scheme at heart, he dealt with her regarding it as diplomatically as if he were an ambassador at a foreign court, instead of the master of his own household. She was disappointed in him, and she disapproved of him; but, having her own pursuits, she suffered less keenly than another woman might have done. She had been born to endure, but certainly not to suffer; and she liked to think and to say that, with all her defects, she was not of the suffering kind.

The part that Bruni had played, in the breaking of Miss Bromfield's engagement, touched her more deeply than she was willing to confess. She had always said that Ambrose was a brute; but her husband had proved it, and had turned his knowledge to account in the most sagacious way. And, when she tried to tell him so, he only laughed and said that was her doing. There was something very nice about this. She began to think his methods worth studying, and she wished they were more alike in their tastes. She grew meek and submissive in his presence, and no longer tried to preside over their table as if she were rapping to order at a sewing-circle. She took to breakfasting in the Italian fashion, and bought a foreign cookery-book, to serve up strange dishes full of pounded chestnuts and bits of sausage; and finally, she imported privately a quantity of the sweet cakes the Italians call *biscotti*, that he might soak them in his wine after dinner. He smiled at these attentions; they evidently pleased him; and so, one night when he showed an inclination to smoke his cigar at home, she gave up the most important meeting of the season for his sake, and never told him of the sacrifice. Here was a change indeed!

But Bruni was far from pleased at the apparent coolness between Marvin and Miss Bromfield. He had done more than his share of the work; it seemed only fair to him that they should complete it for themselves. He really expected to see them rush at once into each other's arms. But here was

she reserved, and he indifferent; so that nothing of
the kind happened or seemed likely to happen. It
was too bad! After Ambrose was safely married
and out of the way, he could not rest. Like Sister
Anne in her tower, he scanned the horizon and
found only dust upon it. He brought home heaps
of society papers, and ran his finger down the
columns, stopping it at every hint of a new engagement in the upper circles. But the one he wanted
was never there. Then he would pace the room,
and swear oaths of six syllables; fortunately, all in
his own melodious tongue.

"What *is* the matter, Cesare?" his wife asked, on
one of these occasions.

"Galileo was a fool!" he replied.

"What do you mean?"

"He said the world moves—I say it does not.
That's all."

"I don't understand you," she sighed.

"Those people are not engaged yet. Do you
understand that?"

Yes, she understood that perfectly, and she
laughed at him.

"The world moves slowly—give it time," said she.

"Time!" he repeated, angrily. "What does he
want with time? Why doesn't he walk straight up
and ask her, instead of making the tour of the
seven churches? They ought to have come
together long ago—you know they ought. And I
say the world stands still—at least with these
idiot Bostonians."

"She may not love him, after all," suggested Mrs. Bruni.

"Not love him?" he cried, pounding the table violently. "Then why did you break her engagement? It was a crime you committed. Not love him? She is dying for him—that I know."

"Well, then, perhaps he doesn't care for her."

"Then he's a brute—an ass—a *porco!*" and Bruni called a dozen saints to witness that this was true.

"It will do no good to swear," said his wife, soberly. "And I advise you to let them alone. It's the way with Boston men and women. They either wait till they are old before marrying, or they never marry. All the swearing in the world won't hurry them."

"For what do they come into the world, then?" growled Bruni.

But with this problem his wife declined to grapple.

This was the state of things in Casa Bruni when Helena went there for her final sitting. She was the only guest at luncheon, where Bruni, in his lightest mood, detained them long. After it, they all adjourned to the studio, Mrs. Bruni first procuring a bit of sad-colored embroidery, with which to occupy herself, while the artist went up before them to arrange the light. He placed the portrait upon his easel, and then drew the curtain across the great, recessed window. In doing this, he carelessly knocked down an old unframed canvas, that stood near. It proved to be an unfinished picture that he had half forgotten, and he smiled as he looked at it, and began to brush the dust from it with his sleeve. At that moment the others came in.

"Do you remember my attempt at landscape?" he said to Helena. "See!"

It was the sketch of the oaks at Waverley, that he had shown her long ago. She looked at it over his shoulder for a moment, without speaking. "I painted the figures out, as you advised," he went on.

"Did I?" she asked, absently. "Yes, I remember. It is better so. Have you sold it?"

"This? Oh, no. I shall make a present of it, some time, to a friend, who is very fond of the place —my friend, Mr. Marvin."

"Oh," said Helena; and she walked away to the platform, and dropped at once into her pose.

As Bruni put down the sketch, he could not help glancing mischievously at his wife. She frowned back at him severely.

He turned away to the little platform, where Helena sat with her face in strong relief against the background of the dark-red curtains. He looked from her to his easel, from his easel back again to her.

"It is not so very bad, after all," said he. Helena smiled at the pardonable weakness for his own work, that this speech rather thinly veiled. She gave him just the expression that he wanted. He dashed at the picture with his brushes, walking backward now and then, and turning to consider his results in a great mirror, that covered the bit of wall behind him from floor to ceiling.

Mrs. Bruni worked quietly on in her corner. Helena did not dare to speak; the long silence that followed was almost oppressive to her after their noisy luncheon; but she preferred not to be the first to break it.

It broke itself, as it were, suddenly, with the sharp ringing of a bell, that echoed through the little house. Bruni pricked up his ears; and then, with palette, brushes, and all, he rushed out upon the landing. In a moment he came back and took down the portrait hastily. "It is Marvin," he said. "He is coming up."

Helena rose, instantly. "I would rather not meet him," said she. And she started toward the door, where she would have met him face to face.

"Quick, then; go that way," said Bruni, pointing to the crimson hangings.

All studios are confusing places, and Helena had never seen the window. For the moment she welcomed it as a means of escape—a door leading to another room. She stepped behind the curtains. Before her was the open river; behind her only those swaying folds, through which she could hear the others talking. It was a shelter at all events.

Bruni meanwhile had put away the portrait, and had set up in its place the unfinished oak trees. Now he saluted Marvin, who was already shaking hands with his wife. Over his friend's shoulder, Bruni bent upon her a fierce Italian scowl of the true *cinquecento* pattern. She did not wait for a second hint, but folded her tent like a crushed Arab, and silently withdrew.

"Your note came this morning," began Marvin.

"Yes," said Bruni, with a queer, embarrassed look. Then he pointed to a chair, and began to mix the colors on his palette with one of his brushes, abstractedly.

"Yes," repeated Marvin. "I inferred that you wanted to see me. But if you are busy—"

"No, no!" said Bruni, laughing himself into composure. "My note meant that I had not seen you for a small eternity. Do sit down; I will go on with my work, and you shall talk to me."

"The wretch!" thought Miss Bromfield in her mouse-trap. "Does he mean to keep me shut up here for an hour or two?"

"Is that the way you work?" asked Marvin, whose eyes had followed Bruni to his easel. And the latter, in the recesses of his heart, let off a muffled volley of Italian oaths. His oaks were planted there before him, upside down.

He was not to be disconcerted by such a trifle. What did Marvin know about art? "Why not?" he replied, soberly. "It is the true way to crystallize effects." Then he stretched his arm out rigidly, and gave the sketch a stroke or two, but with a dry brush. "Do you think of setting yourself up as critic of the plastic arts?" he continued, with bitter sarcasm.

"No," said Marvin, finding that he had really ventured beyond his depth. "But a cat may look

even at a king, I suppose. I didn't know you painted
landscapes. May I see what you are doing ? " and
he jumped up, without waiting for permission.

" There is no harm in that," said Bruni, reversing
the picture with a fine condescension, as if to suit
it to his lower level. " There you are ! "

There Marvin was, indeed ! In a flash, he recalled
his walk of the year before under those very trees.
To think of that was to remember Bruni's master-
stroke at the club afterward, when awkward dis-
closures concerning the walk threatened him. He
thought of these things, and forgot to give the
artist a word of praise.

" How did you happen to do that ? " was all he
said.

" I did it for you. I knew you liked the place,"
explained Bruni.

" Thanks," said Marvin, looking about to make
sure they were alone. " How did you know ? "

" I saw you there—once," Bruni replied.

There was a pause, during which Bruni dabbled
at the sketch with a brush dipped in oil. They
were alone. Why should not he have the tardy
thanks that were his due ?

" That was a clever thing you did once at the
club," said Marvin ; " you remember ? " Bruni
nodded. " I understood your motive perfectly.
You saved me in the nick of time. The matter,
though, was not so serious as you imagined."

" I imagined nothing," retorted Bruni, curtly.

Marvin was annoyed, both at the tone of this

speech and at the shallowness of Bruni's mind implied in it. There had been no opening chapter of romance woven about him, after all.

"So much the better, then," he said, somewhat coldly; "I thought you took me for a blighted being—a cast-off lover of Miss Bromfield."

A nice turn their talk was taking, under all the circumstances! Bruni slapped away at his canvas, savagely.

"Oh, no," he said; "I comprehended the situation. You were pleased at the engagement. *Buon Dio !* You asked nothing better than to go to church and see her come out of it Mrs. Ambrose !"

He was a deep fellow, this Italian. Marvin looked at him in surprise.

"I don't say that," he replied.

"Then why not say it? It is a good thing when a girl marries the man of her choice. You ought to be glad to see her Mrs. —— anybody that you please !"

Marvin strode up and down the room solemnly. "I hope she will take the right man, certainly," said he.

"The right man ?" growled Bruni, backing away from the picture. He looked at it a moment critically; then he turned on Marvin.

"Look here !" he said; "your hand on the table! Don't try to play false cards with me, Marvin! you are the man !"

"I !" said Marvin, with a laugh; "I ! What stupid nonsense ! She treats me as though I were

a pickpocket. I said six words to her the other
day, and was well frozen for my pains."

"Bah! You don't understand women."

"Who does, Signor mio ? "

"No man. I have studied my own wife for years,
and am no wiser. But what you say proves nothing."

"No," said Marvin; "it only proves that if I
am the man, she must speak first and tell me so."

"You are a fool—I mean a Bostonian!" Bruni
answered.

Marvin stopped his walk at the easel and faced
Bruni, who had retreated, crab-like, nearly to the
opposite wall. The two men looked at each other
for a moment in silence. Marvin spoke first.

"Bruni, old man! For Heaven's sake don't take
me for one of those reserved idiots with a secret
sorrow! Don't go about thinking that I am in love
with her!"

"It is the truth!" cried Bruni, in despair. What
else could he say ?

"You wish me to swear then that I do not love
her?" Marvin asked, with irritation in his voice.

"You dare not say it!"

Marvin looked down at his coat, and with his
hand brushed away a thread, as if its weight oppressed him. "But I do say it! I shall never
marry her!" he returned.

"It is a lie!" yelled Bruni, in a storm of rage.

Marvin looked up in mingled anger and surprise.
A slender line of light flashed out in the great mirror
behind Bruni. The curtain at his own back had

swayed a little. It might have been a draught of air; but he saw that Bruni was looking at the curtain, and not at him.

He tore it away furiously, and found Miss Bromfield there, in tears—sobbing to herself, for he had heard no sound. The next moment she was in his arms.

Bruni went down stairs to find his wife. She was writing, at her desk in the drawing-room. He could hear the scratch of the quill, as he stole in on tiptoe. He went up and leaned upon her chair.

"'*Eppur si muove,*'" he whispered.

She dropped the pen, making a great splash of ink upon the page.

"What do you mean? Have they—have you—?"

He nodded, smiling like a chimpanzee. "*Si, madonna; è cosa fatta!* Galileo was a wise man, after all."

And then—O marvel! He put his arm around her neck and kissed her.

A little more than five years afterward, one evening in the early summer-time, Jack Elliston and Dr. Dudley sat alone on the balcony of the "Ægean." The sun was setting, and they looked at the rose-colored light, as they had done often and often in the years gone by. There was no one in the rooms behind them; the house seemed deserted.

"How this place has changed!" said Jack, tilting his chair back against the wall, with a yawn that he made no attempt to disguise.

He had grown stouter, and looked as if he were

rather too fond of dining. He was not rich, as the term goes nowadays—not even so rich as his mother had fondly hoped he would be. Nevertheless, his uncle, after endowing numerous worthy institutions, had provided for him.

Dr. Dudley answered rather mournfully. "Yes," he sighed, "three years in a club are a generation. Look at our old crowd! Married or dead almost to a man!"

"For better, for worse," said Jack, laughing.

"Very much for the worse—some of 'em!"

"You think this better. I am not so sure about it," Jack continued. "By the way, I hear the divine creature has applied for a divorce."

"Mrs Ambrose—yes," Dudley answered.

"Good! They say he beats her," said Jack, who had completely forgotten the rumor of his friend's early attachment to Miss Feathering.

"Possibly. He drinks like a Roman emperor."

"Yes, that's his type." And here Jack brought his chair forward with a thump. An open victoria passed the house, and in it were Marvin and his wife. Jack bowed to them cordially. He and Marvin would never be intimate, but they had become friends again.

"Speaking of angels," went on Jack, as he resumed his attitude of luxurious ease, "that was a lucky escape for her. Wasn't it?" And he indicated the retreating carriage.

"From Ambrose, you mean—yes. Marvin looks happy enough," said Dr. Dudley, gloomily.

" He is happy," Jack asserted, confidently. " Dudley, why do you and I sit here alone? There is but one thing for us—to make a happy marriage!"
And yet he has never married.

THE END.

BRIEF LIST OF BOOKS OF FICTION

PUBLISHED BY CHARLES SCRIBNER'S SONS

George W. Cable.

THE GRANDISSIMES. *New edition.* 12mo, . . $1.25
OLD CREOLE DAYS. *New edition.* 12mo, . . . 1.25
The same in two parts. 16mo. Cloth, each, 75c.; paper,
   each, ...30
MADAME DELPHINE. 12mo, ...75

Edward Eggleston.

ROXY. A Tale of Indiana Life. Illustrated. 12mo, 1.50
THE CIRCUIT RIDER. A Tale. Illustrated. 12mo, 1.50
THE HOOSIER SCHOOLMASTER. Illustrated. 12mo, 1.25
THE MYSTERY OF METROPOLISVILLE. Illustrated.
   12mo, ... 1.50
THE END OF THE WORLD. A Love Story. Illustrated.
   12mo, ... 1.50
Complete Sets (in box), ... 7.25

J. G. Holland.

SEVENOAKS. Small 12mo, ... 1.25
THE BAY PATH. Small 12mo, ... 1.25
ARTHUR BONNICASTLE. Small 12mo, . . . 1.25
MISS GILBERT'S CAREER. Small 12mo, . . 1.25
NICHOLAS MINTURN. Small 12mo, . . . 1.25

Frances Hodgson Burnett.

THAT LASS O' LOWRIE'S. Illustrated. 12mo. Paper,
   50c.; cloth, ... : 1.50
HAWORTH'S. Illustrated. 12mo, ... 1.50
LOUISIANA. 12mo, ... 1.00
SURLY TIM and Other Stories. Small 12mo, . . 1.25

EARLIER STORIES.
   LINDSAY'S LUCK. 16mo. Paper, ...30
   PRETTY POLLY PEMBERTON. 16mo. Paper, ...40
   KATHLEEN. 16mo. Paper, ...40
   THEO. 16mo. Paper, ...30
   MISS CRESPIGNY. 16mo. Paper, ...30

SCRIBNER'S LIST OF BOOKS OF FICTION.

Frank R. Stockton.

RUDDER GRANGE. 12mo. Paper, 60 cents; cloth, $1.25
THE LADY OR THE TIGER? and Other Stories. 12mo.
Paper, 50 cents; cloth, ...   1.00

George P. Lathrop.

NEWPORT. 12mo. Paper, 50c.; cloth, . . .   1.25
AN ECHO OF PASSION. 12mo. Paper, 50c.; cloth,   1.00
IN THE DISTANCE. 12mo. Paper, 50c.; cloth, .   1.00

Saxe Holm's Stories.

FIRST SERIES.

"Draxy Miller's Dowry," "The Elder's Wife," "Whose
Wife Was She?" "The One-Legged Dancers," "How
One Woman Kept Her Husband," "Esther Wynn's
Love Letters." 12mo, Paper, 50c.; cloth, . .   1.00

SECOND SERIES.

"A Four-Leaved Clover," "Farmer Bassett's Romance," ·
"My Tourmaline," "Joe Hale's Red Stocking," "Su-
san Lawton's Escape." 12mo, Paper, 50c.; cloth, .   1.00

H. H. Boyesen.

FALCONBERG. Illustrated. 12mo, ...   1.50
GUNNAR. A Tale of Norse Life. Square 12mo, .   1.25
TALES FROM TWO HEMISPHERES. Square 12mo, .   1.00
ILKA ON THE HILL TOP, and Other Stories. Square 12mo, 1.00
QUEEN TITANIA. Square 12mo, ...   1.00

Edward Everett Hale.

PHILIP NOLAN'S FRIENDS. Illustrated. 12mo, .   1.75

Augustus M. Swift.

CUPID, M.D. A Story. 16mo, ...   1.00

Howard Pyle.

WITHIN THE CAPES. One vol. 12mo, . . . $1.00

E. T. W. Hoffmann.

WEIRD TALES. 2 vols. 12mo. With portrait, . 3.00

Erckmann-Chatrian Series.

FRIEND FRITZ. 16mo, ... 1.25
THE CONSCRIPT. Illustrated. 16mo, . . . 1.25
WATERLOO. Illustrated. 12mo, ... 1.25
MADAME THERESE. Illustrated. 16mo, . . . 1.25
THE BLOCKADE OF PHALSBURG. Illustrated. 16mo, 1.25
THE INVASION OF FRANCE IN 1814. Illustrated. 16mo, 1.25
A MILLER'S STORY OF THE WAR. 16mo, . . 1.25

Jules Verne.

GODFREY MORGAN. Illustrated. 8vo, ... 2.00
MICHAEL STROGOFF. Illustrated. *New edition*. 8vo, . 2.00
A FLOATING CITY, and THE BLOCKADE RUNNERS.
Illustrated. 8vo, ... 2.00
HECTOR SERVADAC. Illustrated. 8vo, ... 2.00
DICK SANDS. Illustrated. 8vo, ... 3.00
A JOURNEY TO THE CENTRE OF THE EARTH. Illustra-
ted. 8vo, ... 3.00
THE MYSTERIOUS ISLAND. Illustrated. 8vo, . . 3.00
FROM THE EARTH TO THE MOON DIRECT IN NINETY-
SEVEN HOURS, TWENTY MINUTES. Illustrated. 12mo, 1.50
STORIES OF ADVENTURE. Comprising " Meridiana," and
"A Journey to the Centre of the Earth." Illus. 12mo, 1.50
THE DEMON OF CAWNPORE. (Part I of the Steam
House). Illustrated. 12mo, ... 1.50
TIGERS AND TRAITORS. (Part II of the Steam House).
Illustrated. 12mo, ... 1.50
EIGHT HUNDRED LEAGUES ON THE AMAZON. (Part I
of the Giant Raft). Illustrated. 12mo, . . 1.50
THE CRYPTOGRAM. (Part II of the Giant Raft). Illus-
trated. 12mo, ... 1.50

SCRIBNER'S LIST OF BOOKS OF FICTION.

The King's Men.
A Tale of To-morrow. By Robert Grant, John Boyle O'Reilly, J. S. of Dale, and John T. Wheelwright. 12mo, $1.25

Virginia W. Johnson.
THE FAINALLS OF TIPTON. 12mo, . . . 1.25

Mrs. E. Prentiss.
FRED, MARIA, AND ME. With illustrations. 12mo. *New edition,* 1.00

J. S. of Dale.
GUERNDALE. An Old Story. 12mo. Paper, 50 cents; cloth, ... 1.25
THE CRIME OF HENRY VANE. By the author of "Guerndale." 12mo, ... 1.00

Mary Adams.
AN HONORABLE SURRENDER. 16mo, . . . 1.00

Count Leo Tolstoy.
THE COSSACKS. 12mo, ... 1.25

Donald G. Mitchell.
DR. JOHNS. 12mo. *New edition,* . . . 1.25

Julia Schayer.
TIGER LILY and Other Stories. 12mo, . . . 1.00

Mary Mapes Dodge.
THEOPHILUS AND OTHERS. 12mo, . . . 1.50

A. Perry.
THE SCHOOLMASTER'S TRIAL. 12mo, . . . 1.00

H. C. Bunner and Brander Matthews.
IN PARTNERSHIP. Studies in Story-Telling. 12mo, 1.00

Across the Chasm.
One vol. 12mo, ... 1.00

SCRIBNER'S LIST OF BOOKS OF FICTION.

Stories by American Authors.

A collection of the most noteworthy stories written in recent years, not hitherto printed in book form, now published by arrangement with the authors.

I.—WHO WAS SHE? Bayard Taylor. THE DOCUMENTS IN THE CASE, Brander Matthews and H. C. Bunner. ONE OF THE THIRTY PIECES, William Henry Bishop. BALACCHI BROTHERS, Rebecca Harding Davis. AN OPERATION IN MONEY, Albert Webster. 16mo, ... $ .50

II.—THE TRANSFERRED GHOST, Frank R. Stockton. A MARTYR TO SCIENCE, Mary Putnam Jacobi, M.D. MRS. KNOLLYS, J. S. of Dale. A DINNER PARTY, John Eddy. THE MOUNT OF SORROW, Harriet Prescott Spofford. SISTER SILVIA, Mary Agnes Tinker. 16mo, ...50

III.—THE SPIDER'S EYE, Lucretia P. Hale. A STORY OF THE LATIN QUARTER, Frances Hodgson Burnett. TWO PURSE-COMPANIONS, George Parsons Lathrop. POOR OGLA-MOGA, David D. Lloyd. A MEMORABLE MURDER, Celia Thaxter. VENETIAN GLASS, Brander Matthews. 16mo, . . .50

IV.—MISS GRIEF, Constance Fenimore Woolson. LOVE IN OLD CLOATHES, H. C. Bunner. TWO BUCKETS IN A WELL, N. P. Willis. FRIEND BARTON'S CONCERN, Mary Hallock Foote. AN INSPIRED LOBBYIST, J. W. DeForest. LOST IN THE FOG, Noah Brooks. 16mo, ...50

V.—A LIGHT MAN, Henry James. YATIL, F. D. Millet. THE END OF NEW YORK, Park Benjamin. WHY THOMAS WAS DISCHARGED, George Arnold. THE TACHYPOMP, E. P. Mitchell. 16mo, ...50

VI.—THE VILLAGE CONVICT, C. H. White. THE DENVER EXPRESS, A. A. Hayes. THE MISFORTUNES OF BRO' THOMAS WHEATLEY, Lina Redwood Fairfax. THE HEARTBREAK CAMEO, Mrs. L. W. Champney. MISS EUNICE'S GLOVE, Albert Webster. BROTHER SEBASTIAN'S FRIENDSHIP, Harold Frederic. 16mo, ...50

VII.—THE BISHOP'S VAGABOND, Octave Thanet. LOST, Edward Bellamy. KIRBY'S COALS OF FIRE, Louise Stockton. PASSAGES FROM THE JOURNAL OF A SOCIAL WRECK, Margaret Floyd. STELLA GRAYLAND, James T. McKay. THE IMAGE OF SAN DONATO, Virginia W. Johnson, . . .50

VIII.—THE BRIGADE COMMANDER, J. W. DeForest. SPLIT ZEPHYR, Henry A. Beers. ZERVIAH HOPE, Elizabeth Stuart Phelps. THE LIFE MAGNET, Alvey A. Adee. OSGOOD'S PREDICAMENT, Elizabeth D. B. Stoddard, . .50

IX.—MARSE CHAN, Thomas Nelson Page. MR. BIXBY'S CHRISTMAS VISITOR, Charles S. Gage. ELI, C. H. White. YOUNG STRONG OF THE CLARION, Millicent Washburn Shinn. HOW OLD WIGGINS WORE SHIP, Captain Rowland F. Coffin. "—— MAS HAS COME," Leonard Kipp, . . .50

X.—PANCHA, T. A. Janvier. THE ABLEST MAN IN THE WORLD, E. P. Mitchell. YOUNG MOLL'S PEEVY, C. A. Stephens. MANMAT'HA, Charles de Kay. A DARING FICTION, H. H. Boyesen. THE STORY OF TWO LIVES, Julia Schayer, ...50

Complete Sets, 10 vols. in a box, $5.00.